it's

raining

men

USA TODAY BESTSELLING AUTHOR
JULIE HAMMERLE

Entangled Publishing, LLC
10940 S Parker Road
Suite 327
Parker, CO 80134
rights@entangledpublishing.com

Amara is an imprint of Entangled Publishing, LLC.

Visit our website at www.entangledpublishing.com.

Edited by Stacy Abrams
Cover illustration and design by
Elizabeth Turner Stokes
Interior design by Toni Kerr

ISBN 978-1-64937-028-0
Ebook ISBN 978-1-64937-041-9

Manufactured in the United States of America

First Edition July 2021

10 9 8 7 6 5 4 3 2 1

an imprint of Entangled Publishing LLC

ALSO BY JULIE HAMMERLE

For John, my partner in quarantine.
Thank you for a year of walks, food experiments,
franchise Fridays, and hot tub happy hours.

For all the lonely people.

It's Raining Men is a hilarious, heartfelt rom-com about finding love when you least expect it and discovering your own inner strength, however the story includes discussions of death of a loved one, mention of cancer treatments, and one scene of a character drinking to excess, so readers who may be sensitive to this, please take note.

CHAPTER ONE

Teddy Ruxspin Doctors

"Okay, what's wrong?" Gayle Gale asked after I'd finished listening to her heart and lungs.

"Well, your chest sounds good, but your blood pressure is higher than I'd like it to be." I wrapped my stethoscope around my neck.

"I was talking about you, Annie, not me. What's with the weepy eyes?"

I asked all the patients in my concierge practice to call me Annie. I found it lowered the doctor-patient barrier in our relationship, making them more likely to contact me with potentially serious symptoms.

It also, unfortunately, had the side effect of encouraging them to ask me about my personal life.

I wiped my eyes with one hand as I made a note on her chart. "It's just allergies." I glanced up at my patient, whose furrowed brow illuminated the usually masked wrinkles on her light brown, sixty-something skin. She wasn't buying a word out of my mouth. All day long at work, my eyes had been welling with tears for no reason, which was completely unprofessional and not at all like me. I'd been telling my patients I had seasonal allergies, but Gayle Gale, the Chicago news anchor legend, the badass woman who'd gotten a former mayor to admit live on camera to tax evasion, naturally saw right through me.

"No, it's not. Spill it."

"I honestly don't know. It's been happening out of the blue for no reason," I said, chuckling. "Maybe it actually is allergies. Or maybe I'm extra sensitive to Tina's new cleanse." My assistant, despite my efforts to insist that she was a healthy young woman who already looked gorgeous, was trying a new fad she'd found on TikTok involving something like onions, garlic, cayenne pepper, saffron, and fish broth. That would make anyone's eyes water.

"That's not it." My patient narrowed her gaze. "Man trouble?"

"Only if you count *not* having a man as man trouble." I shook my head as I remembered I was in my office and not on my friend's living room couch. Maybe I should rethink my stance on formality and make my patients call me Dr. Kyle. This whole overfamiliarity thing was blurring too many lines, even for a consummate professional like me. "Your high blood pressure—"

"Family health issues?"

"Yes, well," I said, "obviously hypertension can be hereditary."

"I meant *your* family," Gayle said. "Is everyone well? Your mom, your brother, your adorable niece and nephew?"

"They're all fine." At a previous appointment, Gayle had charmed me into telling her about my family. She'd even watched a video of my niece dancing to that one song from *Frozen*. I helped Gayle lie down on the exam table. "Now, we have several medical options for hypertension, but equally important—"

"How about your roommate?" Gale said as I palpated her abdomen. "What was her name? Kerry?"

"Kelly," I corrected her, "and she's fine." My face tightened, and I realized I was smiling. Dang it, she'd hit the bull's-eye. Gayle was good. Too good. "She's coming home tonight, actually."

"Where's she been?"

"She moved out to Galena with her parents for a few months to help her dad after knee surgery." I paused. "Hey, by the way, did you know Kelly's dad also has high blood pressure?"

"Many people do," Gayle said. "That will be nice for you to have your roommate back in town. I'm sure you've missed her."

The now-familiar sensation of my eyes stinging returned. I blinked away the tears as I helped Gayle sit up.

"Annie, sweetie." Gayle squeezed my hand. "Tell me all about it. I'm listening."

I was fighting a losing battle here. "Gayle, if I tell you about it, will you finally let me say my piece about the dangers of high blood pressure?"

Gayle steepled her hands and nodded seriously. "I will."

I sat down and rolled my chair closer to the exam table. "Okay. Kelly left a few months ago, and, as I'm a fairly introverted person, I didn't think it would bother me that much. But I've spent most of the past twelve weeks either working or lying on my couch watching mind-numbing television, eating by myself, doing everything by myself, and honestly, the fact that she's coming home, and it means I no longer have to feel this crushing loneliness, is a relief." I wiped my eyes again. "Hence the tears."

"And that's it?" Gayle asked.

"That's it," I said, smiling at her. "As much as I enjoy spending most of my time with you and my other patients, I'm just really looking forward to seeing my friend again." I grabbed a prescription pad. "For the hypertension, I want to start you off on—"

"Have you heard of Man on Main Street?"

I dropped my pen in my lap. I could feel my own blood pressure rising. "Of course." Man on Main Street was a recurring segment during the news on her station, WTS TV.

"Darius is always looking for new, interesting people to interview around Chicagoland. Would you be interested in talking to him about being a concierge doctor?"

"I'm sorry?" I'd lost the conversation thread. We'd been talking about Kelly coming home, and then I was trying to get back on the high blood pressure topic, and now she wanted me to talk to her coworker about…?

"I think it would be great," she said. "Whenever I tell people about your practice, they're both confused and intrigued. I think you should let Darius do a segment on you."

"If I agree to this, will you finally—*finally*—let me tell you about how your job stress and sodium intake might be affecting your health and how I'd like you to make sure you get regular exercise while also taking a thiazide diuretic?"

"Yes," she said.

Even though going on TV was the absolute last thing I'd ever consider, a promise was a promise. And after Kelly came home tonight, I knew everything would be okay again. Life would get back to normal, and the two of us could joke about the utter absurdity of *me* going on television to talk about my practice. "Okay, then. Fine. Tell your coworker to call me about an interview."

The things I was willing to do for my patients.

CHAPTER TWO

Crimpin' Ain't Easy

"Alexa," I said in the odd, authoritative voice I always used when I spoke to my virtual assistant, "shuffle songs from Phil Collins."

No one could tell me I didn't know how to party.

As the opening strains of "In the Air Tonight" pumped through my speakers, I made sure the house was ready for Kelly's homecoming. I placed a vase of daisies (her favorite) on her bedside table. I made sure the entire bottom floor of my converted three-flat, which had served for the past five years as Kelly's apartment, looked clean and tidy. I shoved my recently acquired stationary bike into an empty corner and artfully draped a throw blanket over it, and I arranged the TV remotes in a little basket to look like an inviting bouquet.

On the first floor, in the main part of the house, I set out guacamole that I'd purchased at Whole Foods on my way home from work and set two bottles of wine—white and red—on the living room coffee table next to three glasses and a wine opener. My phone buzzed in the pocket of my pajama pants—yes, we were going extra casual tonight—as

I surveyed my handiwork.

"Yessi?" I said. I'd invited my other BFF from college, Yessi, over tonight to help welcome Kelly back to the city. I hadn't spent much quality time with Yessi in the past few months, either. She had a baby about six months ago and was now back at work, juggling her child, her marriage, and her career as a high-powered corporate attorney. But tonight she said she'd be here for Kelly.

"Annie?" Yessi's voice sounded panicked. "Olivia has a fever."

"Oh no." Yessi often called me with baby-related medical questions, and I was always happy to help—when I could. It had been way too long since I did my pedes rotation. "How high?"

"One hundred and one," she said, "rectally. Since her doctor's office is closed, Polly and I are taking her to the emergency room."

"Hi, Annie!" I heard Polly, Yessi's wife, a veterinarian, say on the other end.

"Hi, Polly!" My brain scanned through all the information I'd retained about infants and fevers. "How is Olivia behaving?"

"She's crying a lot." As if on cue, the baby let out a wail in the background on Yessi's end.

"It's most likely something simple," I said reassuringly. "You're doing the right thing taking her in. The doctors will get the fever down and will be able to tell you exactly what's going on."

"Thanks, Annie," Yessi said. "I'm sorry I won't be able to make it tonight."

"Say hi to Kelly!" Polly shouted.

My heart sank. Yessi and I kept missing each other these days. "Will do!" I said as cheerfully as I could muster. "We'll get together another time soon. Please keep me updated on Olivia and call if you have any questions."

I set the phone down with a sigh and turned off "Sussudio." Worried about Olivia and sad about not getting to see my friend, I was no longer in the mood for Phil. I grabbed one of the three wineglasses on the coffee table and returned it to the dining room hutch.

The doorbell rang.

"If this is a sales call..." I muttered to myself as I made my way over to the door. But when I opened it, I found Kelly standing there, eyes down on her phone.

She looked up, surprised, as if she hadn't just rung my doorbell. "Annie!" she said finally, shoving her phone in her pocket and shooting me a dimmed-down version of the thousand-watt, toothy white smile I'd known since the very first day of college. Petite Kelly, with the big, curly blond hair and sun-kissed bronze face like a California surfer girl, fell into my arms, sobbing.

I squeezed her tight, resting my head on the top of hers, as her body convulsed against mine. "Oh my gosh, Kelly, what's wrong? Is it your dad?"

She shook her head and mumbled something against my shoulder that I couldn't hear.

I pulled away, holding her at arm's length. "Say it again?"

She opened her mouth to speak just as my phone buzzed again in my pajama pants pocket. I held up a finger to stop. "Pause," I said, "one second. Yessi's taking Olivia to the emergency room." I checked the caller ID on my phone. "Shoot." I wrinkled up my nose. "It's a patient. I have to take this."

I answered the call—a former Chicago Bulls player who now did color commentary for one of the radio stations in town. He hurt his knee playing a pickup game with his kids in the driveway. I told him to ice it tonight and call an orthopedic specialist I knew in the morning if it wasn't feeling better.

"Ugh," I said, shoving my phone back in my pants and heading back into the living room. "I know it's silly, but I always feel guilty when I have to send patients to a specialist. It's like, what are they paying me for? Maybe it's time I recognize I'm not superhuman."

I paused in the doorway and watched Kelly down almost a full glass of red wine before wiping her mouth with the back of her hand.

"Kel?"

She turned toward me, eyes pink and bloodshot. Finally able to get a good look at her, I realized that she was a more muted and monochrome version of her usual self tonight. Kelly normally wore dresses and cute tops in bright, bold colors—reds, pinks, blues, yellows, sometimes all at once. She'd dress up every outfit with chunky jewelry and fun shoes. Tonight she wore a pair of boring black jeans under a faded pink sweatshirt. (A *sweatshirt*!) She hadn't put on a stitch of makeup, and her only hint of bling was a modest gold pendant around her neck.

"What's going on?" I asked.

She sat up straight, shoulders back. "It's nothing," she

said. "I guess I miss my mom and dad. I'd spent so much time with them over the past few months—" She let out a huge sob, and I dashed to sit next to her on the couch. I took her hand in mine.

"I get it," I said. "I was emotional all day at work today, knowing you were coming home. I've been...lonely." I grinned at her. "But now we're reunited, and things can finally get back to normal. For both of us."

She burst into tears, dropping her head into her hands.

Crap. This was completely new and unexpected. Kelly loved her mom and dad, but the three of them had their issues, too. When she left home for college, she left for *good*. I had a hard time believing they were the real source of this despair.

"You want to put on a movie or something?" I asked.

She shook her head, her blond curls flopping around her shoulders.

"Play a board game?"

She scrunched up her nose.

I knew what I had to do. I wasn't trying to make my introverted self feel better. I had to think like Kelly—suggest something she might want to do.

"Um...there's a new bar nearby..."

Her eyes lit up.

"Maybe we can put on makeup, get dressed up, and...do that?"

Kelly leaped off the couch and right into my chest, wrapping her arms around my neck. "Yes, Annie. Thank you! I think a night out is just what I need."

I guess I was changing out of my comfy pants.

CHAPTER THREE

We Didn't Start the Bonfire of the Vanities

"Oh my god!" Kelly grabbed a flyer off the table just inside the bar. "They have trivia on Thursday nights! We should totally go next week. Remember when you, Yessi, and I used to do trivia all the time?"

"I do," I said, yanking down the hem on the very short hot pink dress I'd agreed to wear because Kelly said it would make her happy to see me in something, quote, "not the color of decomposition."

"What was our team name again?" she asked.

"It's a Headband." The name was something I'd pulled out of my butt one night, a very random quote from the TV show *Felicity* that no one ever understood. We were excellent at trivia, but eighties and nineties throwbacks were our specialty.

"Why did we stop playing again?" Kelly's now fully lashed-up and glitter-ized eyes narrowed. "Oh, yeah, because you and Yessi are assholes."

"That's…not exactly fair." Yessi and I both hated losing, and once we may have gotten into a very loud fight because she thought she was right on a question about Queen Victoria when I knew she was wrong, and the bar we used to go to back then may have banned us from trivia for life. If that made us assholes…well, yeah, I supposed that made us assholes.

I glanced around the bar and suddenly longed for my usual going-out uniform of jeans, Converse All-Stars, and whatever clean ancient concert tee I could find in my drawer. Everyone in the pub was dressed down except Kelly and me. We looked like Romy and Michele on the way to their high school reunion.

But I was here to make my friend feel better, and my dressing like a birthday clown was apparently working for her. Her mood had already perked up dramatically.

As Kelly stopped to chat up some guy who'd quickly caught her eye, I wobbled toward the bar in a set of platform heels I'd bought back in the early aughts for a Halloween costume. I set the lavender beaded clutch my sister-in-law made me carry in her wedding on the counter and hopped—not gracefully—onto a stool.

The bartender, a tall guy in his twenties with dark hair, tattoos, and a five o'clock shadow darkening his tanned complexion, set a coaster in front of me. His ice-blue eyes gave my outfit the once-over, and I caught a hint of amusement on his lips.

I waved a hand down my Barbie-clothed body. "Drink it in."

The smirk disappeared. "Oh, I wasn't—"

"Sure you were." I glanced over at Kelly, who was now leaning over to talk to a different random guy, her cleavage on full display. This wasn't like her. She was fun and bubbly and friendly, but never this friendly. Never "shove my boobs in a twentysomething stranger's face" friendly. "I'll have an old-fashioned," I told the bartender, keeping my eyes on my friend.

Something was going on with Kelly—something more than her simply missing her parents. When the bartender set my drink in front of me, I grabbed it and my purse and went over to where Kelly was now whispering sweet nothings into the ear of someone who had probably been eating paste in kindergarten back when we were in college.

"Kel," I said, smiling, "want to move over to the bar with me? We can catch up there."

She stood up straight, and though she'd been laughing with the young dude, her eyes lacked any joy.

"Come on." I wrapped an arm around her shoulders. "Let's chat."

At the bar, I ordered her a glass of sparkling rosé. The bartender, who'd apparently learned his lesson about appraising his customers' outfits, barely even glanced at Kelly's purple, pink, and teal pants and lavender eye shadow.

"Okay." I squeezed my friend's hand. "Please tell me what's going on with you. I know it has to be more than you just missing your mom and dad."

"It is," she said. "It's—"

A loud crash and the sound of glass shattering cut her off, and my head snapped toward the bar. Our bartender, the guy with the eyes, was leaning over, gripping his leg. Blood trickled toward his ankle, and shards of the broken bottle surrounded his feet in a puddle of fizzy pink wine.

I leaned over the bar. "Are you okay?" I shouted.

He looked over at me. "I'm bleeding."

"I see that." I glanced at Kelly, looking for permission.

"Go," she said, waving her hand. "Be the superhero. We'll talk later."

"No." I grabbed my purse and headed toward the injured patient. "Come with me. We'll talk while I clean him up."

The bartender's eyes widened in shock and concern. "What?"

"I'm a doctor." I motioned to one of the waiters working the tables. "Can someone clean this up, please?"

The bartender tilted his head in disbelief as his eyes scanned my ensemble.

"She *is* a doctor," Kelly said, glancing at her phone, "and a damn expensive one, too. Consider yourself lucky."

"Where's the manager's office?" I asked, glancing around.

"That way." The bartender nodded toward a closed door in the hallway off to the right of the bar.

Kelly and I each wrapped one of the bartender's arms around our shoulders—which had to look pretty laughable, because he had a good five inches on me and way more than that on Kelly—and walked him toward the office. People called out, offering to help, but I waved them off. I didn't need their assistance. Asking to help me with a little cut was like volunteering to help LeBron James with his dribbling.

"What's your name, by the way?" I asked. "I should probably know it, if I'm going to do surgery on you."

"Surgery?" he said.

"She's exaggerating," Kelly said.

"Dax," the bartender said.

"Nice to meet you, Dax," I said as I opened the office

door. "I'm Annie."

"And you might as well know that I'm Kelly, since we're bonded for life by blood now."

I felt Dax shudder under my arm. I calmly patted his hand. "It's okay. You're going to be fine. It's just a little cut." I was very used to big strong men getting squeamish around blood, needles, or knives. One of my patients—a Cubs third baseman—once fainted in my office when I had to lance a boil on his foot.

Kelly and I eased Dax into the desk chair. Then I ducked into the private bathroom and washed my hands. There was a first aid kit on the shelf above the sink.

I snapped on a pair of latex gloves from the first aid kit and stepped out of the bathroom. "I'm going to take good care of you, Dax, but I can multitask. I want to hear what my friend was about to say right before you smashed a bottle into your leg."

"I didn't smash a bottle into my leg."

I ignored him. "Kelly?"

She snuck a peek at Dax. "You really want to talk about this now?"

"Of course." I sanitized a pair of tweezers with alcohol and knelt on the floor to see the wound better. "This should be no problem." I'd slipped into full doctor mode. "The glass is right at the surface." I glanced up at my friend. "Go ahead, Kel."

She folded her arms across her chest.

I patted Dax's knee. "You're doing great."

Dax drew in an audible breath and held it.

I slowly extracted the sliver of glass and dropped it into

the garbage can next to the desk. "Hard part's done."

"Great. So I can get back to work now?" Dax moved to stand, but I pushed him down, resting my hand for a hot moment on his ample pectoral.

Butterflies invaded my stomach, but I tamped them down. I was a professional, and this guy was way too young for me to even think about behaving unprofessionally with.

"You're almost done," I said, and he grunted in annoyance. "Just need to clean out the wound and bandage it. Seriously, Kelly. Talk."

"No."

I looked over at her. She still had her arms folded in annoyance, and she kept tapping her foot like she was urging me to hurry up. Kelly didn't normally get pissed at me—not like Yessi did. The two of us were so alike, we often butted heads. But Kelly was supposed to be the easygoing member of our trio.

I dabbed some antibiotic ointment on Dax's leg. "Did I do something, Kel?"

"No," she said, "of course you didn't do anything. I'm going to head home. I'm not in a bar mood anymore." Before I could stop her, she rushed out of the office.

"You definitely did something."

I glanced up at my patient. A scar bisected one of his eyebrows, and I wondered for a moment what happened there. "Thanks. Yeah, I know."

"You know what it is?"

"Not a clue." I carefully placed a bandage on Dax's ankle. "She just got home—we're roommates; she lives in my basement—and I was so excited to have her around again, because I'd been so lonely while she was gone, but now she won't even talk to me, and I'm not even sure what I did." I paused.

"Am I good here?" Dax asked after a beat.

He actually didn't care about any of this, not that I could blame him. I patted his ankle and stood. "All better."

He slowly rose from the chair, and his blue eyes met mine, knocking the breath right out of me. God, he was pretty. If I were ten years younger...heck, who was I kidding? If I were ten years younger, I still wouldn't have the guts to go for a guy with that many tattoos. He'd probably think I was a huge dork. But, then again, was I just imagining it, or was he looking at me like he wanted me for a snack? I tucked some hair behind my ear. *I think he might kiss me.* I subtly licked my lips.

"Thank you, ma'am," he said.

Thud. That sound was my ego crashing to the ground.

I was in a bar, made up and dressed to the nines (or, well, maybe like the six-point-fives) with my Julia Roberts in *Pretty Woman* legs on full display, and this twentysomething bartender called me *ma'am.*

Cool.

"You're very welcome, *sir*," I said as he limped toward the door.

With his hand on the knob, he turned around and said, "You know, maybe your friend isn't responsible for your loneliness."

"Okay, pal," I said sarcastically. Who said something like that to a stranger? "Thanks for the tip."

He left the room, and I finished cleaning up and putting

the first aid kit away. How dare this young guy give me life advice? He didn't know me. And besides, Kelly and I were fine. She was simply having a hard time tonight, readjusting to her old life.

Tomorrow was another day, and we'd be back on track.

CHAPTER FOUR

Women of Questionable Morals

"Thank you so much for coming with me," I told Kelly as we got out of my car and headed up my mother's front walk.

"No problem," she said. "You know I love your mom." Kelly grinned like the Cheshire cat. The midday sun glinted off her sparkling eyes. "And she loves me."

"Too frickin' true." My mom did love Kelly, who was bubbly and sweet and not quite as uptight as her firstborn child. My mom loved Kelly so much, she'd even tried hard to set her up with my brother when we were all in our twenties. Thank goodness it didn't work out. I wouldn't have been able to live with the image of the two of them together seared upon my brain.

After all the drama at the bar last night, things had mellowed today to a "strained family Thanksgiving dinner" comfort level. Like we'd all tacitly agreed we weren't going to mention Uncle John's conspiracy theories while we politely passed the mashed potatoes and discussed the weather.

When I came downstairs this morning, I found Kelly

humming while making coffee in the kitchen. When she cheerfully handed me a mug, I decided I wasn't going to question it.

Carrying a bag from Tony's Deli and an iced coffee from Dunkin' for me, I yanked open the front door of the house where I grew up. "Mom, we're here!" No answer.

This was my normal Saturday routine—wake up, check messages for work or sometimes put in a few hours at the office, and then head over to my mom's house for lunch. I knew she was expecting me. She was always expecting me.

Kelly and I walked toward the back of the house. "Mom?" I called again. Were we at the point where I needed to get her one of those buttons to wear around her neck in case she fell? "Mom!"

"Annie!" The voice came from outside. "We're in the backyard!"

Phew. No Life Alert today.

I set the lunch bag on the kitchen counter, and Kelly and I headed out back. My mom, in her early seventies with close-cropped gray hair and not a stitch of makeup on her lined, olive-toned skin that matched mine, sat on the patio with another woman about her age—a woman who'd grown small and frail since I'd last seen her.

"Kelly, my dear!" My mom, ignoring me, popped up from her seat and wrapped my friend in a gigantic hug.

"So good to see you, Mrs. Kyle," Kelly said, winking at me over my mom's shoulder.

I beamed at her. That teasing smile had been the most normal moment between us since she got home.

My mom finally let Kelly go. "How are your parents?"

"They're fine."

I turned my attention to my mother's guest, letting my mom and Kelly continue their little chitchat. "Mrs. Casey," I said, doing a quick assessment. She'd lost quite a bit of weight, and her pale skin had taken on a translucent, papery quality. "Nice to see you. How are you?"

"I'm fine, dear," Mrs. Casey said.

No, she wasn't. I could tell. My doctor spidey senses were tingling.

"Regina," my mom said, "you remember Annie's friend Kelly?"

Mrs. Casey narrowed her eyes, thinking. "I believe I do. It's good to see you again."

"Nice to see you, too, Mrs. Casey."

"Regina," she said.

Kelly grinned, sipping her coffee. "Of course. Regina."

I stared at her in disbelief. She had really done a one-eighty since last night when she'd been mad and weepy. This morning, she'd adopted the persona of a Disney princess—all rainbows and sunshine. Maybe she'd just needed a good night's sleep.

"Annie"—my mom, having returned to her seat, pushed one of the patio chairs toward me with her foot—"Regina stopped by for coffee this morning." She frowned, glancing at her friend, who nodded an assent. "Her cancer is back."

That was my fear. Damn it. "Mrs. Casey, I'm so—"

"Regina." She reminded me to call her that every time I saw her, but I just couldn't do it. She had been my next-door neighbor and school principal growing up, and she'd always hold a position of authority for me, even thirty years later.

"How are you feeling?" I asked, purposefully avoiding using her name. "Who's your doctor?"

"Dr. Stucco at Lutheran General," she said.

I made a mental note to do some research on this doc... the name wasn't familiar. "You like them?" I asked.

"Yes," she said. "He wasn't my main doctor the last go-round, but he was on the team."

Kelly sipped her coffee. "Dr. Annie is on the case." She squeezed my mom's hand. "No reason to worry. Superwoman over here will take care of everything."

Blushing, I turned to Mrs. Casey. "Are you doing chemo? Radiation?"

"I start chemo this week."

I nodded, taking it in. "You know you can call me with any questions or concerns. I *want* you to call me." I looked pointedly at my mother. "You, too—keep me updated on everything, and I'll intervene if necessary."

I wasn't an oncologist, but at least I knew how to work the system if necessary. And if this Dr. Stucco turned out to be a bust, I could refer Mrs. Casey—*Regina*, sorry, still couldn't do it—to someone whose reputation I knew better.

"Thank you, Annie," Mrs. Casey said. "I appreciate it." She patted my mom's hand, and I realized then that a silent tear had trickled down my mother's cheek. She and Mrs. Casey had been best friends for four decades, and the thought of losing her had to be too much to bear. They were like Kelly and me—thick as thieves, friends forever, each other's person. And since my dad had died, my brother had moved to Texas, and I was busy with work, Mrs. Casey had been the one daily constant in my mom's life. No wonder she'd chosen to stay in this house instead of moving in with me when I offered the bottom floor of my three-flat to her. Her person lived right next door.

"How's Rob taking all this?" my mom asked, wiping her eyes and shoring up her shoulders, attempting to appear fine and strong for her friend.

"Rob?" Kelly whispered to me. "Who's Rob?"

"Mrs. Casey's son." I blushed. "You remember..." My entire face was on fire now.

Kelly nodded knowingly. "Oh, yeah. I remember." She waggled her eyebrows. "Mr. Boob Honker."

Kelly knew the entire story of my life, one chapter of which included Rob taking me, a junior, to his senior prom, which was quickly followed by some hand stuff in the back of his car, the first time I'd ever made it past first base.

Mrs. Casey chuckled. "I think Rob's in a bit of denial, but I'm so lucky to have him around." Her grin morphing into a frown, she glanced over the fence, toward her own house. Rob had moved back in with his mom after his dad died a few years ago.

"What is it, Reg?" my mom asked.

"Nothing." Eyes bright, Mrs. Casey shook her head. "It's nothing. You know how it goes. Sometimes I just have those moments of realization that things will be ending for me— sooner or later," she added quickly. "It's a symptom of being over seventy more than anything."

My mom squeezed her hand. "Regina, you're going to be okay."

"You *are*," I said. "We're all going to take good care of you."

"I know." Mrs. Casey smiled. "It's just, any brush with mortality like this gets you thinking, that's all." Her lip quivered. "I'm worried about leaving Robbie alone."

My mom jumped up from her chair, ran to Mrs. Casey, and hugged her from the back. Once again, my chest tightened at the thought of Kelly and me like this, in our seventies, one of us on the verge of losing the other. After three months without her in the house with me, I honestly wondered how I would survive if I were the one left behind. Being alone did not suit me.

"Don't talk like that!" my mom said. "You're going to be fine, and no matter what, Rob will be, too."

"I know, I know." Mrs. Casey shrugged her off. My mom took the hint and went back to her seat. "It's silly. I know that Robbie has his friends and his business—he has a very full life—but I'd like to see him settled down, you know, to leave with the knowledge that *someone* will be there for him, no matter what."

"His friends will be there for him." I didn't know Rob very well as an adult—we were just Facebook friends—but I could tell he had a large group of long-term buddies who always had his back. "He'll be fine."

Mrs. Casey shook her head. "His friends have all settled down. They have families."

I was about to say it didn't matter that they all had families of their own now, that their friendships would stand the test of time, but, no, Mrs. Casey did have a point. Yessi and I were still close, but she had Polly and Olivia now, not to mention her career. Naturally, she couldn't be there for me and Kelly like she could back in our twenties.

"I want to see him married again," Mrs. Casey said. "Maybe that's selfish of me, but…it's how I feel."

My mom squeezed her friend's hand. "I totally get it, Regina."

I shot Kelly a "kill me now" look. I'd heard this song and dance not infrequently from my mother—that she wanted to see me settled down and married, as if that would signal the end of my story, like people didn't grow or change or get divorced or die or anything like that, like marriage was the final nail in someone's coffin. I was a doctor with a very successful practice—a job that kept me busy seven days a week. People paid a hefty fee for me to be at their beck and call. Maintaining romantic relationships had always been tricky, and my mom knew that. Still, none of that counted for anything in her mind. She'd only be fully proud of me when I had a ring on my finger.

And now they were discussing poor Rob behind his back, making assumptions about what he wanted. He owned his own construction business and worked a ton, too. From what I could ascertain on Facebook, he seemed happy and content. He'd already tried the marriage thing once, and apparently it hadn't worked out.

Maybe Rob was fine on his own, like me. And Kelly.

For me, marriage had never been the be-all and end-all. It had never been a priority. I knew at a young age that I didn't want kids, and so I never felt that urge to partner up. Having a spouse was great for some people, but I had something equally great—a best girlfriend who was also perpetually single and who'd be my ride-or-die companion through our adult lives. We'd been talking about it for years—traveling around the world together after retirement, buying a home down in Florida, drinking daiquiris, and carrying on affairs with various pool boys.

I nudged Kelly gently in the side, and she shot me a smile tinged with sadness. She was so sensitive, Mrs. Casey's story was probably hitting her right in the feels.

Then, suddenly, her eyes lit up mischievously. "Maybe Rob and Annie should get together."

I glared at her. I expected that kind of comment from my mom, but not from my traitorous best friend.

"I've always thought you and Rob would make a great couple. Annie, you know that." My mom's eyes turned dreamy. *Thank you so much, Kelly, for putting this particular bee in her bonnet. Now I'll never hear the end of it.*

"Rob always has such nice things to say about you," Mrs. Casey said.

"I haven't talked to Rob in a long time," I said, "but he was always nice to me when we were kids." I tactfully left out the part about losing my hand virginity to him.

"You *are* both single and about the same age," my mom said.

I laughed off her comment. "Like that's all it takes, Mom. We're not pandas at the zoo."

"Circumstance is a powerful thing." Kelly looked as dreamy as my mom now. She was probably trying to imagine which of Rob's groomsmen she'd hook up with at our wedding.

"Okay, so why don't *you* go out with him?" I said, smiling sweetly. "You're here today. That's as much circumstance as me being here."

"We were talking about you, not me."

"I appreciate that, but I'm fine on my own. You all know this." I had the dating apps on my phone. Sometimes I even looked at them. I wasn't utterly useless, dating-wise. "I understand this is all coming from a good place, but it's making me uncomfortable."

"Annie, we're just trying to help," my mom said.

"I get that, but it feels a little like you're ganging up on me," I said.

Kelly snapped out of her daydream. "We're not ganging up on you, Annie. We love you and want you to be happy."

"I am happy," I said, shrugging, "and the only reason you guys are pushing this is because Rob is single and I'm single. That's it. I think I've spoken to him twice in twenty years. Why on earth do you think Rob Casey is the key to my happiness?"

"And why are you one hundred percent sure he isn't?" Kelly asked.

Well, I didn't have an answer for that.

"You and Rob should exchange numbers, at least," my mom said, pulling out her phone.

"Mom—" I warned.

"I'm not trying to start anything, Annie. Seriously." She tapped on her phone.

I chuckled. "Sure you're not."

"I mean it. You're right that we were only trying to push you two together because you both happen to be unattached right now. I'm sorry, and I won't do it again."

I narrowed my eyes, watching her carefully. I didn't buy it. She never gave up this easily.

She scrolled through her phone. "I'm just saying, Rob

should be able to reach you in case Regina needs anything, or if Rob has any questions about her care."

Damn it. She'd played me like a fiddle, and she knew it. She pretended to drop the whole dating-Rob scenario and tapped into my doctor gene, knowing that I'd never be able to live with myself if I didn't do all I could to support Mrs. Casey. "Okay. He's welcome to contact me if he has any *health-related* questions."

My phone pinged, and I looked down. My mom had already sent me Rob's number. That woman worked quick. I loaded his contact info into my address book.

"But that's it." I raised my eyebrows at my mother and Mrs. Casey. "He should call me only in my official doctor capacity."

All three women stared at me, wide-eyed and innocent. Kelly blinked.

"Of course, Annie." Mrs. Casey winked at my mom, who passed it on to Kelly.

Shaking my head, I stood. I had to get out of here and away from the three matchmakers trying to orchestrate a love connection. "I'll bring out our sandwiches," I said, leaving the three of them to plan my imaginary future nuptials to one Robert James Casey.

CHAPTER FIVE

Lights, Camera, Questions!

J en the producer smiled at me reassuringly. "Just act natural. Do doctor stuff."

I haltingly reached for my iPad, which sat next to me on the large, round counter in the middle of our office space. I held the tablet as if it were a foreign object I'd never encountered before. With one barely functioning hand, I attempted to push my glasses up over the bridge of my nose.

"Annie," my physician's assistant, Tina, hissed into my ear. "She said act 'natural.' You have heard that word before, right?"

"Of course I have." I gave up on the iPad, setting that back down. Dealing with any kind of modern technology right now was not going to end well for me. Instead, I went analog, grabbing the nearest pen and pretending to scrawl some very important words on a pad of paper.

"She's doing fantastic," boomed a deep, melodic voice from the doorway.

I glanced up and found a very familiar face grinning at me, a face I had seen hundreds of times before—not in person, but on TV and on massive billboards splashed all over I-294. Hand out and ready to shake, he strode across the room toward me.

"Doctor Annie Kyle." He took my hand in both of his large, warm, smooth ones. "So delightful to finally meet you." He winked.

Little points of heat formed on my cheeks. "Nice to meet you, too, Mr. Carver."

He patted my hand. "Darius, please."

As he wandered over to speak to his producer, Tina got right up in my face and started whisper-squealing in my ear. "Oh my god, he is hotter than he looks on television I am going to faint I swear to you right now I am going to faint prepare yourself for that eventuality."

"Tina," I said calmly, mentally trying to reroute the blood rushing to my face. "He's just a human being. And it's not like he's the first famous person to step into this office."

"No, but he is the most beautiful. I mean, even you with your weak eyes can see that." She flicked the side of my glasses.

Yes, I could see through my nearsightedness and astigmatism that Darius Green, Man on Main Street reporter for WTS TV, was a very good-looking human being. I wasn't kidding when I said that we were used to having famous people in this office—my clients ran the gamut from a former *Top Chef* contestant to, of course, the lead anchorwoman at Darius's station, Gayle Gale, an icon in Chicago if ever there was one.

But Darius did outshine them all, objectively, looks-wise, even if he was a little plasticky for my taste. I'd gone out a few times with another TV newsman, who gave off the same aura of perfection. Darius's teeth were whiter and straighter than the laws of nature allowed. His dark brown skin glowed in a way that suggested a bathroom cabinet full of expensive creams and serums.

And, besides, he was here in a professional capacity, so even thinking about his looks was out-of-bounds.

"Annie." Darius returned to me, and a whiff of spice and wood hit my nostrils. "Jen showed me the footage so far, but I need a bit more. Can we get you into an exam room with a patient?"

I checked the clock. I'd blocked out an hour for this interview. My next patient wouldn't be here for another forty-five minutes. "We'd have to wait…and I'm not sure my patient would be okay with that. They're very private."

He glanced at his watch. "I have to depart before then anyway. Maybe you know someone who can pose as a patient?" His high-wattage smile tractor-beamed right to Tina, who nearly melted into a puddle. She reacted to Darius the same way she reacted to her favorite K-Pop acts, or whatever they were called, on YouTube.

But she rallied quickly, and her hand shot up. "Me," she said with authority. "Yes, I will do it." She reached behind the desk and grabbed her gym bag. "Call me 'Mrs. Chestnut,' heir to a generations-old beverage company, who has been carrying on an affair with a member of the British royal family."

"You are aware you won't have any lines," Darius said.

"I still need to get in character."

As Tina left the room, I said, "She started out as a theater major."

"What happened?"

I winced. "She can't act."

Darius chuckled, and the sound of his titter resonated off the office walls. "While she's preparing herself, why don't you and I sit down for the interview."

I led Darius, Jen, and their cameraman to my private office. After I took the seat behind my desk, Jen came around and helped me with a microphone. "I'm a little self-conscious about appearing on camera." I shot Jen a shy smile as she pushed my long, brown hair over my shoulder. I usually wore it up in a ponytail, but today, because of the interview, I tried to style it myself, with curlers and everything. I'd even put on mascara, only managing to poke myself in the eye twice. A new record! Normally I would've had Kelly do the whole beautification thing for me, but she'd been scarce since the weekend—probably making up for lost time at work. "I wouldn't normally do something like this, but Gayle convinced me it'd be the right move for my business."

"She's right." Darius unbuttoned his suit jacket and settled into the guest chair on the other side of my desk. "I've interviewed all kinds of people, from teachers to research scientists to busboys. This particular series is all about highlighting folks with various jobs around Chicago. When Gayle told me about you and your practice, I knew we had to talk. I'd heard about concierge medicine but didn't know much about it. This is our chance to educate the public"— his white teeth flashed my way, his handsomeness sending a giddy thrill down my spine—"and give your business the publicity it deserves."

I took a deep breath as Jen and the cameraman checked

my lighting and did some other video-related stuff that I certainly didn't learn in med school. I smoothed down my baby blue button-down shirt under my pristine white lab coat. I could feel my brain swirling and a bout of lightheadedness coming on. I knew it was just nerves, but the sensation unsettled me.

"Okay, Annie," Darius said. "You ready?"

I nodded, swallowing, trying to quickly dissolve the dry knot that had developed in my throat. I was going to blow this. I was about to make a fool of myself on national television. Okay, not "national" television, but WTS was a superstation, right? People from here to Nebraska would tune in to watch me make a jackass of myself.

Very cool and exciting. Thank you for goading me into this, Gayle Gale.

I felt my lips pull into something I hoped resembled a smile.

Darius leaned across the desk. "Just act natural," he whispered.

There was that word again.

"Pretend we're just two people having a conversation."

His warm smile did ease my nerves a bit. The gorgeous man was right. I'd do fine. This was just a simple chat on a topic I knew well.

"Let's go," I croaked. "I'm ready."

I grabbed a sip of water from the mug on my desk as Darius did a quick intro.

"We'll do the voice-over later, but for now, I'll just say I'm here today talking to Dr. Annie Kyle, a Chicago physician, who has a very unique kind of job." He smiled at me again, and I almost forgot about the microphone on my lapel. "We're going to edit this down for time, so you and I can keep our banter casual here. Don't worry about going too long or too in depth on your answers." He paused and drew in a breath. "Dr. Kyle, why don't you start by telling us what kind of doctor you are."

Just a conversation. Just a conversation. A chat all about me. This is a test I can't fail because I know all the answers. "I'm a concierge doctor."

"A concierge doctor?" He chuckled, and I knew it was a laugh of faux surprise because Gayle had told him exactly what I did for a living and he'd just mentioned it a few minutes ago. "Concierge? Like at a hotel." He nodded slightly, urging me to go on, to give him more to work with.

Easier said than done.

"Yeah." I looked right in the camera, and the cameraman shook his head fiercely. *Come on, Annie.* My eyes shot back to Darius. "Yeah. Like the hotel thing, but not…"

I noticed him glance at Jen as if sending an SOS message. *Great.* "Can you explain exactly what a concierge doctor does?"

"Yes," I said, then nodded. My body parts had stopped cooperating with one another. It was the iPad all over again. "A concierge doctor…" I straightened my torso. "A concierge doctor is a regular physician, but patients pay me a monthly fee…"

"And what does that get them?" He smiled encouragingly.

"It gets them…" Again, my eyes snapped to the camera; again, I had to pull them away. I touched the inside of my wrist. My pulse was racing. I drew in a deep breath. *Just a conversation. Hardly anyone is going to see this—just the millions of people in the greater Chicagoland area. I'm only here to explain what I do. That's it.*

I straightened my shoulders. "It gets them access," I said with more confidence. "I take on a smaller patient list, so I'm on call for them twenty-four seven and it's much easier for them to get in and see me when they want to. I'm available to my patients, whenever they need me."

There. That wasn't so bad. Darius and his team of editors could do something with that. Probably.

"So you're on call constantly?"

I scratched my neck and accidentally moved the microphone. Jen ran over to fix it. I folded my hands tightly in my lap to keep from making that mistake again. "Um... yes. I'm the only doctor in the practice right now—my mentor, who brought me in, retired about a year ago—which means I'm officially on call all the time."

"That must be tough on your social life." Darius winked.

A blush crept up my neck, and I checked myself before I said *What social life?* "It's okay," I said. "My patients don't really abuse the situation. But, yeah, my time is never really my own. There's always that looming responsibility. I can't let go and unwind like other people."

"If you were to unwind," he said with a smirk, "what would you do with your time?"

"Um..." I frowned. What did anyone do with their time? "I like running. I watch a lot of TV and movies."

"That's fun." He smiled encouragingly. "Do you travel?"

"I haven't been on vacation in years," I said.

"Because you can't take time off, or...?"

"Because I *choose* not to. Because my job is what I do with my time. My mentor, Katherine, brought me into this practice because she knew how seriously I would take the job." I leaned forward, feeling a bit more secure. "I could bring in another doctor or someone to cover for me once in a while, and maybe I'm a perfectionist, but I don't feel comfortable doing that. This is my vocation, and I'm fully committed to it. Besides, with a practice like this—" I clamped my mouth shut.

"With a practice like this…?" Darius raised his eyebrows, encouraging me to continue.

"I just meant that in a practice like this, I have a lot of VIP clients. I mean, to me, all my clients are VIPs, but some of them are also, quite literally, very important people, even outside the doctor's office." I chuckled. "I don't feel comfortable handing their care off to just anyone."

My moment of levity appeared to encourage Darius. "You won't name any names?"

"Oh, of course not." Shocked that he would even ask that, I felt my eyes widen.

He tapped his note cards on the desk. "So, in this series, we obviously like to find out all we can about the subjects' jobs, but also how those careers affect the rest of your life." He flashed his megawatt smile again, along with a quick wink. "I'd like to go back to the social life thing. Are you married?"

"No," I said.

"Dating anyone?"

I shook my head.

"Is it safe to assume that it's pretty tough to date when you're on call so much of the time?"

"Well, yes," I said. "And also it's hard to find a guy who

understands that my job and my patients come first. I worked hard to get to where I am, and I need to find someone who's okay with—"

My phone buzzed, and I glanced down.

"'Okay with...'" Darius prompted me.

"I'm sorry." I snatched my phone off the desk, holding it close to my chest, shielding the screen from his eyes as well as the looming camera lens. One of my patients was contacting me with an urgent question of a very private persuasion. "I need to return this call."

"Ironic that we were just talking about how your job affects the rest of your life."

"Just how it goes." I stood, and Jen rushed over to remove the microphone from my shirt collar. "I'm so sorry that we have to cut our interview short, but you wanted to know what being a concierge doctor was like." I grinned, shrugging.

"You're right. I did want to know all about your career." Darius glanced at his watch. "And I think I want to know more. I *need* to know more. I know our time is almost up today, but can I come back early next week?"

Shit. And here I thought I'd escaped. "I'll have to check my schedule."

"Fine," he said. "Do that and get back to me." My phone buzzed again. This time it was Darius sending me his contact information.

"Okay," I said. "Will do."

Darius held out his well-manicured hand again, and I shook it. "Nice to make your acquaintance, Annie. We'll talk again soon." The overhead lights glinted off his teeth, and again my knees buckled slightly. I didn't normally go gaga over celebrities, but I actually watched Darius on the news, and he was just as impressive in person.

Sending a quick text back to my patient, I headed toward the door. "It was really nice talking to you."

"Next time, I want to dig deeper into your need to find someone who understands the rigors of your career."

I turned around.

He shrugged, looking vulnerable for the first time today. "That really hit home with me." He flashed a smile. "Call me to set up a time to talk again."

"I will." Swallowing the knot that had developed in my throat, I held up my phone. "I really have to handle this, though. Goodbye." Then I pulled open the door, stepped into the lobby, tripped on the rug, and nearly fell flat on my face.

CHAPTER SIX

The One With All the Trivia

After a long day of regular work stuff on top of the Darius interview—after which Tina kept reminding me about how I face-planted onto the floor by saying over and over again that this was a life lesson for her that she should *always* keep her phone camera on, always—I wanted nothing more than to head home, put on sweatpants, and curl up in front of the TV. But Kelly, who'd been fairly absent all week, had insisted that I meet her for trivia tonight, for, as she put it, "old times' sake."

Since I got to O'Leary's Barn a little early, I grabbed us a table, pulled out my phone, and settled in. Kelly'd said she'd be here around six fifteen, and it was only about six now.

Dax the bartender came over and wiped down my table. "What can I get you?"

"You're waiting tables now?"

He nodded back toward the bar. "There's a new guy. Our boss wants him to train behind the bar tonight. One of our usual waitresses called in sick, so here I am." He smiled and held up his order pad and pen. I ignored the whiff of a butterfly in my stomach. It had only popped up because he was wearing a Talking Heads T-shirt. Nothing Dax-specific. People who appreciated David Byrne were my kind of people, generally. It wasn't like I'd ever be interested in a way-too-young guy who'd *ma'am*ed me.

"How's your leg?" I asked.

He tapped on his thigh with his pen. "Good as new."

"I'll have an old-fashioned, thanks," I said.

"You got it." He turned on his heel and went back to the bar.

I played around on my phone for a few minutes—returning some emails and texts—until Dax came back with my drink. I checked the clock. Six sixteen. Still no Kelly.

"Thanks," I said as Dax set the drink in front of me.

"Where's your partner in crime?" he asked, dimples flashing. Where Darius, the superstar news guy, was all polish and sheen, Dax was more rugged and unkempt. He had what appeared to be a perpetual five o'clock shadow, unrelenting bedhead, and that scar bisecting one of his eyebrows. But all that was just me objectively noticing people's physical characteristics. As a doctor, it was my job to pay attention to details.

"You're being extra chatty today."

"You left me a thirty-dollar tip last week," he said. "Your bill was ten."

"Ah." I sipped my drink. "So this friendliness is economic."

"Sure."

"Kelly's on her way," I said. "We're doing trivia tonight."

"Well, good luck." Solemnly, he nodded toward the spot near the front of the bar where the quiz master was setting up his trivia paraphernalia. "No one beats the Very Stable Geniuses."

"The who?" I narrowed my eyes.

"The front table. They're the reigning champs."

I followed his finger to where he was pointing and found a table of younger white guys, probably in their twenties, who'd come to the bar dressed in button-down shirts and ties. "They're babies. They won't be able to compete with Kelly and me." I could feel my competitive spirit rising. The Very Stable Geniuses hadn't met me yet.

My entire life, I'd never been the hottest girl in the room, but I'd always managed to shine in this kind of environment—whether quiz night at a bar or Academic Bowl in high school. The Very Stable Geniuses wouldn't know what hit them. I knew shit. Lots and lots of random shit.

Dax glanced at his watch. "They may be competing against just you, if your friend doesn't make it."

"Oh, she's on her way." I checked the phone again. Six twenty. No Kelly. No texts. "This was her idea."

Dax leaned down, and I drew in his scent of spice and hops. "I know, no cheating, but if you need help on any of the questions, I'm pretty good at trivia."

"Is this about the tip again?"

"Yes," he said, "but I also know a shocking amount of useless info." He smirked. "I can pretend to be delivering you a fresh drink or a bowl of nuts…"

"I'll be fine, thanks." Blushing, I picked up my phone and pretended to check a very important text. I couldn't tell what his angle was yet, beyond the tip thing, but I knew somehow he was messing with me. And I, Dr. Annie Kyle, would not be messed with.

Dax took the hint and went back to the bar.

I scrolled through Facebook for a few minutes, getting into a quick fight with my cousin, who believed everything he saw on whatever his preferred confirmation-bias news source was at the moment. When I sensed the door to the bar opening, I glanced up eagerly. Kelly. It had to be. We were going to kick ass and take names tonight.

But it wasn't her. A woman with thick, curly, brown hair up in a knot on top of her head and a cheeky chipmunk smile on her freckled face stepped in and glanced around.

"Yessi! Oh my goodness!" I jumped up and ran to my friend, pulling her into a hug, her chin hitting my collarbone. "What are you doing here?" I released her from my clutches.

"Kelly invited me." Yessi glanced around, searching for our mutual bestie. "Where is she?"

"Not here yet." I gestured toward one of the chairs, and Yessi took a seat. I couldn't suppress my smile. "This is so fun!"

Yessi narrowed her serious dark brown eyes. "This isn't going to end in you and me yanking each other's hair out during the sixth round again?"

I laughed. "No! This time we have a mutual enemy." I nodded toward the table at the front. "The Very Stable Geniuses."

Yessi appraised them and turned back to me. "Oh, screw those guys. They won't know what hit them."

I beamed. "I'm so glad you're here." My heart swelled in my chest. Kelly had put this together—a fun evening, just the three of us girls, like back in our twenties. Excitement and joy pumped through me. I hadn't realized just how much I needed a night like this.

I rose from my seat. "Let me get you something to drink."

"A beer," Yessi said. "They say it's good for milk production or something." She cupped her hands around her heavy breasts.

"How's Olivia doing, by the way?" Yessi had texted me after the emergency room. Olivia just had an earache.

"Back to her old self," Yessi said. "Complaining about everything, but she's fever free."

"You want a Green Line?" I asked. "I think they have it on draft."

She smiled. "You know me too well."

Taking a few deep breaths, I pushed through the crowd and up to the bar. Dax was on the other side, talking to some other woman—some pretty young thing with reddish-blond hair and an eager smile. He leaned across the bar, resting on one elbow, eyes wide. He was chatting her up. It only proved that whatever he was doing talking to me a few moments ago wasn't flirting or anything more than acting as a waiter looking for a good tip. I was—and always would be—way too old for him. There was power in recognizing that.

With each step I took toward forty, I became more and more invisible. Dax had probably offered to help me with trivia as part of a Boy Scout's instinct to practice kindness to one's elders.

"A-hem," I said impatiently. I would not wait around for whatever...*this*...was.

A few seconds later, he slowly turned and beamed when he saw it was me. "Annie, what can I get you?"

"Green Line," I said. "Draft, please."

He grabbed a glass.

"It's for my friend Yessi."

As he poured the beer, he looked over at my table.

"Kelly's still on her way. She invited Yessi to come do trivia tonight, like we used to do back in our twenties." I didn't normally ramble on like this to strangers, but since I now understood Dax saw me less as a person and more as a well-tipping patron, I really didn't care if I literally talked his ear off. "Yessi and I haven't hung out for real in months. She's married and has a new baby."

He set the glass down in front of me.

"And she's a big-shot lawyer, so she's always super busy. I'm so excited she's here."

His bisected eyebrow arched. "You want me to put this on your tab?"

"Just so you know, I won't need your trivia services tonight," I said, ignoring his question. I'd spent the past three months talking to essentially no one other than my patients and my mother, so I was in it to win it. "Yessi's just as competitive as I am, and we complement each other's weaknesses. Like, I'm really good at geography, pop culture, history, and biology, but Yessi knows sports, music, and literature, which are my biggest blind spots."

He blinked.

"Kelly doesn't quite have the breadth of knowledge Yessi and I do, but every so often she'll come in with an answer about something really specific that happened to the Kardashians."

"Tab?" he said.

"Yeah, tab." He turned to add the beer to my bill.

"You know what?" I said. "I'll take a sparkling rosé, too. Kelly should be here any minute."

He grabbed the bottle and wineglass, too.

"Don't break that one on your leg," I said.

He chuckled as a gust of hot wind hit us. My eyes traveled to the door just in time to see Kelly flouncing in, blond hair bouncing around her shoulders. She waited in the doorway for someone coming in behind her—a man, probably in his mid- to late-forties, with graying brown hair, tortoiseshell glasses, and a polo shirt. The milky white band of skin from his ankle down to where he wore his boat shoes with no socks suggested a golf tan.

Kelly grabbed the dude's hand and kissed it playfully—intimately.

My eyes bugged out at Dax, but he'd seen an out from my conversational clutches and had moved on to wiping down glasses and chatting with the young strawberry-blond woman across the way.

"Annie!" Kelly yelled to me with a wave. Then she dashed over to the bar, still clutching the guy's hand. "Yessi, you too! Come here quick."

Yessi ran over, and Kelly thrust out her left hand, which now sported a massive diamond solitaire on the ring finger. "Yessi and Annie, this is Mark. The two of us are getting married!"

CHAPTER SEVEN

Marky Mark and the Trivia Bunch

Mark was bringing our team down.

I kept trying to send silent signals to Yessi to say something—she was never the type to worry about feelings when victory was on the line—but she kept laughing and joking with Mark and Kelly like the Very Stable Geniuses weren't about to beat us.

I smiled along as I tried to answer as many questions as I could on my own without soliciting the help of the group.

But during the fourth round, Ronald, the quiz master, asked, "What was the largest contiguous empire in the history of the world?"

The four of us put our heads together, keeping our voices down so the other teams couldn't hear our debate.

"Not Rome," Yessi said.

"Definitely not Rome," I said, recording my answer on the sheet. I always liked to confer with my friends to keep up the veneer of being a good, collaborative teammate, but when I knew something, I knew it. "I'm pretty sure it's the Mongol Empire. In fact, I'm positive it is."

"Or is it the British Empire?" Mark asked, brows furrowed under his thick-framed glasses.

"Contiguous," I said, putting my fingers together. "Touching. The British Empire may have been the largest overall, but it was pretty spread out. Genghis Khan kept his conquests confined to Asia." I pushed my own glasses up on my nose. I knew my history.

Mark squinted. "I think this is a trick question. I'm pretty sure I heard something about the British Empire being the biggest."

I looked with frustration at Kelly, who was watching her new fiancé with big doe eyes. "Kel?" We'd been competing in trivia competitions together for years. She knew better than to oppose me when a question about maps was on the line.

"Let's go with Mark's answer," she said, squeezing her beau's hand.

"I agree with Kelly," Yessi said. "Let's give Mark this one. He seems pretty sure."

My jaw dropped. Yessi was supposed to be on my side. Did she actually expect me to go with a wrong answer simply to coddle a grown man's feelings? I didn't like thinking it, but motherhood had changed her.

Still, I caved to peer pressure and begrudgingly went along with the group. I erased my absolutely correct answer from the line and wrote "British Empire" next to number five, knowing full well this was one answer our new team—Wine O'Clock (Mark's idea, since he owned a wine shop in Galena)—would be getting wrong.

I wouldn't let this get under my skin. I barely knew Mark.

If Kelly loved him, it probably meant he was a good guy. I was the asshole who hated to lose. "Are you a big history buff, Mark?" I asked.

Sipping his wine, he grinned. "Nah," he said, "but you know, sometimes you just hear something and remember it." He tapped on his temple.

Or, you know, you hear something and remember it completely incorrectly.

Stop it, Annie. It was just one itsy-bitsy question out of a hundred.

I leaned back in my chair and sipped my drink, watching Kelly and Mark together—playing with each other's fingers, making goo-goo eyes. Kelly had always been the romantic among us. Before she moved in with me five years ago, she'd lived with three different serious boyfriends, but she hadn't introduced us to anyone in years. I knew she dated casually and had been on a number of first dates, but nothing more than that. How had she gone from the odd fling to engagement without telling anyone about it?

I glanced at Yessi, trying to read her reaction to the situation. My no-nonsense lawyer friend had to have strong opinions about this, but she was leaning toward Mark, eyes as big and rapt as Kelly's, hanging on his every word.

After the quiz master's assistant, Meghan, had collected all the papers, Ronald started going through the answers for this round. Wine O'Clock got the first four right, boom, boom, boom, boom. "Number five," Ronald said dramatically, "the largest contiguous empire in history?"

"The Mongol Empire," shouted one of the Very Stable Geniuses up near the front.

Of course they knew it.

"That is correct." Ronald made a note on his paper.

Mark smiled sheepishly. "Sorry, Ann," he said. "Looks like you were right."

Ann. He called me "Ann." I checked Kelly's reaction to see if she was messing with me—if she'd told her fiancé to call me "Ann" as a joke, since she knew how much I loathed my formal first name. That was certainly the kind of prank we'd play on each other. But no, she was too focused on lacing her small, thin fingers between Mark's broader ones.

So, he just honestly didn't know. My roommate and very best friend in the whole world had told her fiancé so little about me that he didn't even know my preferred name. I felt my throat starting to close up with tears.

"I go by Annie, actually," I said brightly, forcing my tone to stay light. "And don't worry about the wrong answer. It happens. Everyone flubs one once in a while."

"Next time, I will defer to you." Mark stood and glanced around the table. "Allow me to atone for my sins." He winked at Kelly, who beamed. "Another round of drinks?"

"Thanks, honey!" Kelly blew him an air kiss as he headed up to the bar.

"I love him," Yessi said when Mark was out of earshot.

"Me too." Kelly grinned.

"How did you two meet?" I popped a fry into my mouth. My best course of action was to keep my mouth full at all times—whether with food or drink—to numb the sad, wistful feelings that had started creeping up and to keep myself from saying anything that might rub Kelly the wrong way. She was currently seeing the world through the lenses of someone who was about to marry a dude who owned a wine shop.

"It's really cute, actually." She examined her ring, watching the light play off the substantial diamond. "I'd just had the most frustrating day with my parents—" She raised her eyebrows, and Yessi and I understood the shorthand. As much as she loved her mom and dad, the three of them didn't see eye to eye on much. Living with them for a few months had to have been tough on her.

So that's what this was. Mark had gotten her through a tough time. Their relationship was like Keanu and Sandra Bullock at the end of *Speed*—based on an intense experience. Kelly was now back to her real life in Chicago, far away from Galena. Soon she'd no longer need Mark. Suddenly I pitied the guy. He was about to be cast aside, and he had no idea.

"I had to get out of my mom and dad's house for a little while," Kelly said, "so I drove into town and found this adorable little wine shop, and I started chatting up the owner." She gestured toward Mark at the bar, and I turned to find him laughing with Dax, just two guys enjoying each other's company. I frowned. Poor Mark. I gave their engagement a month, tops.

Kelly kept going. "I told Mark all about my family situation, and he helped me pick out the perfect wine to get through the night with my parents. Then he told me to come find him if I needed someone to talk to later." She grinned. "I took him up on that."

"How long ago was this?" I asked. "I mean, did you guys get to spend a lot of time together in Galena?"

"You met him right away, didn't you?"

My mouth fell open as my eyes traveled to Yessi, who

was tapping away, unbothered, on her phone. "You knew about this?"

She looked up at me, wide-eyed. "I… No." She clamped her mouth shut.

"You did," I said, my chest about to cave in on itself. I'd assumed Kelly had kept Mark a secret from everyone, but nope. Just from me.

"Annie." Kelly reached for me, but I pulled my arm away and shoved four fries into my mouth. Three months. She'd been seeing this guy—seriously, as there was a ring involved—for three months and had not said one word about him to me, though she'd told Yessi all about it, apparently. The lack of balance in our relationship turned the crispy potatoes to glue on my tongue.

Yessi squeezed my hand. "I haven't known that long," she promised. "Mark had been looking for some legal advice, and Kelly came to me."

I nodded slowly, taking that in.

"She was kind of forced to tell me about their relationship." Yessi laughed. "She couldn't call me up and be like, 'Hey, Yess, here's a random guy from the street who has a question about a rental lease.'"

"Sure." I supposed that made sense, but it still didn't explain why no one, over the course of three months, had ever let it slip that Kelly was seeing someone. And the fact that both Kelly and Yessi knew while I didn't made it sting even worse. It was one thing for Kelly to have a secret on her own. She was allowed to have her private life. But two of us should not hide information from the third one—unless for the express purposes of a surprise party.

Yessi grabbed one of my fries. "I think what we need to talk about now is getting Annie to join the club."

"What club?"

"You're next." Yessi's eyes glinted mischievously, and she pointed to the wedding ring on her left hand.

"Ha-ha." Since when had my dating life become an acceptable topic of discussion? First my mom and Kelly, then Darius today, and now Yessi. "You both know I'm fine on my own." Besides, I wouldn't be "on my own" for long. This thing between Kelly and Mark would play out, and then our lives would go back to normal.

"We know you are, Annie," Kelly said, glancing at Yessi, "but wouldn't it be fun for all of us to be able to get together with our significant others? You all can come out to Galena—"

I held up a hand to stop her. "Wait, what?"

Kelly's face grew pale. "Galena," she said. "I'm...well, I mean, I'm moving there, of course. It just makes sense. Mark's business is really taking off, and my mom and dad will need me around more and more as they get older. I can do real estate from anywhere." She grinned. "It will actually be great. You guys can come stay for the weekend. Mark has this huge, beautiful house in the Galena Territory."

I stared at Yessi. "I suppose you knew about this, too."

She squirmed under my gaze and pretended to check her phone.

I chewed another tasteless fry as Mark came back to the table with a bottle of wine and four glasses. "This is an excellent vintage," he said.

"None for me," I said, shaking my empty cocktail vessel. "I'm one and done." Probably another tidbit of information about me Kelly hadn't yet shared with him.

An urge to bolt hit me, but I fought it. And I blinked back tears that stung my eyes. My friends had been keeping two huge secrets from me, and as much as I wanted to believe this Mark thing was a phase, Kelly was moving to Galena for him. She was packing up her life and leaving me.

I tried to drum up some happiness for her, but any sympathetic joy I felt was muted by my own fear, sadness, and uncertainty.

For more than twenty years, ever since we met on day one of our freshman year of college, Kelly and I had been there for each other. We'd watched boyfriends come and go, together. But now she'd gone and met someone, and, though she'd opened up to Yessi, she had kept him a secret from me for three whole months.

The walls of certainty about my own life crumbled around me.

I started to rise, ready to make a break for it, but Ronald announced the next category: movies. I had to stick around for that. I knew even more about movies than I did about history and geography. I had a duty to my team and to the honor of quiz night itself, and I would not let them down.

"Make sure you have your sheets for the fifth round." After a brief pause while we gathered our things, Ronald said, "Question number one: Which two twenty-first century Best Director Oscar winners each won twice for movies that did not win Best Picture?" Ronald paused. "Bonus points if you can also name the movies."

I tapped my pencil against my teeth, thinking, running through the last twenty or so years of Oscar nominees and winners. At least this was a good distraction from the sinking pit of despair growing in my stomach.

"I know this!" Mark whispered. "Steven Spielberg and Martin Scorsese!"

"Yay, Mark," Kelly said, clapping her hands.

"Wrong." With authority, I wrote the correct answer on the line. They would not pressure me into throwing Mark a bone this time. Not on a movie question. "Martin Scorsese won for *The Departed*, which also won Best Picture. He's out. Spielberg won for *Saving Private Ryan*, which famously did *not* win Best Picture, but his only other win was for *Schindler's List*, which obviously did. And both of those movies were made in the nineties, anyway, so he's automatically disqualified." I showed my team the paper. "The correct answer is Ang Lee—*Brokeback Mountain* and *Life of Pi*—and Alfonso Cuarón for *Gravity* and *Roma*."

Mark grinned. "Wow, Annie. You really know your stuff."

"I do." I waved off his praise and listened hard for the next question, ready to crush the competition and show everyone in this room who was boss.

CHAPTER EIGHT

Tequila Mockingbird

We lost to the Very Stable Geniuses.

The young suits at the front table fist-bumped each other and downed shots of Malört in celebration, because of course they did. I watched their puckered faces as they pretended to enjoy the taste.

"We'll get 'em next time," I told my teammates as I stacked papers and collected our pencils to hand back to Ronald. I avoided mentioning that we only lost by one point—one point that could've been made up if they hadn't insisted I listen to Mark on the Mongol Empire question. But that was water under the bridge. I'd already practically moved on.

"We definitely have to do this again." Yessi draped her purse over her shoulder. "I loved getting out of the house for a while."

"For sure." Kelly gave her a hug. "I will definitely make a special trip in for this."

A frown overtook my forced grin. "Special trip?"

"I mean…" Kelly glanced nervously at Mark. "I'm moving out to Galena as soon as possible. Why keep trying to sell houses here when I won't be around to see the sales through to closing?"

"Right," I said.

She wrapped an arm around my shoulder. "But I'll still be back a ton. It'll probably take me months just to get all my crap out of your house." She laughed.

"Yeah," I said, imagining her space in the basement—bare and cold and lonely. What would I do with it? Set up yet another TV-watching station in my house? Maybe I'd try again to convince my mom to move in with me. Still, I plastered on a happy face and said, "Your crap is welcome to stay as long as you need."

Kelly beckoned Yessi and me to her. "Ladies," she said. "I want to ask you something."

I drew in a deep breath. Here it came—the inevitable question, the one I knew was coming since the moment she flashed that ring: the bridesmaid inquiry.

Smiling shyly, Kelly asked, "Will you two be my maid and matron of honor?"

And there it was.

I'd been maid of honor in Yessi's wedding, too—or, well, Kelly and I had been co-maids of honor, standing solidly as a unit in our singleness. We got a little drunk together (this was back when Katherine was still at the practice and I could afford to let loose once in a while), made fun of all the pomp and circumstance and hearts and flowers, and then she went and hooked up with one of Polly's brothers that night while I passed out alone in my hotel room with *Frasier* blaring on the TV.

It'd probably be more of the same for me this time, but

without a similarly perpetually single girlfriend to back me up. I'd be forty by then, the last unattached woman standing, forced to do shots—probably of Malört—in the corner with Kelly's college-aged cousins.

Still, I pulled her into a hug, because what else could I do? "Kel, of course I'll be your maid of honor." She was my best friend forever. In sickness or in health. Through a dating drought or a marriage, I would be there for her.

I glanced over my shoulder at the bar. We needed to commemorate this moment somehow. Our era was ending, while the Mark and Kelly dynasty was just beginning, and, though my world was crumbling around me, I would buck up and do my solemn duty as maid of honor. "You guys want to do a shot or something to celebrate?"

"I really have to go," Yessi said. "I've got to get home to pump and dump before I explode."

"Understood," I said, knowing better than to argue with a woman sporting a pair of engorged mammaries. "Kel?"

She took her fiancé's hand. "Mark and I had better head out, too. We've got a long drive back to Galena. I'm staying there through the weekend."

Galena. Tonight. So, she really was basically living there. "You're driving the three hours tonight? You guys know you can crash at my place."

"Mark has to open up the store early tomorrow," Kelly said. "But we'll definitely take you up on that another time."

"You know you'll always have a room in my house." I forced another smile. "Well, it was good to see both of you. Mark, nice to meet you." Barely looking at him, I nodded toward the new guy, the man only I hadn't known existed until tonight.

"Nice to meet you, Annie." I knew the kinds of guys Kelly usually dated—sullen artsy types with tattoos, like Dax, honestly. Mark seemed more my speed—safe, responsible, ink-free. I couldn't imagine what had drawn Kelly to him. It was the kind of thing I would've loved to discuss with her, if she had bothered to tell me she'd met someone special before it became "ring official," but now I felt like I had to keep my mouth shut. She hadn't trusted me enough to let me in before the engagement, so why would she want my opinion after the fact?

When the door had closed behind my friends, I finally fully exhaled the breath that'd been stuck in my chest for hours and headed up to the bar. I parked myself in front of the new redheaded bartender. "Hi," I said. "What's your name?"

"Peter." He shot me a sweet, gap-toothed grin on his pale, freckly face. He looked like Opie on *The Andy Griffith Show*, and not much older. Peter was even younger than Dax—maybe fresh out of college. He probably saw me and wondered how many grandchildren I had.

"I'm Annie."

"Nice to meet you, Annie." He flashed me a kind smile. "What can I get you?" He wiped down the counter in front of me.

Sucking in my bottom lip, I scanned the shelf of liquor behind him. I'd already had my allotted drink tonight. I had to stay in peak shape in case any of my patients needed me. But, hell, what was one more? I never did this kind of thing, and what were the chances that someone would need me tonight of all nights? "Give me a shot of something, please."

"Tequila?" he said.

"Sure, because no one's ever made a bad decision on tequila."

Peter set a glass and a lime in front of me, and Dax, who had been listening in, pushed a shaker of salt my way.

I wet my wrist, poured on some salt, and licked that off. Then I held up the shot as a toast and downed it, finishing up the ritual with a lime. Damn, that tasted like regret. "Another one," I told Peter.

He obliged.

"So, your friend's getting married," Dax said, coming up next to Peter.

"I suppose so." I drained another shot and twirled my index finger in the air, indicating I'd like another round.

Instead Dax set a glass of water in front of me. Buzzkill.

"You like the guy?" Peter asked.

I rolled my eyes. "No, but what does that matter?"

"Seems cool to me," Dax said, as if anyone had asked his opinion. "Knows his stuff about wine."

"Yeah, because that's what truly matters."

Dax, probably realizing his rookie mistake of wandering into this conversation, turned away and focused on glasses that needed wiping.

As I downed my third shot in short succession, the guilt started settling in. I was too responsible not to worry about the ramifications of my actions. I was the good girl, the A-student. I didn't shirk my responsibilities. I pulled out my phone and texted my assistant Tina. *Hey! Sorry this is last minute. Are you available to take calls from patients tonight?*

My BFF got 💍 and we're 🎉 🥂 .

OMG, she wrote back almost immediately. *Forward everything to me. I'm just 🐿️ 🐟 🏋️ . No problem!*

I had no idea what any of those emojis meant, but I wasn't about to question it.

Tonight I, a single woman nearing her forties who had just gotten very disappointing news, would doff her doctor hat and behave irresponsibly for once in her life.

"My friend kept her new fiancé a secret for three months," I told Peter. "Three months." I scoffed. "Though she told our other friend about him."

He frowned. "Why do you think she did that?"

"I honestly don't know." I glanced at the door, holding out hope that Kelly would rush back into the bar to admit she was wrong—that she hadn't meant anything by telling Yessi and not me. "She and I... We were supposed to grow old together, to travel the world after we retired. I even brought that up this week with her. I feel like a fool. She had so many opportunities, but she never mentioned she'd met someone."

"You're mad she told your friend and not you." A little wrinkle appeared between Peter's eyes, like he, the new guy here, was trying to catch up to my little personal soap opera.

"Yeah, Peter." He didn't get it. He probably lived in a one-bedroom apartment with his six best pals. He had a good ten to fifteen years before he knew how it felt to be the one left behind.

Dax wordlessly set one of his stellar old-fashioneds in front of me, wiped his hands, and walked away.

With stinging eyes, I squeaked out a "thank you." My throat had closed up.

One of the guys from Very Stable Geniuses sidled up next to me at the bar. "Good game tonight, Wine O'Clock," he said.

"Annie," I choked out. My old-fashioned had gone down the wrong pipe.

"Nice to meet you," he said. "I'm Brad."

Of course he was.

"You doing the citywide tournament?"

I shook my head, the alcohol and my mood and the Kelly of it all hindering my comprehension of this conversation. My brain had started to grow very fuzzy. "The what?"

"The Great Chicago Trivia Championship," he said, brow furrowed. "You don't know about it?"

"No...I've been away from the trivia scene for a while."

He pulled out his phone. "Give me your number."

I rolled my eyes. Okay, well, this was a new one. I awarded him a few points for ingenuity.

"To send you the info," he said, annoyed. "I don't want to be competing in this thing against a bunch of losers." He smiled. "I only want to beat the best."

Flattery would get him everywhere. "Ugh, fine." I rattled off my number. A few seconds later, a photo of a flyer popped up on my phone. Starting a week from Tuesday, for six weeks, a bunch of different bars around Chicago would be hosting a massive, citywide trivia tournament. Teams could have no more than eight people. It cost two hundred dollars to enter, with a five-thousand-dollar grand prize. "Dang," I said. The grand prize for trivia tonight at O'Leary's Barn was twenty-five bucks off your bill.

"Exactly," Brad said. "It's kind of amazing. Teams

compete from all around the city. It culminates in a big event on the final night for the top four teams. This bar is one of the host sites."

"Cool." I shut off my phone.

"There's a big trophy, too."

My ears perked up. "A trophy?" I had the perfect spot for it, too: right on the back of my baby grand piano.

"Do you think you and your friends might be interested?"

At the mention of my friends, I downed more of my drink. Yessi couldn't get out of the house that often, and Kelly was living in Galena now. "I don't think so."

"Too bad," he said. "I hope you find someone else to play with. The competition needs talent like yours."

A lump formed in my throat. A big part of me wanted to do it. I hadn't felt as alive as I had answering those questions tonight in I didn't know how long, but I didn't have a team. I couldn't think of one single person who'd want to spend the next six Tuesdays with me. "Thanks for the info, Brad."

"I mean," he said, "you have my number now. Feel free to text if you're ever lonely...for trivia."

Somewhat grateful to be able to channel my emotions from despair over my life into annoyance at Brad, even momentarily, I focused on the new shot Peter had just set in front of me.

"Go away, Brad." This was my life from now on: drinking alone in a bar, having no one to compete with me on my trivia team, considering a booty call with an obnoxious younger man just for something to do. I downed the shot.

"I think you're done now," Dax said, clearing away my shot glass and plate of limes.

"I think you don't know what you're talking about, my friend." I flashed a twenty and motioned to Peter to get me another drink. He, my hero, obliged me.

CHAPTER NINE

Inglourious Astirds

By the time I woke up in bed the next morning, the inside of my mouth had taken on the consistency of a gym sock—fuzzy and stinky—and I could feel the beginnings of a headache marching outward from the depths of my brain.

One by one, memories from last night popped into my head like still images from a slideshow: Kelly flouncing into the bar with a spectacular engagement ring on her finger, Mark making us lose at trivia, Peter plying me with shot after shot after shot, me talking with Dax, fighting with Dax, smelling Dax's leather jacket as he put it on at the end of the night...

For some reason I could feel the supple leather against my cheek. I brushed the sensation away and kneaded my throbbing temple.

I hadn't gotten sloppy like that since the day after I finished med school, because I rarely ever, even pre-concierge practice, allowed myself to let loose to the point of forgetting chunks of the night. As I told Darius the day before, I had responsibilities. I was a mature, adult woman.

A sad numbness lurked behind my hangover. Last night had been anything but fun and celebratory. I'd allowed myself to be overserved in order to drown out an impending sense of dread and doom. My vision blurred, and not just because I hadn't put my glasses on yet.

Kelly, my perpetually single best friend, was getting married, and I was the last spinster standing.

Not really. I mean, I didn't see it that way—not exactly. I knew neither a ring nor a mate determined my worth, but I still couldn't shake this sensation of being left behind, especially since I was the last to know Mark even existed. Yessi and Kelly were part of the "couple club," and I wasn't.

It was like back in high school when all my girlfriends suddenly started dating, and I found myself at home alone on Friday nights, watching *Boy Meets World* with my mom and dad.

Did ABC still host a TGIF lineup on Fridays? Well, I was about to find out.

No, Annie. Stop it. No more wallowing.

I'd allowed myself one night of being a pathetic, blubbering cliché. It wasn't a night I was proud of, but it was over. Now, in the light of day, I could go back to being a kick-ass concierge doctor who was fine on her own, who didn't need a man or anyone else to fulfill her, and who didn't even need a mother-sucking plant in her big empty house to keep her company.

I swung my legs over the side of the bed, pausing a moment to let my pounding brain catch up. I was never drinking like that again.

Never, ever, ever, ever. *Ever.*

I patted my bedside table, hunting for my glasses, but they were nowhere to be found. My dress from last night formed a blurry puddle in the corner of the floor, and I had fallen asleep in my bra and underwear—black lace, theoretically my "I'm feeling fun and flirty" lingerie, though I had only put it on because it happened to be clean and it had been quite some time since anyone had actually seen my underwear. I was on a bit of a dry spell.

From the counter in the adjoining bathroom, my phone buzzed, jolting me into action. After a night of foolishness, I was back on the clock now, ready to serve my patients who needed me. I had made them a promise to be there whenever they had a question or concern, and I'd shirked that duty, handing it off to Tina for the night. I wouldn't let them down again.

I just hoped nothing too emergent had happened while I was indisposed.

I padded into the bathroom, the cold tile waking up the bottoms of my bare feet, and picked up my phone. I squinted at the screen, holding it away from me and closing one eye to see better.

Fifteen messages? Crap. This couldn't be good.

Immediately I imagined all my patients in the hospital at the same time after a coincidental pileup on the Kennedy.

I clicked on the first one, from someone listed in my phone as "John the plumber." It said, *Annie, I'm flattered, but I'm married.*

An unpleasant tingling sensation snaked its way up my neck.

I looked at the next message. From Brad, Mr. Very Stable

Genius. *lol. Not for me, Annie, but you know I'm game for a hookup. Text me next time ur up late.*

My chest tightened, and my ears burned. What. The. Fuck. And "ur?" No. Absolutely not. Who was he kidding?

I scrolled to the top as a slab of lead settled in my stomach. I closed my eyes and counted to three before reading the text I had sent at 2:34 a.m. to…I counted…thirty-nine men in my contacts.

Hi, everyone! This is Annie Kyle, and I am letting you know that I am serious about settling down. Yes, that means getting married. I'm sick of playing games and pretending to be someone I'm not. I am a doctor, which means I work a lot but make a ton of money. If that scares you, that's your problem. I love TV, and I love to run. I hate coconut, but I will drink a piña colada. I don't want kids, but I may be open to, like, a turtle. If this interests you and if you are serious about marriage with me, Annie Kyle, please respond to this text. Everyone else, thank you for your time.

A pained squeak escaped from my throat, and I couldn't decide whether to run or lock myself in the bathroom forever.

As a compromise, I hurled my phone as hard as I could at the bedroom wall, watching as it slammed against the plaster. I prayed that I had smashed it to smithereens, as if that'd erase the embarrassment of last night—like fifteen men hadn't already read and responded to my embarrassing messages—like the goddamn Cloud wasn't a thing.

Oh, but it *was* a thing.

Out of nowhere, my bedroom door flew open, and who should appear but Dax. Still wearing his black jeans from last night and a white T-shirt, his dark hair shot up at all angles, and dark circles rimmed his blue eyes. "What happened? Are you okay?"

"Oh my god, what are you doing here?" I lunged for my bed and grabbed the first thing I could find—a large unicorn-shaped pillow my niece had given me for Christmas—and attempted to hide my underwear-clad body.

Dax's eyes traveled from the floor up to where the unicorn horn rose like a spire between my breasts. "I told you I would stay here."

"What? *Why?*" A little flicker of a memory popped into my head, but it was attached to Dax putting on his leather jacket, and its smell was the only thing I could recall about that moment.

"Because you drank about a gallon of tequila, and I didn't want to leave you alone."

Oh. That.

He reached down and picked up my phone, dusting it off. "I'm assuming someone responded to your text?"

I hugged the unicorn tighter. "You knew about that?" I squealed.

He held up his hands in surrender. The sunlight through the window glinted against my phone's screen. "Don't shoot the messenger. I tried to stop you."

My nostrils flared. "Why didn't you?"

His shoulders rose to his ears. "Because...I'm not your keeper, and I barely know you."

"You overserved me."

"That was Peter," he said, "and, again, not your keeper. Plus Peter and I started watering down your drinks after a while, anyway." He glanced at the phone. "How was the response?"

I reached for the phone, accidentally dropping the unicorn in the process. Oh well. What did I have to hide? I placed one hand on my hip and held the other one out expectantly. "Give it to me."

Eyes squarely on my chest, Dax passed me the phone. "What did the guys say?"

"I don't know. I only read two of the messages—both rejections, thank you very much." I stepped over to my dresser and buried the phone under a pile of my underwear, where it would live for eternity. I grabbed my robe and wrapped it around my nearly naked body.

"You're not going to look at them?"

"What's the point, Dax?" I said. "If I don't look at them, I'll never know. I'll go buy a new phone today and get a new number, and then I'll move to Wyoming and go full *Doc Hollywood* or something, and everything will be fine."

"Sounds like a plan to me." He turned to leave.

"Besides," I said, stalling him with his hand on the doorknob. "Nobody worth considering would respond to a message like that. If anyone wrote back saying they'd be up for settling down with me after one drunken text, that would be a huge red flag to avoid them."

"You're right." He pulled open the door.

"And, I mean, how would any of this even work?"

Dax turned slowly back around.

"Like, what?" I shrugged, chuckling. "Would I call one of them and say, 'Hey, yeah, person I barely know. Let's do this. Let's get married.'"

Dax's eyes narrowed. "Are you...considering this?"

"No!" I laughed. "No. Could you imagine us telling people

how we got together? That I sent a drunk text to a million guys, and this one responded? That's ridiculous."

"Yeah," he said, arching his bisected eyebrow. "It is."

I reached into my underwear drawer and pulled out my phone. "Or...is it?"

"Are you still drunk?"

I scrolled through my phone, looking quickly at the responses. A few guys actually had responded affirmatively. These were all men I at least had some rapport with. I knew what they looked like and what they did for a living. I was almost forty, and I'd never been good at the dating thing. Any time I'd tried online dating, it had been a disaster. An arrangement like this could be more my speed.

I didn't "need" a husband, but...maybe I wanted one? "These guys had the courage to respond and tell me point-blank that they feel the same way," I said. "I shouldn't reject them out of hand."

"Okay..." Dax said, hand back on the doorknob. "I'm gonna go..."

I waved him off and looked back down at the phone, focusing on the red circle with an *8* over my message icon. Kelly had met her new fiancé in a chance encounter at the wine shop he owned. Yessi had met Polly while out celebrating the night she made partner. My mom and dad had known each other back in kindergarten. Everyone had a unique story about meeting their spouse. One wasn't better than the next.

And maybe someday, my future husband and I would find ourselves, happily traveling the world, telling all the folks on our cruise ship about the day I sent out a drunken mass proposal and he responded.

CHAPTER TEN

A Team Has No Name

After Dax left that morning, I made myself some coffee, sat down at my kitchen table like I was about to pay bills or do my taxes, and read through each and every one of those responses. On a legal pad, I listed the names of all the eligible bachelors and created columns for pros and cons.

When all was said and done, one man stuck out: Robert James Casey.

His pro list was long. I found him attractive. He owned his own successful business, and he was good to his mother. Having grown up together, we already knew a lot about each other and could skip over the whole "getting to know you" phase.

Cons, I wasn't so sure about. He'd been married before, but that wasn't necessarily a bad thing. And, if I remembered correctly, he liked watching sports a lot, which was one of my least favorite recreational activities, but we were talking about marriage here, not fusing our bodies together. He could watch sports on his own time.

One item straddled both lists: my mom loved him.

If I ended up marrying Rob, I would never, ever, ever hear the end of it.

At lunchtime on Saturday, I headed out, as usual, to my mom's house. Already things were not going as planned. I'd wanted to get out to Edison Park early, to get my chat with Rob over and done with before lunch, but I had several patient calls I had to take.

No problem. Mom and I would eat together, assuming I could choke anything down, and then I'd head over to Rob's.

As I pulled into my mom's driveway and shut off the engine, my eyes traveled to Rob's house, right next door, a big, old, yellow-brick Chicago bungalow with a mossy green awning across the front windows. I saw no lights on in the house, but that didn't mean anything. It was midday, and the sun was out.

I hadn't even considered that he might not be home. Frick. I'd been going for the element of surprise. I should've planned this better. Damn it.

Oh well. Couldn't dwell on that now. I grabbed the bag of sandwiches from Tony's Deli and headed into my mom's house.

Voices came from the back of the house. Probably my mom watching the news on TV. She kept it on all day, every day, whenever she was awake. "Mom!" I called.

"In here!" she responded.

I tossed my heavy purse on the wingback chair just inside the front room and headed back toward the kitchen. "Something smells good," I said. "Did you ba—"

I stopped short as I realized my mother was not alone. Sitting at the island in the middle of the room was a very

familiar-looking man about my age, with blond hair that had
dulled slightly since our teen years, sun-tanned skin, and
muscular arms peeking out from under an old Cubs T-shirt
with Greg Maddux's name and number on it. Back when we
were kids, he'd always reminded me of Johnny Lawrence
from *The Karate Kid*, in a good way. I'd always found Johnny
much hotter than Daniel LaRusso.

"Hi, Rob." My throat nearly closed up. We were supposed
to meet at his house, not here. At least that was the way I
had planned it in my head while also foolishly neglecting to
relay that plan to anyone else.

He smiled, looking just as nervous as I felt. "Good to
see you, Annie."

"Robbie came over to help fix my sink." My mom passed
him a plate of homemade chocolate chip cookies. "It started
leaking yesterday."

He raised one of the cookies, smiling. "This is my pay-
ment."

"Thank you so much, Rob," I said sincerely. I let that
sentence do some heavy lifting—thanking him for being there
for my mom when I couldn't be and expressing my gratitude
in advance for him not saying anything embarrassing in front
of her while he was at it.

"Maybe you want to join us for lunch," my mom said.

Both of our heads snapped to her. Lunch. With Rob
Casey. And my mother. I'd never survive it. Not today. "I'm
sure Rob has—" I started to say.

He stood and chimed in. "I do," he said. "I'm meeting a
client about a kitchen remodel."

"Next time, then," my mom said as Rob leaned down to

kiss her on the cheek.

I knotted my fingers together as I worked up my nerve. "Hey, Rob," I said, nodding toward the back door, "can we...?"

Avoiding my mother's gaze, I led him out to the backyard and onto the patio, away from the windows and the prying eyes of my mother.

He grinned sheepishly. "So..." Rob folded his arms, as if looking for something to do with them.

This was my cue. "Rob," I whispered, taking a moment to make sure my mom wasn't hiding on the stoop or that his mom wasn't just beyond the bushes, spying on us, "first of all, about that text: I'd just found out my best friend got engaged out of nowhere, and I was overserved at the bar—"

"So you didn't mean it?" His face darkened.

"I...didn't," I said, "or, well, at least I didn't think I did, but then I read some of the responses..."

"Mine?"

"Yeah."

An airplane sailed over us, and my breath caught in my chest as Rob stepped closer, probably just to hear me better. His fresh, soapy scent made its way to my nostrils, and I was transported back a million years to when he took me to his prom, where we swayed to "Crash Into Me" by Dave Matthews Band in the middle of the Notre Dame High School gym floor before leaving together and making out in his car in the alley next to Brooks Park.

Now that guy, who'd been my first...not everything, but some things...was looking at me with fear and uncertainty, like he did that night so, so many years ago. I was pushing forty, but I could still so easily access those high school feelings. My brain kept them in a folder at the front of the old neural pathways filing cabinet.

"And?" he said.

"And, Rob…" I straightened my shoulders, preparing myself to give the speech I'd been practicing since I finished my pros and cons list yesterday. "I know we don't know each other well as adults, but we do have history together. Our families have history together." I paused, ready to drop the bombshell. Rob would either be open to it or would run away screaming. "I'm open to giving it a shot."

"Giving what a shot?"

He was going to make me say it. "Like…" I swallowed. "Marriage."

He shot me a crooked smile that sent me back twenty years. "Well, you are almost forty."

"What?"

Rob chewed his lower lip. "Didn't we once, back when we were kids, agree to marry each other if we were both single at forty?" He grinned.

I shook my head. "I don't—"

"I was probably about ten, so you were nine," he said. "We kissed behind the big oak tree…"

The memory came flooding back to me. We'd kissed in his backyard and vowed to be man and wife. Blood rushed to my cheeks.

"You're coming up on your fortieth birthday, aren't you? In August?"

"Oh my gosh, I am." My cheeks flushed. I couldn't believe this guy was actually on board with my ludicrous proposition. "Are we really seriously agreeing to this?"

"Honestly, yeah. I'm willing, if you are." He smiled nervously. "Your message the other night was like a sign from the universe. I'd just come home from another really bad first date, and—*ping!*—there was a text from Annie Kyle. It seemed like fate." He reached for my hand, and I let him take it. His rough, hardworking hands felt like heaters against my ice-cold ones.

"How do we do this?" I asked, grateful to actually have a partner in this—someone who hadn't been completely scared off and horrified by my text, *Dax*.

"We don't have to rush into anything today. Let's make a plan to go out—say we're open to getting to know each other as adults." He chuckled. "You know, at least a little bit, before we head over to the church and talk to Fr. Paul—or get our mothers involved, for that matter."

A large truck barreled down Touhy Avenue, just two houses down from my mom's place, shaking the ground below my feet.

Rob's hand caught my elbow. "What do you say?"

I gazed up at him, Rob Casey, with his soulful blue eyes and mature crinkles on his ruddy, Irish skin. He was a man who owned his own business and cared deeply for his mother—and mine, for that matter. I didn't know him well as an adult, but I did know that he was a bit of a homebody who enjoyed watching sports and hanging out with his friends at the local pubs.

I...could actually see myself getting used to all that.

I could imagine our wedding—officiated by Fr. Paul, the priest to whom I'd made my first confession. (I had crumpled up my little brother's prized possession—a two-dollar bill—

and I'd been certain I had boarded the Hell Express for that.) I could see us at our reception afterward, Kelly, my now-matron of honor, giving a toast and explaining how Rob and I got together. "He was the boy next door," Kelly would say, "and after Annie sent him an embarrassing text, Rob didn't make fun of her. He told her it was okay and that he'd thought the text was fate's way of telling him to go for it."

That wouldn't be so bad.

"Okay," I said, squeezing his hand. "Okay, let's do it. Let's go out and see what happens."

"Excellent." A smile of relief spread across his face. "Why don't you check your schedule and text me later to set up a date."

"Sounds like a plan."

Rob, still holding my hands, pulled me closer, leaned down, and kissed me softly on the cheek. My insides fluttered, as they used to when I was a young girl who had a bit of a crush on her slightly older next-door neighbor.

"Oh my goodness!"

The spell broken, I dropped Rob's hands and spun around. My mom stood on the top step, looking down at us from just outside her back door. Her hand had gone to her lips, and her eyes glistened with tears.

"Oh my goodness," she said again, "I knew it! You're in love!"

CHAPTER ELEVEN

Lavish Display of Ignorance

Welp. I supposed our mothers were now involved.

While I knew this arrangement with Rob was what I wanted, the amount of delight my mom displayed at seeing Rob and me together dizzied me. It pressurized the whole situation. She'd hummed and buzzed as she put out the food for our Saturday lunch.

"You and Robbie," she kept saying like it was her new mantra.

"Mom, we're going on a date. *A date*. As in 'one.' As in 'don't get your hopes up'—or Mrs. Casey's, for that matter."

No doubt my mom would scurry right over to her best friend with this salacious gossip as soon as my car left the driveway. My mom would get over the potential disappointment of me not marrying Rob, but Mrs. Casey didn't need that kind of stress on her already taxed system.

"You and Robbie." Her unfocused eyes gazed out at the backyard, and I knew she was picturing a bridal shower with all her relatives and church friends.

"We barely know each other," I said. "Stop planning our

wedding." Though that was where all this was headed, wasn't it? Rob and me spending time together was just a formality before we made it official? My mind raced. Two days ago, I'd been alone and sad and drunk. Today, I had a guy—a very nice, attractive, professional, and age-appropriate guy—who wanted to marry me.

My mom pinched my cheek. "This is how it happens, though." She took her seat at the table and placed her napkin on her lap.

I passed her the container of macaroni salad from Tony's Deli in an attempt to end this ridiculous conversation. If we crammed food into our mouths, at the very least it'd slow down the dialogue a bit.

My mom waved me off. "None of that for me. I'm on a diet now."

"What?" I said, wrinkling my nose. "You love Tony's macaroni salad, and, besides, you don't need to lose any weight, Mom."

"I sure do, if I'm going to look good in wedding photos." She hacked off a sliver of submarine sandwich about the width of my thumb. "This doesn't have any oil on it, does it?" She appraised the sandwich critically.

"Oh good lord, Mother. You need to stop this nonsense." I shoved a quarter of my sandwich into my mouth and stared out the window. I had to eat my lunch and get out of there. This was why I never discussed my private life with my mom. There was no such thing as "just a date" or a "casual relationship." Every man I met was potential marriage material; every innocent interaction represented an opportunity for lasting love. And this time she wouldn't be alone in her gossiping and theorizing. This time she'd have her BFF on board, equally invested in seeing me and Rob coupled up.

This would be a disaster.

On Friday afternoon, Gayle Gale came in masked up and wearing disposable gloves. She'd even wrapped a cashmere scarf around her neck, despite the eighty-degree summer weather. "My throat feels scratchy, Annie."

"Let's see." I mimed removing the scarf, and Gayle did so. I felt her neck. "I'm not feeling anything on the outside. Your lymph nodes aren't swollen, so that's a good thing." I grabbed my tongue depressor and flashlight. "Let's check out the inside." She pulled down her mask, and I flashed my light around. I pulled away and made a note on my chart.

She replaced her mask and her scarf. "What do you think? My husband and I just had dinner with my brother, who got back from a trip overseas last week. I heard there's a new flu..."

"I'm not concerned," I told her. "Your throat looks irritated, but that could be from overuse or allergies."

"I've never had allergies."

I wrote her a note on my pad for some over-the-counter remedies. "People can develop new sensitivities later in life, and with the changing climate, I'm seeing more and more of it. Plus, I think that these days, we're all just a little more hyperaware of how we're feeling." Smiling reassuringly, I handed her the paper. "Try this and see if you feel better.

Drink some hot water with honey and lemon to soothe the throat. With no other symptoms, I think it's most likely a combination of the weather and your job." I smiled at her. "You do have to talk a lot, professionally."

"That's true. Thanks, Annie." She glanced at the paper and tucked it into her purse. "I'm sorry to bother you with this."

"Don't worry about it." I led her toward the door. "I'm glad you called. Allergies are frustrating and present symptoms that can be scary, especially when you're already on the lookout for things like coughs and sore throats. Try the over-the-counter stuff, a little vocal rest, and we'll go from there. If anything changes, do not hesitate to call me."

"Never do."

"And keep taking your blood pressure medication."

She saluted me.

I opened the door and found Darius standing in the middle of the common area, leaning against the desk, checking his phone. My stomach lurched. He, too, had been on the text, though he hadn't responded. I guessed a guy like him received goofy messages every day from desperate women trying to get his attention. What was one more?

"Hello, Darius." Gayle swanned across the room and gave her coworker a friendly peck on the cheek. "What are you doing here?"

"Following up on my interview with Annie." He winked at me behind dark-rimmed glasses that made him look like Clark Kent, barely concealing his Superman alter ego.

I glanced at my watch. Crap. I *had* told him to stop by. And, *oh shit*, he probably wanted to mention that text in his story about me. That had to be it.

Jen and the cameraman had set up in one of the exam rooms, where Tina, in an elaborate outfit—complete with a fascinator—perched on the table.

"Well, good luck, everyone." Gayle waved and left the office.

My legs like lead, I ushered Darius into the exam room with the camera, where we found Tina musing about finding her best light while Jen and the cameraman ignored her.

"Hi, Annie," Jen said brightly but authoritatively. "This shouldn't take long. We only want to get a little video coverage of you interacting with your 'patient.'" She put that word in air quotes.

"Great." This I could do. I understood my motivation. I had to pretend to perform my duties on Tina—just run through my usual checklist of items. I tried to ignore Darius's looming presence on the guest chair just inside the door or the potential reaction of my patients when they found out about the drunken and desperate text their doctor had sent to most of the men in her contact list.

At least I'd somehow had the good sense, even in my intoxicated stupor, not to solicit any of my patients. Thank the universe for small favors.

I stepped over to Tina and listened to her heart with my stethoscope.

"What do you think, Doctor? Will I make it?" Tina asked dramatically, her lip quivering.

"Nope," I told her. "You have minutes to live. If you're lucky."

A tear formed in the corner of her eye.

"Maybe I was wrong about you," I said. "Maybe you actually do have acting chops."

"You doubted me?" Tina's eyes went wide.

"Never." I checked out her eyes, ears, and throat.

After I got through testing Tina's reflexes and checking her lymph nodes, Jen called cut. "I think that's plenty," she said, peering into the camera as it played back the footage. "Thanks, Annie. That's a wrap."

"Great." I removed my lab coat and felt a cold breeze under my arms. My pits had sweated through my button-down. Super. I pressed my arms tight against my sides as I stepped over to Darius. "Jen thinks she got enough." My upper arm still stuck to my side, I stiffly offered him my hand, and he shook it, holding on for a few beats too long.

"She has, but I'm not quite finished with you," he said, a sly grin spreading across his lips.

My stomach plummeted. Here it came.

"Can we talk for a second?" he asked. "In your office? I just have a few follow-up questions. No camera necessary."

"Sure," I croaked. My mouth had gone dry. I put my lab coat back on to hide my pit stains as I led Darius across the common area to my office.

I shut the door, and the two of us took the same seats we had the other day when he'd come in to interview me the first time.

"I'm happy to answer any of your questions," I said brightly. "I'm sure you have many about the practice—"

"I'm not here to talk about that." Darius, eyes down on the desk, pointedly pushed my stapler a centimeter closer to me. "I got your text message the other night."

Crap, crappity, crap, crap.

"Please don't say anything about that in your segment. It could ruin me. Please. I'm begging you."

He took off his glasses and wiped them on a handkerchief. "I'm not going to include that in the piece."

"You're not?"

"Of course not. That's not my style." He placed the Clark Kent glasses back on his face.

"Okay...thanks." I let out a sigh of relief until I remembered that this conversation wasn't over. He'd brought me in here specifically to talk about the text. "Is there...anything else?"

"Yeah..." He shot me a more muted, slyer version of his high-wattage smile. "I've been thinking a lot about that text the past few days."

My stomach sank into my feet as a wave of nervousness rolled through me. "You have?"

He touched my stapler again, this time moving it back to where it had been in the first place. "I think it's a great idea."

"Yeah?" Ice flowed through my veins. I instinctively glanced at the door, looking for Jen or the cameraman. This had to be a prank. I was on *Punk'd*. Or Darius had been tricky when he said he wouldn't use the text. Maybe he wouldn't use it in the official piece about my practice, but he'd save it for some gotcha segment for the news program that would paint me, an accomplished doctor, as a pathetic, man-hungry old maid.

"Yeah." His grin expanded this time, fully revealing that set of perfect teeth—gleamingly white and straight. "You put it right out there, no mincing words—'I'm sick of playing games.' I thought it was refreshing and brave."

He was messing with me. This Grown Man—capital letters—in a suit with a pocket square was screwing with me right now.

"And I think," he said, shrugging. "Let's do it. Let's get married."

CHAPTER TWELVE

The You Got It, Dudes

"Let's get...married?"

"I know what you're thinking, and I know we just met," Darius said, "but I'm a very decisive person, and you and I could be good together." He smiled confidently, even through this ridiculous conversation. "Maybe dropping 'marriage' into our second conversation ever seems a bit out there, but I think ultimately we're looking for similar things."

He pulled his phone out of his jacket pocket and pulled up the text message. Goodie. He'd saved it.

"The part where you said you make a ton of money and if that scares you, that's your problem." He glanced up at me, his brown eyes soft. "Women aren't intimidated by my job," he said. "Generally, it gets me in the door, so to speak. But it ends up being the thing that drives a wedge through my relationships—I never know if someone wants me because of me or because of who I am, what I have, and what they believe I can do for them." He frowned.

Maybe Darius had a point. He and I had high-powered, well-paying jobs, and that did affect other people's behavior when they were around us. He and I were kind of in the same boat.

"My thing's a little different," I said. "My job does often get me through the door, like you said, but it usually ends there."

I recalled one of my most recent first dates—the one where the guy kept trying to trick me into saying how much I made, like all he wanted was to know that he brought home more than a female doctor.

"Usually, in my experience, the guy spends the entire date either explaining to me why I shouldn't make as much as I do or trying to prove that he's superior to me in some way."

"Buffoons," Darius said.

I chuckled—this time from actual, genuine relief. It was nice to talk to someone who at least kind of knew where I was coming from and who had the same issues of trust when it came to meeting new people. "They are buffoons."

"So." He rested his large, perfectly manicured hands on the edge of my desk. "What do you think?"

My mouth dried up. "Well, I'm intrigued."

He smiled. "Good."

"But two things." I folded my hands in my lap and clutched them hard. "One, I think we should go out once or twice, just to make sure this is what we want." I grinned at him. "I mean, I barely know you."

"True, though I feel like I know you." He grinned. "At least a little bit, after editing all your footage."

I cleared my throat. "And the other thing is…there's another guy in the mix."

He nodded, taking that in. "Fair enough."

"He's someone I've known my entire life. Our moms are best friends—"

"So, he's in the dependable, boy-next-door lane." Darius steepled his fingers, resting them against his lips.

"Yes," I said. "I suppose that's what he has to offer."

"Well, let me tell you what you get with Darius Carver." He stood and paced from one end of my office to the other. "I get in to all the best restaurants and hottest clubs, VIP sections. I can get us tickets to any concert."

"I'll admit, I'm not a huge club person. Or concerts, for that matter."

He winked. "You haven't done clubs or concerts the Darius way. Just wait."

My stomach bubbled with excitement. Being with Darius could be pretty cool. With Rob, my life wouldn't change much, and that idea comforted me, but maybe I needed a push into something a little more thrilling. I had never been to a concert with a famous news guy. It'd be worth a shot, anyway.

He sat back down and folded his hands on my desk. "I'm going to be perfectly honest with you. My line of work, if I want to go beyond where I am now—which I do—having a significant other by my side would be an asset, especially if it's someone poised and impressive."

"A doctor," I said.

"Absolutely, a doctor." He smiled. "Someone close to my age. Someone professional, who understands life and how the game is played."

"What game?" I asked.

"The promotion game." His hands grasped for mine.

We sat there, hand in hand, staring at each other, like Meg and Mr. Brooks in the Marches' hallway. But Darius wasn't professing his undying love and affection. He was making a business proposition—something that my very analytical mind understood and appreciated. We weren't all that different, Darius and me. "When I saw your text the other night, I thought, *Annie gets it*. She is looking for stability and companionship. A permanent plus-one. That's what I need."

"A permanent plus-one."

"Exactly," he said, as if I hadn't simply repeated his own phrasing. "I'm old enough that I no longer believe in soul mates or love at first sight. I understand that passion fades. Been there, done that. Going into a relationship with eyes wide open, with an understanding that this is a mutually beneficial arrangement, is the mature and modern way to date."

"Mutually beneficial...?"

"You go with me to my events, I go with you to your events, and we never have to show up anywhere alone again."

Alone. There was that word I'd come to despise.

Darius got it. The two of us would be agreeing to not much more than mutual companionship. Maybe we could even live mostly separate lives and arrange to meet up only when we needed to. That had always been an issue for me with relationships—the expectation that I needed to be available to the other person twenty-four seven. I couldn't promise that with my job, and neither could Darius. Our relationship would be much more transactional, which worked for my busy, independent lifestyle. I was looking for a plus-one, not a soul mate.

"You want us to be like *Holidate*," I said eventually.

He narrowed his eyes and shook his head. "I don't know what that is."

"It's a Netflix rom-com—"

"Oh, I don't watch those kinds of movies."

I mentally started a con column for Darius. "*Holidate* is a rom-com about two people who decide to be each other's perma-date for all holidays and large events."

A slow smile invaded his face. "I like that. A 'perma-date.'"

I kept my gaze focused on his left cheek, avoiding those eyes and that smile. "But it didn't work. They ended up falling in love."

Darius didn't miss a beat. "Maybe we will, too."

CHAPTER THIRTEEN

Soylent Moon Fries

Kelly had been in Galena all week with Mark, but we had plans to meet up for trivia at O'Leary's on Thursday night. For once I actually had something besides work to talk to her about. I had two guys who were serious about settling down (with me) and two upcoming first dates with those men. Kelly and I had been missing each other recently—I tried to call her while she was out for dinner with Mark's family, and she tried to call me when I was busy with a patient—but tonight, we'd finally get to spend time together one-on-one, and things could get back to normal.

When I got to the bar at six o'clock, I sat facing the door at the table we'd sat at last time. Dax immediately brought me an old-fashioned.

"Thanks!" I grinned up at him as I took a sip. "Fantastic. Are you waiting tables again?"

"Nah," he said. "But I didn't want to make you get up and lose your spot."

"Wow. Thank you," I said, clearing the lump that had settled in my throat. "That was really nice of you."

"Well, I expect a good tip. I saw you waving that twenty at Peter last week, and I don't want to chance you giving your drink orders to him." He winked, and heat tingled my spine. God, I was hard up for attention and affection, for anyone at all to acknowledge my existence—even this young guy, with the scruff and the tattoos. How pathetic could one person be?

"You know I always tip well." My eyes dropped to my phone and a notification about an upcoming heat wave.

Dax retreated to the bar.

I opened up my text convo with Kelly, which stretched back years, since I bought my first iPhone. I normally deleted conversations, preferring to keep my digital footprint tidy and organized, but I saved every interaction with Kelly, my mom, and Yessi.

I'm excited for tonight! I texted Kelly and set my phone down.

I grabbed the answer sheets Ronald left on our table and wrote "Dorothy and Blanche" across the top of all ten. I'd come up with the name earlier today. I figured whenever Yessi could join us, we'd just add a "Sophia" to that. I chuckled to myself. *She is such a Sophia.*

I took another sip of my drink as my phone buzzed.

Grinning, I checked the message from Kelly. *Crap, Annie! I totally forgot. I'm stuck in Galena right now. I got my first client here, and they want to see every house in existence.*

I pressed my lips together and shoved my phone into my purse. I folded my hands in front of me on the table as my eyes started to water slightly. Dax came by and dropped off a plate of French fries.

"The cook made too many," he said.

I gazed up at him and tried to force myself to smile. "Looks like you really are angling for a better tip."

"Going for the record." He paused. "You okay?"

"Yeah," I said brightly, grabbing my drink and focusing all my attention on stirring that. "Doing great."

A beat later, Dax said, "Okay," and walked away, leaving me alone—the way I wanted it.

Hand shaking, I picked up one fry, dipped it in the house-made ketchup, and shoved it into my mouth. I barely tasted anything but the sharp tang of the sauce against my tongue. I chewed and chewed and chewed. Kelly was still in Galena. She knew we had concrete plans tonight, and she was still in Galena. She hadn't even thought to text me earlier to let me know, because Kelly, my best friend in the whole entire world, had forgotten all about me.

My nose stuffed up, and I blinked and blinked, trying to focus on anything but Kelly. The weather. The grain of the wood on this table. *Bozo's Circus* and the Grand Prize Game. I drew a cube on my answer sheet. Splat! A tear moistened the paper. I wiped another one away. With a wobbling hand, I drew the drink to my lips.

"Good evening!" Ronald bellowed from the stage.

I wiped my eyes and my nose, straightened up, and focused hard on the quiz master.

"Welcome to the last Thursday night trivia for a while," he said. "Remember, starting in two weeks, O'Leary's will be hosting the big citywide trivia tournament on Tuesdays. We hope you'll join us for this very exciting event."

Oh, yeah. The big tournament. I glanced up at the Very Stable Geniuses table, where the guys were giving each other high fives, ready to crush the Annie-free competition all across Chicago.

I took a big swig of my drink.

"Round one!" Ronald said as his assistant passed out the questions. "Geography. Get ready."

Instinctively, I pulled the first answer sheet toward me, and I crossed out "and Blanche" at the top of the page. It'd just be Dorothy tonight. Blinking through tears, I read the questions and filled out the entire sheet in about two minutes. Then, with a pit in my gut, I gave my answer sheet to Ronald, avoiding his pitying eyes the whole time, and headed right to the bathroom, where I could use my phone. Ronald had threatened to disqualify anyone caught looking at a screen during the quiz.

I smiled as I passed a twentysomething woman in a cute purple dress, wondering how her night was going—if she could rest assured that her best friend was still her best friend. Just inside the door, I turned on my phone and opened my Kelly chat.

You could have texted me earlier to let me know you weren't coming. I'm sitting at the table by myself playing trivia alone like a jackass.

I read the words over and immediately deleted them. This wasn't a conversation to have over text. Kelly and I would need to hash this out face-to-face when we were together again. If we were ever together again.

When I got back to my table, Ronald was already starting the second round—an oral literature round; not my best category. I scrambled into my seat, wiped my eyes, and readied my pen.

"In the New Testament, which book comes after the four gospels?"

"Crap." I stared at the blank paper, thinking. Bible stuff was never my strong suit. Kelly was much better, since she was raised in an evangelical household and had to recite psalms, chapter and verse, in order to have dessert after dinner. My family was Catholic, not super devout, and we were considered Bible scholars if we knew the gospels were Matthew, Mark, Luke, and John.

"It's Acts," a voice above me said.

I glanced up as Dax slid into the chair across from me.

He pointed to the blank spot on my paper. "Acts of the Apostles. Write it down."

"What are you doing?" I hissed, glancing up at Ronald, feeling like a high school kid who just got caught passing notes during a test. "This is cheating."

"It's not. I took the rest of the night off, and now I'm on your team."

"Jeez, you'll do anything for that tip."

"Yes, I will." He grabbed the pen and wrote "and the Tin Man" next to my "Dorothy." "Now let's win this thing."

"You're pretty darn good at trivia," I said as Dax poured each of us a water behind the bar. I'd already reached my one-drink maximum, and, after last weekend, I would not be exceeding that anytime soon.

He set the glass in front of me. "Don't act so surprised."

"I'm not surprised," I said. "I'm impressed."

Our new little team, Dorothy and the Tin Man, performed

pretty well for our first time out. We managed to come in close second to the Very Stable Geniuses.

Brad the Genius, speaking of, now sidled up next to me, like Nagini the snake approaching Harry Potter, making me choke on my water. "Hey there. You know, you two are going to be tough to beat in the citywide competition." He held up two fingers. "Two beers, please." He squinted at the menu above the bar. "Antiheroes," he said to Dax.

"I'm off the clock." Dax tossed his towel on the counter. "Peter will get those for you." He tapped his fellow bartender on the shoulder and came around to the customers' side of the bar.

"Seriously," Brad said. "You guys are smart, and it makes me kind of hate you, honestly."

"Thanks, I guess?" I glanced at Dax, who had taken the open barstool next to me and was checking a text on his phone. We did make a good team. And right now trivia was the one thing in my life that brought me any joy. Maybe we should team up and kick the rest of Chicago's ass? "What do you say, Dax?" I asked.

Dax glanced up from his phone. His expression, usually bored and vaguely mocking, had turned worried. His brow furrowed. "Huh?"

"The trivia tournament. The big citywide thing on Tuesday nights," I said. "Do you want to be teammates?"

His eyes flitted to the door. "Oh, no. I don't want to do that."

Right. Of course. I was nothing but a big-tipping old lady to him.

I sipped my water, trying to drown the disappointment

in my stomach. "That's fine. I wasn't sure I wanted to do it anyway. I'm not always free on Tuesday nights. I have"—I struggled to make something up—"a standing thing with my mom."

No, I didn't. If anything, if I showed up at her house on a Tuesday night, she'd shove me right back out the door. Tuesday nights were her Bunco nights with her friends, and I was not allowed to intrude.

"You can join our team," Brad said.

"Thanks, Brad," I said. "But if we teamed up, we'd ruin the tournament. We'd be too dominant."

"You're right about that." Brad picked up his beers and headed back to his friends.

Dax and I sat in silence for a moment.

"You okay?" Now it was my turn to ask him that question. He kept acting fidgety and upset.

Dax looked down at me as if he'd forgotten I was there. "Oh," he said. "Yeah. I'm fine." He looked at his phone again.

Annoyed, I pulled out my own phone. I'd always heard about women becoming invisible as they got older, though I never truly believed it would happen to me. I was tall and fit and looked younger than I was—or so I thought. But now here I was, abandoned by my best friend, being ignored by a twentysomething bartender. Choosing to pursue pure, unadulterated commitment with either Darius and Rob had been a smart, mature decision. As far as I could tell, no one else would ever look at me as a desirable being again. I kept thinking about that video with Tina Fey and Julia Louis-Dreyfus, about their "last fuckable day."

I'd apparently reached mine.

CHAPTER FOURTEEN

I Am Smartacus

I started to stand, ready to leave and go home to my empty, lonely house and make a date with my trusty vibrator, Timothy Olyphant (who'd never abandon me!), when the door to the bar flew open and in rushed a young woman with long, wavy, honey-brown hair. She wore the same nervous expression as Dax, whom she approached breathlessly.

"Dax, I am so sorry about this."

I sat right back down in my chair. Might as well use my newfound invisibility to spy on people and get the gossip. Maybe this new superpower wouldn't be so bad. At least I'd be able to entertain myself. It was like watching live television.

"What am I supposed to do, Lily?" he asked, eyes flashing with anger.

She took the spot on the other side of Dax. "I know, seriously. It sucks, and I'm so, so sorry."

I turned my head under the guise of checking the score on the TV—Cubs two, Cardinals zero—and in the process, nearly fell off my barstool.

Dax caught my arm without looking at me. "Hey, Peter, can you get Lily a beer?"

"A Miller Lite," she said.

"Get something better," he told her. "It's on me."

"Dax, I like Miller Lite."

"Many people do," I said.

Annoyed, Dax gestured toward me. "Lily, this is Annie. Annie, this is Lily, my sister."

Oh, *sister*. Interesting. The plot thickens. I reached across Dax and offered her my hand. "Nice to meet you."

"Are you…?" Lily, blue eyes wide, looked from me to Dax.

"No," Dax and I said at the same time. A giggle bubbled up in my throat. As if.

"She's becoming a regular here," he added, rubbing his temples.

"What's wrong?" I asked.

"Nothing," Dax said sharply.

"Obviously it's not nothing," I said. "Is it a headache?" I rummaged in my purse. "I always have ibuprofen…"

"It's not a headache."

Lily accepted her beer from Peter with a brief smile. "I just told Dax—"

"Lily, I've got it." Dax glanced at me. "It's really no big deal. I've been staying at Lily's…for a little while," he said, covering up some secret bit of information he evidently didn't want me to know, "but now I have to find a new place to live. Immediately." He sighed.

"Not you," Lily said, frowning. "You can stay, but she has to go."

She? This conversation kept getting more interesting.

"Who's she?" I asked.

"Joanne," Lily said.

"My dog," Dax said.

"You know I love Joanne." Lily placed her hand on Dax's forearm. "She's the sweetest girl in the world, but Travis is super allergic."

"You said Travis would be down in Atlanta," Dax said.

"They lost their funding." Lily looked at me. "Travis is my roommate. This situation was supposed to be perfect—Dax and Joanne needed a place to stay, Travis's room was going to be available for a few months while he shot a movie down south—but now—"

"Travis is back," Dax deadpanned.

"Yeah." Lily frowned. "Again, Dax, I'm so, so sorry."

"I know you are." Dax cuffed his sister lightly on the arm. "But now what am I supposed to do?"

"Where's Joanne now?" I asked, trying to imagine what a dog named "Joanne" might look like. I kept picturing a standard poodle with curly blond tufts of hair.

"Right outside." Lily nodded toward the door. "In my car." Her face brightened, and she turned to Dax. "Hey, maybe Mom and Dad can take her. Or Mur—"

"No," he said sharply, cutting her off. "She's my *dog*, Lil. I've had her for six years. I'm not just going to leave her in Wisconsin with Mom and Dad or hand her off to someone who's not going to take care of her the way I would."

"I'll take her," I said, not even thinking about it.

Dax and Lily looked at me as if I'd grown a second head.

"Annie, what are you talking about?" He picked up my water glass and smelled it.

I snatched the glass back. "I mean it. I have a huge, empty house," I said, "and I love dogs." At least I thought I did. I'd actually never had one of my own. My parents always refused to let us get one, no matter how much my brother and I begged. And then I was in med school, and interning, and doing my residency. The time never felt right, but now, with Kelly moving out, maybe having a dog could actually work. Why not try it out with someone else's pet? Joanne could be my training pooch. "I'd be happy to have Joanne."

"Maybe this is a good temporary solution," Lily said. "Joanne can stay with Annie for a little while, until you find your own place."

Dax glared at his sister for a moment before fixing his eyes on me. "You're busy," Dax said. "You're a doctor with a very demanding job. Weren't you the one telling me that you're on call all the time?"

He had a point. My day-to-day schedule was mostly pretty fixed, but sometimes I did have to rush in, if someone needed me in the hospital. I hadn't thought this whole Joanne thing through, probably because I'd been grasping at any straw that would prevent me from being alone right now.

"Besides," Dax said, "this isn't any different than shipping her off to live with Mom and Dad. I still wouldn't get to be with her."

A ludicrous, half-baked idea popped into my head. I brushed it off. But it persisted. Maybe it wasn't so half-baked. Maybe it was an amazing, perfect idea. "Dax, you can move in, too."

Now the siblings looked at me as if I'd added a third head to my previous two.

"I know it sounds ridiculous, but your timing's actually good. My friend Kelly—you've met her—"

"The one who got engaged."

My stomach soured. "Yes. She's moving out to Galena to start her new life with Mark, and her room is empty." Or it would be, after I chucked all her things into the guest room on the top floor. "It's not even a room, really. It's a whole apartment. You and Joanne could have the entire garden-level floor to yourself." I snapped my fingers. "And it's really perfect because you and I work totally different hours. You can watch Joanne during the day, and I'll be around in the evenings and at night. She'll be the happiest, most spoiled dog in the world." I paused for a breath. "What do you say?"

Dax gawked at me. "What do you get out of this?" he asked. "I can pay you rent, obviously."

I shook my head. "I don't want the money."

"Then what do you want?"

I raised my eyebrows. "I want a Tuesday night trivia partner."

CHAPTER FIFTEEN

Paw Posse

"This place is really nice." Rob jogged down the steps from the second floor. "Who was your contractor?"

I set the chips and salsa Rob had brought over on the kitchen island. He'd shown up bearing food. I awarded him major points for that. "I used a Lincoln Square guy," I said. "Greg Tillman?" My cheeks flushed. He'd been on the text and had responded that he was married but that his wife wouldn't mind if he and I hooked up once in a while. "I won't be using him again."

"Well, you won't have to. You'll have me." Grinning, Rob ran a finger along the counter. "He did do a good job." He glanced around. "Though I'd change a few things."

"Oh, yeah?" I sat down at the counter with a glass of white wine, which Rob had also brought with him. Mrs. Casey had taught him well. "Like what?"

I cringed as he opened one of my kitchen cabinets—okay, maybe Mrs. Casey still had some work to do. "I can't believe you're looking in there." I covered my face with my hands. The cabinet in question was right above the fridge and was chock-full of mismatched storage bowls and lids.

"It's okay. I'm a professional." He smiled back at me. "And, believe me, I've seen worse than a disorganized Tupperware cupboard."

"How would you fix it?" I asked in a flirty, lilting voice. I kind of wished he'd worn his tool belt tonight. It would've completed the picture.

"First of all," he said, "I'd add some dividers to one of the deep drawers down below for all your bowls and lids, and then I'd put vertical dividers in this cabinet for things like baking sheets and cooling racks."

I sipped my wine. "It's cute that you think I have and use those things."

"And then over this way—" He beckoned for me to follow him.

"I can see you from here," I said, raising my wineglass.

I watched him in his well-fitting jeans travel to the far corner of the kitchen/family room where I spent most of my time in the house. "In this corner, I'd put in a huge, state-of-the-art pantry with a place to store root vegetables, a dedicated coffee bar, a refrigerator drawer just for keeping drinks cold—"

"You know I don't cook, right? I order out, like, six times a week."

He smiled at me. "I'm just saying what *I* would do. A big pantry is my dream. I keep trying to get my mom to knock out the wall between the kitchen and her bedroom."

I gasped. "You want to take away your mother's bedroom?"

He came over and sat next to me at the counter. "There's another bedroom on the first floor. You know that." He winked at me. Yes, I did. I'd been in the Caseys' house a million times. "And three upstairs—not that she'd be up for going up and down steps right now." His tone turned somber.

My mom had told me that Mrs. Casey was having a rough time with the chemo. She'd been quite sick. I squeezed Rob's hand.

"So, you like to cook?" I asked, veering the topic away from cancer.

"Love it," he said. "Cooking, baking, grilling, canning, you name it."

"Canning," I said. "Impressive."

"Well, I have to do something with all the tomatoes and cucumbers my mom and I grow." He glanced over at me. "What about the other guy? Does he like to cook?"

"Honestly? Don't know yet." I had been up-front with Rob and told him about Darius. He said he understood that I needed to consider my options, and I think he saw it as a challenge, which I respected. I loved a person with a competitive spirit.

The doorbell rang, and I jumped up to get the pizza. "Go on into the TV room, and we'll eat there."

After I retrieved the pizza and closed the door, a tantalizing aroma from the Pequod's box filled the room, no doubt making its way down to the basement. Suddenly I heard a jingling noise and the sound of heavy footsteps padding up the stairs. Before I even knew what was happening, Joanne, Dax's massive brindle-colored mutt, emerged from the basement and plopped herself right on the couch next to Rob. Dax must have brought her in through the basement after a walk. She hadn't been home when Rob got here.

"What the...?" Rob asked as Joanne's stumpy snout tried to lick his face. "Who is this?"

"Uh...this is my new roommate." It had been a few days now since Joanne and Dax had moved in, and I was still getting used to them being around. "Joanne," I said, "get off the couch."

She flopped where she was, resting her large head on Rob's lap. Her obedience skills left a lot to be desired.

"It's okay. I love dogs." He scratched her ears. "Your mom never said you had one."

"She...doesn't know." I set the pizza on the coffee table and squeezed onto the couch between Joanne's butt and the arm.

"I won't tell her," Rob said. "If your mom's anything like mine, she'll have a lot of opinions."

I laughed. "You know it." I placed a hand on Rob's as he petted Joanne and kept an ear cocked, listening for sounds of Dax in the basement. He probably had work tonight and wouldn't come up to see what was going on, or at least I hoped that was the case.

Joanne was one thing, but no one needed to know that I had invited a strange man to live in Kelly's room. If my mom had opinions on me housing a dog, she'd no doubt have thoughts about a single woman shacking up with a mysterious young bartender.

And I suspected Rob would, too.

CHAPTER SIXTEEN

Cindaf***in'rellas

At around six thirty Monday evening, I stood in my front bay window, watching a white stretch limousine pull up in front of the house and attempt to park next to the curb.

Darius had arrived in style, and I added that mental note to his pro list.

I grabbed my purse and a light sweater and made my way downstairs and out to the car. I had never been picked up like this before, in a limo—not when Rob and I went to his prom; not when I went to my own prom. That year, I'd picked up my date in my parents' Dodge Caravan.

I waved to Darius as I approached the car, and the limo driver opened the door for me. "Thank you," I said, sliding into the backseat.

Darius shimmied back down into the limo and took the spot next to me. He handed me the bouquet of sterling roses. "Sorry I'm a little late. An interview ran long. Sometimes my time is not my own."

"Well, that's certainly something I understand." I sniffed the flowers—sweet and strong—and set the bouquet gingerly on the seat across from me. "The roses are beautiful, and this is quite the car."

"Only the best for Annie Kyle." He squeezed my hand. "We have an exciting dinner ahead of us."

"Good!" I grinned nervously as the car started moving. "I'm starved."

While I'd invited Rob over for simple pizza delivery last night—we spent the entire evening on the couch, watching the new Matthew McConaughey action movie while separated from each other by a big mutt, though we did hold hands across her back there for a little while, and it was definitely nice—Darius had proposed taking me out to one of the hottest new restaurants in Chicago.

"So, what is this place?" I asked. He wouldn't tell me the name of it on the phone.

Even now, he zipped his lip. "Trust me. The less you know, the better. Go into it with your mind wide open to the possibilities."

"Okay." Grinning, I leaned back in my seat. I was so used to always being in control in every facet of my life; I was the boss, the decision maker. It was nice to be with someone else who was willing to take charge. With Darius, I could relax and go with the flow.

He grabbed a bottle of champagne from the limo's mini fridge. "Want some?"

"Sure."

Darius expertly popped the cork, as if he'd practiced this maneuver hundreds of times in front of the mirror to achieve maximum coolness.

It worked.

He poured me a glass.

"Thank you." We clinked flutes, and I felt myself relaxing even further. It was summertime in Chicago, and my date and I were being driven around from place to place. We had champagne. Life was good.

After a few minutes of chatting about the weather and complaining about traffic, I said, "How's your story coming?"

He looked at me, confused. "Which story?"

I giggled. "The one about me!"

"Oh!" He laughed. "Good. I'm retooling it a little bit, trying to figure out the exact right angle." He pressed his lips together for a moment, and his eyes grew serious. "I think we can win an Emmy."

"Really?"

"Well, a local one, obviously, but yes." He smiled, puffing out his chest. "Of course, I approach all my stories with the same vim and vigor—each subject is award-worthy, and each segment must be up to my impeccable standards. Oh!" He snatched the champagne glass from my hand. "Here we are."

I peered out the window at a nondescript, beige building—a warehouse. I checked the other side of the street. Similar view. I spied no other cars in our vicinity. Nerves churned in my belly. This was why I usually was the one who took charge, because when I didn't, I could end up being taken to a murder den or sex dungeon. I was about to become a skin suit.

"Where are we?" I asked, hoping Siri would catch the name of this place, praying I hadn't turned off the location services on my phone.

Darius's eyes lit up. "We're at Jam."

"Jam?" Definite sex dungeon.

He flashed me his pearly whites. "The hottest new restaurant in Chicago."

"I've never heard of it."

"You wouldn't have. It's that new and that hot."

The limo driver opened the door, and Darius slid out. I followed, and he offered me a hand. Gravel crunched under my only pair of high heels—gunmetal Michael Kors pumps from a few years ago. We were in an alley. "This is where the hottest new restaurant in Chicago is located?"

"Yes." He grinned excitedly.

He had to be lying. There wasn't even a fast-food restaurant here, let alone a trendy new bistro.

I would not yet rule out my skin suit theory.

CHAPTER SEVENTEEN

The Where's the Beef Ladies

Darius led me toward one of the back-alley buildings, and I glanced at the limo driver, who was now back in the car, fiddling with his phone, no longer paying attention to us. Darius pulled open the heavy, windowless door. The sound of forks hitting plates cut through the tinkling of adult contemporary Muzak, and people bustled about inside, filling up trays and calling for more food.

"This is a…cafeteria?" I said, taking in the scene, feeling a sense of confusion and relief.

"It is," Darius said proudly. "A few years ago, diner chic was the thing. Now the hot trend is college cafeteria gourmet."

"Cool…" It really did have all the trappings of a dormitory mess. We even had to check in at the front desk with an ID card, which Darius happened to have.

"This is the golden ticket." After the hostess checked us in, Darius fanned the card in the air, blowing on it as if it were on fire. "Hardly anyone has their hands on one of these babies."

I glanced at the round tables of eight. "Is this… Do we

have to do communal dining?" I'd come here to get to know Darius, not have to make small talk with six strangers.

Darius smiled at me with a twinkle in his eye. "Nope. I told you I can get us in to all the VIP spots in Chicago. Jam is no exception. Follow me."

Excited and hungry butterflies danced in my stomach as Darius led me toward a room filled with a huge buffet. I grabbed a tray off the end of a conveyor belt and showed it to Darius. "I think the owners took these straight out of one of Northwestern's cafeterias, around the turn of the century."

Darius chuckled. "Entirely possible."

Inside the buffet room, I found a veritable circus of food and drink and novelty. All of the cafeteria workers wore stylized uniforms from the 1950s, but each station was stocked with gourmet vittles and fancy confections. There was a seafood station with artfully designed sushi in every color of the rainbow, plus caviar, lobster, smoked salmon, and king crab legs. I passed by a salad bar filled with daikon radishes, heirloom tomatoes, Spanish olives, and Stilton.

"Oh my gosh." I paused in front of the cereal wall.

The chef had made his own versions of everything from Life to Lucky Charms. A milk dispenser offered whole cow's milk, sheep's milk, oat milk, or almond milk.

"This is…amazing." I felt like one of those kids in Willy Wonka's factory. My eyes were too big for my stomach.

"Grab whatever you want," Darius told me as he passed by. "Normally they ring you up *à la carte*, but our entire meal has been comped."

Comped. Damn. I really could get used to this.

I scanned the room, my tummy rumbling for food. Back

in college, I would've gone for something like a small side salad, a turkey sandwich, and a banana. Those things were all on the table tonight, but the sliced turkey came from a free-range bird, the gluten-free bread had been baked lovingly on-site, and the cheddar had been aged for ten years at a small monastery in Wisconsin.

Finally, because *comped*, I picked out lobster tail, some roasted Jersey Giant asparagus covered in aged balsamic, a massive chocolate chip cookie dusted with pink Himalayan sea salt, and some white wine. Rung up, my plate would have been almost one hundred and fifty dollars. "Well, I guess that's how they stay in business."

Darius passed his magic ID card to the checkout clerk, who let us pass through without paying. "People don't mind shelling out for a once-in-a-lifetime experience."

"I suppose not," I said. "My mom and dad paid for me to have this experience seven days a week back in college."

Darius laughed and motioned for me to follow him to a set of stairs toward the back of the room. "Our table awaits."

The steps led up to a room with big glass windows that looked down on the diners below. There were only four tables in this VIP section, and only one other table was occupied. I paused at the window and gazed down at the crowd for a moment. "I'm not sure if we're in the fishbowl or if they are."

"Oh, them," Darius said. "Definitely."

At our table, I set down my tray. "I want to make some comment about class wars and the haves viewing the have-nots from a distance, but I'm just too happy not to have to share a table with a bunch of strangers."

Darius chuckled. "I get it—believe me. If it eases your

conscience, dining like this, away from people, is the only way I can eat in peace. Down there, we'd have to chat with people we don't know, and as much as I love schmoozing new folks, I came here to get to know Annie." He bit a piece of lettuce off his fork.

Grinning, I set my napkin on my lap. "Good, because I'm here to get to know you." Things had gone quite well with Rob last night, and I had enjoyed the simplicity of the two of us lounging in my house, eating pizza, but this with Darius was new and exciting. I wasn't hip enough to know about new restaurants. I wasn't part of the Chicago "scene." Darius could open up a whole new world for me. And maybe that was what I wanted for my forties and beyond.

I took a bite of my scrumptious lobster. "Since you've already interviewed me, I think it's my turn to interview you."

He set down his fork. "I agree."

"Okay..." I narrowed my eyes. "Where are you from?"

"Ah." He smiled. "My origin story. I'm from a very small town in Kentucky. We had a farm."

"A farm? That's so cool. I mean, I can't quite imagine you milking goats in your fancy suit..." I waved my hand up and down to indicate his entire polished visage.

He chuckled. "I've got a special goat-milking suit." He smiled warmly. "My hometown is actually how I got started with reporting, interviewing the business owners on the tiny Main Street in the town where I grew up, hence the name of my segment."

"That's really sweet," I told him.

"There are many more adorable stories where that came from." He flashed me a smile.

"I'd love to hear them." Probably because he was a famous dude whose face was plastered on billboards all over the city, I thought I'd had Darius all figured out from the jump. But of course celebrities were more complex than their outward personae. I, of all people, should know that. I took their medical histories for a living. I knew about their vices and their sleep patterns and whether or not they were sexually active. "Okay...what were you like in high school?"

He tapped his chin, thinking. "Again, small town, so everyone did a bit of everything. I played some sports but really enjoyed choir and theater." He snapped his fingers. "We should go see a play sometime."

"Definitely. I'd love that." I chewed a bit of asparagus. "In my office the other day, we talked a bit about our love lives—mostly about how difficult it is for us to date—but I'm wondering...have you ever been married? Or in love...?"

He shook his head, smiling, though his eyes had darkened mysteriously. "Let's not dwell on the past." Waving, he flagged down a waiter to ask for some salt.

My stomach sank. The two of us were talking about potentially spending our lives together. I didn't think it was particularly out of bounds to ask about his dating history, but I supposed everyone had stuff they wanted to keep private. I focused on my food.

He squeezed my hand, and I looked up. "All I meant was that we're both adults. I'm sure we've each had a number of relationships, good and bad. All of that is over and done, as far as I'm concerned." His eyes widened. "I'm focused on the future. I'm looking for someone strong, mature, dependable, and willing to commit. Someone who enjoys good food."

Grinning, he raised his fork, which held a bite of steak.

I smiled back. "Focusing on the future sounds like a plan to me." I watched him tuck into his food, with the notion that I might never actually get to know Darius. But who, honestly, really knew anyone? Darius and I were talking about being each other's permanent plus-ones, not soul mates or best friends. I didn't need to know every detail of his life, nor he mine.

I currently had a hot bartender and his pooch living in my basement. We all had our secrets, and maybe that was okay.

CHAPTER EIGHTEEN

Only You Can Prevent Forrest Gump

Joanne quickly inserted herself into my daily routine. Every morning, as soon as she heard me coming down the steps, she'd bound up the stairs to greet me. Then I'd fill her food bowl and turn on the coffee machine. Once she finished her breakfast and while my coffee brewed, I'd clip on her leash and take her for a quick walk.

Dax had told me when they moved in that Joanne wasn't a big walker, but I was determined to prove him wrong. I knew she had it in her. At first she balked at the walks, dropping to the floor, limp, as soon as I put the leash on her. But I could get her to move by bribing her with a small piece of dog biscuit (the only kind of treat Dax allowed Joanne). With the promise of a tasty little nugget as her reward, I'd gotten her to walk two whole blocks. Today was Sunday, and we were going for three.

"Joanne, this walk isn't just for you; it's for me, too," I explained to her outside my house. "I have podcasts I want to listen to, so if you could extend these walks a little bit, I'd be very appreciative."

She made it halfway up the second block before wanting to go home. She did this frustrating thing where she'd turn all the way around before dropping to the ground in a down-dog position, nose pointed in the direction of home.

"Okay, fine. You did a good job," I told her as we headed back toward the house. "It's like I tell my patients all the time"—yes, I was talking to the dog out loud, in public, but it was fairly early in the morning on a Sunday, and Chicagoans had seen worse—"you can't simply jump into a new exercise routine full throttle if you've never been active before. You'll get hurt, and you'll get frustrated. This is supposed to be fun."

She glanced back at me, panting.

I stiffly patted her on the head.

As we neared the house, I pulled out my earbuds, silencing the voices on my favorite podcast, the one where a trio of actor friends interviewed other famous people. The front door to my house stood ajar.

"What the heck?" Had I forgotten to close it? I racked my brain. No, I definitely remembered leaving the house and closing the door on my way out. When I went walking, I never bothered to lock my door, because I wasn't going far. Now someone had broken into—or, well, not broken in to so much as "walked" into—my house.

I started running, but Joanne refused to engage in that much exertion, even if it would only mean jogging one whole house length. I pulled the beast as hard as I could, dragging her toward the house. Suddenly, a woman's voice from inside yelled, "I'm calling the cops!"

That perked Joanne right up. She barked and dragged me the last twenty feet. I dropped her leash on accident, and she dashed up the steps and through my front door. I ran after her.

"Please! Don't call the cops!" a male voice yelled. "I'm supposed to be here."

"Oh my god! What the hell?" came the woman's voice.

I ran down the stairs, into the basement, to what used to be the garden apartment of this three-flat. There I found Dax (naked from the waist up, wearing only a pair of lightweight, gray pajama pants—I averted my eyes from the vee pointing downward from his very toned stomach) facing off against Kelly, who had been knocked backward onto the couch by a wagging, licking Joanne.

Dax rushed to his dog, pulling her away from the intruder. I helped Kelly up from the couch, noting that she was holding her keys in her hand like a weapon, like she'd been ready to attack Dax.

"Annie!" Kelly yelled, shaking me off. "Call the cops! This jerk broke into your house and has been sleeping in my bed." She pointed her keys at him.

I extracted the weapon from her grip. "Kel, it's okay. Dax and the dog are supposed to be here."

Kelly's eyes snapped to Dax. "Dax?" she said, narrowing her gaze. "You're the bartender from O'Leary's."

"Yes, he is. We know him. He's not a random person off the street." At least not *completely* random. I grabbed my friend's arm and pulled her toward the stairs. I glanced back at Dax and mouthed, *I'm sorry.*

"We should let Dax go back to bed. He didn't get home until after three this morning."

"He didn't get home...?" Kelly tried to turn around again,

but I forced her up the steps. "What are you talking about? What's going on?"

I led her into the kitchen. "Dax and Joanne are staying here for a little while."

"Joanne?"

"The dog." I gestured toward one of the stools at the counter. "Why don't you sit down. I'll get us some coffee and explain everything."

Kelly didn't sit. She stood stiff, glaring hard at the basement stairs.

I poured her a cup and set it down at the spot where she was supposed to be sitting. "Kel?" I said. "Take a seat. Let's chat." My eyes stung. "I haven't seen you in..." We hadn't crossed paths since the night she announced her engagement.

"Can't. I've got to go. I'm just here to pick up something for my sister..." She turned toward me, her jaw clenched. "Where are my things, anyway?"

"Up in the top-floor guest room." I pointed toward the ceiling.

"In the top-floor guest room." She stared at me for one more beat, her mouth set in a line. Then she clomped all the way up to the third floor. I poured myself some coffee and sat down on one of the uncomfortable couches in the front room, noting a thin layer of dust across the back of the baby grand piano in my front bay window.

Okay, so maybe I was kind of a dick for moving her stuff upstairs, but what did she expect? She was never around anymore, and she'd announced she was moving to Galena. Was I supposed to leave her room intact, like a shrine to Kelly, for the rest of my life? Even my mom had turned my brother's room into a workout space as soon as he graduated from college.

A few moments later, Kelly stomped back down, mouth set in a line.

"I'm sorry the dog jumped on you," I said. "She's actually really sweet."

"I'm sure she is." Kelly focused on something in her purse, and I got the sense that she was not looking at me on purpose. "We're shopping for dresses today, remember?"

"Of course I do," I said, too cheerfully. She was mad at me right now? Really? After she kept the existence of her serious boyfriend and now fiancé from me for months? After she dropped the bombshell that she was moving out? I was the bad guy here?

"And you won't have to leave in the middle because of doctor stuff?" Now she looked at me, eyes flashing.

"Yes," I said in a measured tone. "It's going to be fine." I didn't know that for sure, but Sunday mornings tended to be slow for me, as far as patient calls went.

"Ten o'clock. Don't be late." She yanked open the door, and then she was gone.

CHAPTER NINETEEN

The I Do Crew

braced myself outside the bridal boutique on a Gold Coast side street off Michigan Avenue.

Kelly had always been known for her fiery temper, but she rarely—if ever—directed it toward me. Maybe I should've alerted her, sent her a text at least, like *Hey, friend, just wanted to let you know that I need your old room for that hot, young bartender from O'Leary's and his big, slobbery dog, so I'm moving your mom's quilt and your grandma's ceramics up to the top floor. I'm sure you won't mind, since you're already living with the guy you kept secret from me for months, and if your grandma's painted Christmas tree from the eighties was so important to you, you would've taken it with you by now.*

I exhaled. No. Not helpful. I had to be the bigger person today. Kelly was under a lot of stress, and I, as her maid of honor, would do my part and make sure dress shopping went smoothly.

I gripped the door handle at Angel Heart Bridal Boutique and readied my most pleasant and agreeable smile. I vowed to keep my opinions to myself unless asked and my sarcastic comments to a minimum.

A bell chimed as I stepped over the threshold. Kelly, Yessi, and Kelly's younger sister, Kendall, sat together on a plush pink couch, poring over a catalog. They looked up as I walked in.

I swallowed, steeling myself for Kelly's rage.

But instead of berating me or biting my head off, Kelly, smiling brightly—*too* brightly—jumped up, wrapped me in a stiff hug, and rushed me over to the couch.

Good. Either she'd gotten over her annoyance with me or she'd come to the same conclusion I had: repress feelings until the anger subsides.

Yessi, grinning, squeezed my hand. "Hi, Annie."

"Hey." I beamed at her. "This will be fun."

She handed me a mimosa and leaned in to whisper, "We are way too old for this shit."

Damn it. Yessi and I had always bonded over our mutual distaste for rituals like this. But I would not be drawn into her web of sassy bitterness today, even though I had not been in a bridal shop in ten years, and even though I'd felt too old for this shit all the way back then. I just smiled and repeated, "This will be fun."

Yessi eyed me suspiciously and backed away.

"Now that Annie's here, we can get to work." Kelly pulled an old photograph up on her iPad. "This is what we're looking for." She passed the tablet to Kendall, who then passed it to me. On screen was a photo of a bride surrounded by seven bridesmaids wearing the same long maroon sheath dress with a plunging neckline, which was covered by a matching feathery overcoat that gave off a lingerie robe vibe. These women looked like they were headed to only the classiest 1970s key party.

I pressed my lips shut.

I passed the iPad to Yessi, whose eyes bugged out.

"Mark has very specific ideas for this wedding," Kelly said. "He'd like us to try and recreate his parents' wedding motif as much as possible, but since we're getting married in August—"

My eyes snapped to her. "Wait," I said. "This August? As in, like—"

"Yes," she said, sighing. "Six weeks from now. You knew that."

I shook my head. "No, I didn't." Another thing she hadn't told me. This was becoming a pattern.

"Sure you did," she said stiffly. "Mark pulled some strings and was able to book us the inn at the resort in Galena on short notice."

"Oh…" *Calm down, Annie. Be agreeable. Don't poke the bear.* I relaxed my nostrils, which were threatening to flare. "Neat."

Kelly rolled her eyes. "Is that a problem?"

I paused and reaffixed my calm and relaxed smile. "Nope. No problem at all."

Kelly turned to Yessi. "What do you think?"

"These dresses are…" I watched Yessi hunt for the most tactful phrase, but all she came up with was, "I'm not sure a dress like that can wrangle in my lactating boobs."

Kelly snatched back her iPad. "They don't have to be exactly the same. *Obviously.*" She studied the picture for a moment. "Mark says maroon isn't a deal breaker, either, if we can't find anything that exact color. Brick red or burgundy would also work fine."

Yessi elbowed me in the side. "Those are all the same colors, right?" she said under her breath.

I folded my hands in my lap and bit my tongue.

"Heaven forbid we accidentally choose a claret red!" Yessi whispered. "Mark would positively perish!"

I snickered. Then I let out an inadvertent snort. Yessi, that comedic temptress, had gotten me to break. I clutched my hands together harder and pressed my lips together, my eyes watering.

Though Yessi had been the one who made the joke, Kelly's eyes shot daggers right at me.

"Sorry." I lowered my gaze in shame and sipped my beverage.

"Do we even have time to order dresses?" Kendall asked, holding an extremely short gold dress up to her lithe twenty-something body. *Oh heck no, my friend*. The almost-forties outnumbered the younger ladies in this group. We'd wear housecoats before we'd agree to a micro minidress. "My best friend got married last summer, and we had to order the dresses months and months in advance."

"We don't have time, Kendall," Kelly snapped. "I'm aware of that. We'll need to find something off the rack."

"In burgundy? That fits everyone?" Yessi muttered. She, Kendall, and I weren't exactly the same size and shape. "You know, this is why Polly and I told our friends to find their own black dresses—"

"Well, we're going to *try* at least," Kelly barked. She

slammed her iPad down on the coffee table and stormed off to the dressing rooms. Kendall followed her.

"Shit," Yessi said. "I haven't seen her like this since she was trying to pass the real estate exam. Is this all wedding stress?"

"I don't know," I lied.

"She's usually good at this party-planning stuff. It's like her version of yoga." Yessi chuckled. "Remember when she organized that surprise party for my thirtieth birthday, and every single thing possible went wrong?"

"Oh my god, yes," I said, smiling. "They put, like, a cup of salt in your cake."

"Kel was cool as Fonzie when that happened."

The two of us glanced at the doorway leading to the dressing rooms. Kelly and Kendall were pawing through a rack of dresses, arguing with each other.

"This whole thing is moving pretty fast," Yessi said softly.

"Well..." I sipped my drink. "We're not getting any younger. I'm not surprised she wants to have the wedding as soon as possible." I couldn't fault Kelly for that. I was currently in two budding relationships that promised to bypass dating altogether. Why waste time?

"But it's like, just take a beat and relax. It's only a party. And if it's going to stress you out that much, just elope." She grabbed another mimosa for herself. "We're almost forty. Who needs a wedding?"

"I'm not sure this is all wedding stress today," I said, glancing again at the doorway. The sisters were still at each other's throats. I stood, motioning for Yessi to follow me away from the dressing rooms, toward the front of the store.

She and her mimosa trailed me to a rack of sale dresses in all colors of the rainbow.

I flipped through the hangers, stopping on a turquoise blue monstrosity with a big taffeta bow in the middle of the chest.

Yessi fingered the fabric. "I don't think that one will pass muster with Mark."

"Kelly came over this morning," I said, "and..." I stopped on another dress, this one red and vampy with a neckline down to there. How to explain to Yessi the scene Kelly had walked in on this morning? I was a nearly forty-year-old woman, who'd just started platonically shacking up with a much younger bartender I barely knew and his dog.

"And...?" Yessi prompted.

I pulled her even deeper into the racks of dresses. Satin and lace surrounded us. I couldn't do it. I loved Yessi, and I respected her opinions, which she was all too happy to give. To everyone. She never, ever minced words. Which was why something had been bothering me. "Why did Kelly tell you about Mark and not me?"

Yessi squeezed my shoulder. "I told you. They had a legal question. It wasn't like she came running to me the day they met or anything." She leaned out of the rack and looked around. Then she returned to me. "I don't think she would've told me if she didn't have to."

"What's going on with her?"

Yessi sighed. "I've been talking to Polly about this, and she just thinks that friendships change, and sometimes they run their course and end." She shrugged, her eyes glassy. "Maybe Kelly is done with us, and she's pushing us away now to make the eventual break easier."

My lip started quivering, so I bit it. "That can't be it," I said. "I mean, we're here right now. She asked us to be in her wedding."

"It could be the swan song for our friendship." She pulled me into a hug. "I know it sucks, but what can you do?"

I straightened up, knocking her off me. I wiped my eyes. "Well, I'm not going to do nothing. We've been friends for twenty years, and she doesn't get to throw that all away for some wine guy from the middle of nowhere."

I marched toward the dressing rooms, grabbing every maroon-ish dress I could find on the way. Kelly and Kendall sat on the couch together, looking intently through a book of dresses. "Kelly," I said, draping the dresses I'd found over the back of the nearest chair. "I'm sorry I moved your things without telling you. I shouldn't have done that."

She blinked. "Thank you. I appreciate that."

"You still always have a room in my house. It may not be the same room—"

Buzz!

"It may not be the same room—"

Buzz again.

"That's your phone, Annie," Kelly said.

"No," I said, "let me finish this."

Buzz!

"Damn it." I reached into my purse and found my phone. A patient had a question about a persistent fever. "I have to call them, but we'll finish our conversation in a minute."

"No, Annie." Kelly's eyes dropped back down to the dress book. "We won't. We never do."

CHAPTER TWENTY

Singin' in the Brain

"Have you ever been in a wedding?" I asked Dax as I wrote our team name—Dorothy and the Tin Man—across the tops of our answer sheets.

"You mean, have I ever been a groomsman?" He sipped his beer. "No."

"Well, this is my third time," I told him, "and it's…um… interesting to see your friends' personalities really come out under this kind of stress. I mean, I get it, I suppose, but I also think, why put yourself through the hassle?"

Kelly had made us try on practically every dress in the store, and she looked miserable the entire time. If the two of us had been in a better place, I would have pulled her aside, hugged her, and told her that the wedding would be great, with or without maroon lingerie dresses. But I was smart enough to recognize how that would've been received. I could do nothing right around her these days.

I checked my phone to make sure it was on vibrate. I'd managed to make it through the last few trivia nights without any patient interruptions, but one could happen at any moment. That was my life. People made sacrifices for their careers all the time. At least I knew Dax could handle things, trivia-wise, if I had to leave and make a call.

"People like to celebrate with their friends and family," Dax said.

"Sure," I said, "I suppose I understand why people like having weddings, but the only reason I'd ever throw one would be to return the favor to all my friends." I popped a peanut into my mouth.

"Like in *27 Dresses*." Dax checked his phone before shoving it back into his pocket.

"Excuse me, what did you just say?" I blinked rapidly, processing the words that had just come out of his mouth.

He glanced up. "The movie *27 Dresses*. Have you never seen it?"

"Of course I've seen it," I said. "Have *you*?"

He shrugged. "Who hasn't?"

"Many people." Darius, for one. But here was my young, hip roomie, using *27 Dresses* to teach a life lesson. "You just referenced a rom-com in real life. I've never felt closer to you."

Laughing, he rolled his eyes and turned his attention to the Cubs game on the TV behind my head.

"I saw an absolutely ridiculous turquoise taffeta monstrosity at the bridal shop the other day. I could make my friends wear that."

He grabbed a handful of nuts. "Did one of those guys you texted propose?"

"Well, kind of."

His eyes slowly lowered to mine. "What? Really?"

I sipped my drink. I hadn't told anyone—outside of

Rob and Darius, of course—about my current romantic situation, so why not start with the near-stranger who lived in my basement? "So, you remember our conversation after I realized I sent those texts?"

He nodded, shrugging.

"Well, I went to my mom's house the next day and had a chat with her neighbor—this guy Rob I grew up with. We both thought, well, we're single, we know each other, we know each other's families…" I shrugged. "Why not give it a shot?"

"Marriage?"

I nodded. "Marriage."

"Well," Dax said, "sounds like you have a long history with this guy, so it's not so out of the bl—"

"But then Darius Carver came to my office."

He held up a hand to stop. "Darius Carver? News guy Darius Carver?"

"Yup," I said. "He's doing a piece on me."

"Man on Main Street Darius Carver is doing a piece on *you*?" I couldn't tell if the look on Dax's face represented bewilderment or admiration.

"Yeah," I said jokingly. "I'm a big deal, Dax. Keep up."

"Sure you are—go on."

"I'd also sent the text to Darius, and he thought, since we were both in similar places financially and in our dating lives, that maybe we should be pragmatic and make a commitment to each other."

"Do you know him?" Dax's brow furrowed.

"We've been on a date."

"Oh, well then," he said sarcastically.

"I'm almost forty, Dax. Last call's coming. Time to pair

up and move on."

"That is…depressing."

That was…really rude. Dax had no idea what it was like to be pushing middle age, watching all your friends couple up and settle down. I was in fish-or-cut-bait territory.

At that moment, Ronald, more animated than usual, grabbed the mic. "Good evening, ladies and gentlemen!" His voice boomed through O'Leary's Barn. "Welcome to the first ever Windy City Trivia Championship tournament!"

The entire pub erupted in applause. Peter, behind the bar, enthusiastically rang the cowbell.

"It's not depressing," I told Dax. "It's being realistic. You'll understand someday."

"I hope I don't."

"Here's how the tournament works," Ronald said. "Tonight, all across the city, at twenty different bars, teams will compete at the exact same time with the exact same set of questions. At the end of the night, we'll add up the total scores and show you the leaderboard. During the final week, the top three teams will compete in a one-night, winner-takes-all championship held here in O'Leary's Barn."

"We're going to win this," I said, my eyes firmly on Ronald, as a rush of adrenaline coursed through me. I'd never win a beauty contest. I didn't have measurable talents that could bring me trophies or fame. But, damn it, I knew useless facts.

Ronald watched the big, new digital clock he'd placed on the stage behind him. "I assume you all know the general rules—the most important being 'no phones.' If we catch you with your phone out, you will be disqualified…and…" His eyes grew intense, and he looked out at all of us. "Grab your answer sheet for round one."

The sound of rustling papers cut through the chatter in the bar, and a feeling of déjà vu hit me. This moment of utter focus and collective concentration mentally and emotionally transported me back to college and med school, right before a huge exam. My palms sweated, and my stomach whirled. *Game time, Annie. Let's do this.*

"Our first round is geography," Ronald said.

"Good." I readied my pen. "I'm killer at geography," I told Dax.

"In honor of the first—hopefully annual—Windy City Trivia Tournament, our initial round will be all about other cities and their nicknames. When I say go, write the name of the city next to its corresponding nickname. And..." A list of questions popped up on the screen behind Ronald. "Go!"

Dax scooted closer to me, and, for a moment before I blocked it out, his spicy scent went up my nostrils. I concentrated hard on the questions at hand. *No time to be noticing anyone's cologne, Annie. It's time to kick ass and take names.*

Dax pointed to the first line. "Indianapolis."

I wrote that down.

"Number two, Baltimore. Number three, Seattle."

"Hold on, hold on." I was writing as fast as I could. Dax continued to rattle off the answers—Milwaukee and New York and Detroit and Louisville. And I was supposed to be the geography buff.

Soon we only had two left, and I'd barely taken a look at the list to check his answers.

"Queen City..." he said, thinking. "That sounds familiar..."

A lightbulb went on in my head. "It's Cincinnati," I whispered.

"You sure?" he asked.

"Absolutely," I told him.

"Okay, what about Bluff City?"

I tapped the pencil against my cheek, thinking. "Bluff City," I kept repeating to myself. "Bluff City," like somehow the answer would come to me.

After a moment, Dax snapped his fingers as if his own mental lamp had illuminated his mind. He snatched the pencil and paper from me and wrote down "Memphis."

"You sure?" I asked, a residual tingle from his hand brushing against mine still clouding my mind.

"Like, eighty-seven percent."

I shrugged. "That's better than I've got."

He, suddenly looking a lot like nerdy me back in high school, jumped up and ran our paper to Ronald at the front of the bar.

Ronald chuckled. "It's not a race."

Grinning, Dax came back to our table and sank into his seat. "I officially get it now," he said.

"What do you get?" I smiled back, relishing the moment.

"This." He waved a hand around the room, indicating the dozens of people still poring over their answer sheets. "This is quite a rush."

"Well," I said, grinning at him, "wait until we win. Then you'll really know what a nerd high feels like."

His eyes darkened. "Hey, can I say something, probably out of bounds?"

My stomach went queasy. "Yeah, okay."

He focused on a spot over my head—maybe the TV, maybe nothing. "Marriage?" His Adam's apple bobbed up and down. "Do it for the right reasons, okay?"

I thought I was, or at least I was doing it for *my* right reasons, but all I said was, "Okay."

"Good." He looked down at me, and the nerdy geek in him had returned. He leaned across the table and whispered, "When I took up our answer sheet, I accidentally saw the next category."

My jaw dropped. "That's cheating!"

"It's taking advantage of an opportunity," he said. "What do you know about Martin Scorsese movies?"

"Oh my god, so much!" And the two of us volleyed back and forth, jogging each other's memories about *Raging Bull*, *The Departed*, *Hugo*, *Goodfellas*, and more.

"Dorothy and the Tin Man!" Dax lifted his water glass.

I clinked mine against it. "Dorothy and the Tin Man!" I repeated and sipped my refreshing beverage, which Dax had thoughtfully flavored with lemon.

Brad sauntered over from the Very Stable Geniuses' table. "It appears you two are ahead of us by one point in the tournament," he said, offering his hand.

I shook it firmly, like a boss. "Good game, Brad."

"We'll get you next week."

"No, he won't," Dax muttered, eyes lowered in a glower, as Brad walked away.

I chuckled. "You really are riding that nerd high."

He shook his head. "No, I'm not."

"Sure you are. I like Trivia Dax."

He rolled his eyes and looked away, but I caught a smile on his usually too-serious face.

I couldn't help grinning. I hadn't felt this good in days. Using my brain power like this really put me in a state of flow. It did the same to Dax, I could tell, even if he wouldn't admit it.

Proof? Almost as quickly as he turned away from me, he swung back and offered me his fist to bump. "Dude, way to get that bonus question in the TV round. That was clutch."

My chest puffed up. (I decided to ignore the fact that he called me "dude"—at least it was better than "ma'am.") In the TV round, I'd figured out after only a few answers that the one thing all the actors listed had in common was that they'd played boyfriends on *Sex and the City*. It helped us narrow down our choices for the other answers, and Dax and I ended up the only team with a perfect score that round. "Yeah, well," I said, sipping my beer, "that was right in my wheelhouse. Wait until they give us a category about YouTubers, and then you'll see Grandma fail."

"Well, that will be fun to witness, anyway."

I stood and hoisted my purse over my shoulder. "Should we head…home?" My brow furrowed. That still felt weird to say. I didn't even know this guy's last name, and he was living in my basement.

"Sure." Grabbing his backpack (he used a *backpack*), Dax waved to Peter behind the bar, and the two of us headed out onto the street. The air outside had cooled a bit since earlier that evening. And just as it occurred to me that rain had been in the forecast for tonight, a big, sloppy drop landed right on the tip of my nose.

"How's the basement working out?" I asked, wiping it away. We were only two blocks from my house—plenty of time to get home before we got drenched.

"It's great, thanks." He offered nothing more than that. The trivia magic had worn off.

I wouldn't allow us to walk the route home in silence. I couldn't do that. "When I bought the place, I gutted the entire building and fixed up the basement as an apartment for my mom. But she refuses to leave her house."

Nothing.

"So, I'm glad someone is putting it to good use."

"Yeah," he said, shrugging.

Maybe it wasn't fair of me to pile all my emotional baggage on Dax tonight, but I was not in the mood to let the guy I'd allowed to stay in my house out of the kindness of my heart not talk to me on our walk home.

He'd just have to suck it up and be my friend, because I was in the market for one.

I opened my mouth to tell him as much when a loud crack of thunder cut through the night and the sky opened up.

"Oh my god!" I squealed, taking off running as the torrent of water hit my head and back.

"Annie, wait!" Dax yelled, laughing, behind me.

I spun around, the rain sloshing against my tennis shoes and soaking my socks. I raised my arms to the air in surrender and waited for Dax as he strolled toward me, rummaging through his backpack like he had all the time in the world. He triumphantly extracted an umbrella, opened it, and handed it to me.

"That's okay," I said, "I'm already saturated. I don't think I can possibly get any wetter."

"Well, I'm still going to use it," he said. "You can join me, if you want."

He lifted the small black umbrella over his head as the droplets beaded across the fabric and rolled to the ground. It'd be silly of me not to take him up on it. What was I going to do, walk home next to him, getting drenched, while a perfectly good umbrella was within reach? I ducked my head shyly and fell into step next to him. Our wet upper arms rubbed against each other, and I took note for the first time of one of his tattoos—a perfect sketch of a single rose near his wrist.

"That's pretty," I said.

He glanced down at me, blinking. A few raindrops had gotten stuck in his long, dark eyelashes. "What is?"

I pointed to his arm. "The rose."

"Oh, yeah. That." He turned his arm awkwardly, as if attempting to hide the flower from view. "I'm going to get that one covered up."

"Why?" I asked.

"Because what's important to you when you're eighteen sometimes isn't so important when you're twenty-seven."

I did the quick math. My age, which I rounded up to forty, divided by two, plus seven. Twenty-seven. Dax was old enough for me. Barely.

Ugh, why had I even thought that? He carried a *backpack*.

I shifted my arm away from his awkwardly, pulling at my T-shirt to make it less clingy. "I think you just described why I decided years and years ago that I would never get a tattoo."

"Really?" he said. "You've never wanted one?"

"Every time I even thought about getting inked, I'd force myself to imagine what it would look like when I was seventy-five. I couldn't come up with anything I wouldn't eventually regret." My lips slammed shut. That wasn't completely true.

There was this one time, when I was in my mid-twenties. Kelly, Yessi, and I had gone on a ski vacation out in Colorado. We spent part of the weekend hanging out with some bikers, and the three of us seriously discussed getting matching tattoos on the inside of our wrists—KAY, for Kelly, Annie, and Yessi. We'd all assumed that, at the very least, no matter what else happened in our lives, we'd remain friends forever. But something had made us chicken out at the last minute.

"You okay?" Dax asked.

"Yeah," I said, not wanting to get into it—not actually wanting to open up about my personal drama when push came to shove. I'd been too hard on Dax about not being so immediately open and candid with me, a near-complete stranger. There were things I didn't want to talk about, either. "What's important to you when you're twenty-seven may not be important when you're forty."

CHAPTER TWENTY-ONE

1.21 Triviawatts

Dax and I walked the rest of the way in relative silence, the only sounds between us our breaths and our footsteps. My need to fill every gap in the conversation melted away as I focused on the drops of rain hitting the umbrella above us, and our walk devolved into a comfortable quiet.

When we entered the house, Dax dropped the umbrella in the hallway as Joanne padded over to greet him. I hopped on one foot as I yanked off my soaking shoes and socks.

Joanne took this as her cue and dashed over to greet me, knocking me backward onto the nearby bench. She jumped on top of me, licking my face and wagging her tail. I laughed while trying to block my mouth from her eager tongue.

"That's too much, Joanne!" I said, giggling.

Dax pulled her off and helped me up. A jolt of electricity hit me when our hands touched, and I dropped his like a hot pot. "Thanks," I said, shaking out my shirt, which had become skintight and see through in the rain.

"She likes you." Dax finished taking off his shoes and socks.

"She has good taste." Joanne padded back over to me, more calmly this time, and I kissed her soft muzzle. "And she's a sweetheart." I was growing fond of this big, lumbering mutt.

He laughed. "I know that, and you know that, but a lot of people are scared of her size. I think she senses their nerves and tries to overcompensate by being way too friendly."

"Makes sense," I said. "But that's fine with me. I'll take all the Joanne attention I can get. I don't need to share with anyone else."

I watched Dax wander into the living room and over to the piano. He ran his hand across the back, and I winced, knowing how much dust he'd just tracked his fingers through. "Sorry about that," I said. "It's dirty—"

"Do you play?" He pulled out the bench and sat down.

"No," I said. "I bought the piano, promising myself I would learn, but I haven't gotten around to it yet."

He lifted the fallboard, revealing a set of pristine, gleaming black and white keys. Yes, I knew all the lingo. The guy who'd sold me the piano had been sure to go over everything with me. I'd filed it all away in my memory because that was what I did. I remembered useless facts. I figured maybe it'd come up in trivia someday.

It hadn't…yet. But I'd be ready.

Dax pressed softly on one of the white keys, eliciting a whisper of a note.

"My dad used to play," I said. "When I was a kid, my mom said we never had room in the house for a real piano, at least not when my brother and I were living there, but he always swore that he'd get a baby grand for the front window someday."

Dax grinned. "Did he ever get it?"

I shook my head, swallowing. "But I did."

A surge of understanding passed between us.

He opened his mouth to say something else, but then lightning flashed in the window behind him, and thunder boomed a moment later. The lights in the living room flickered, and Joanne went scurrying.

"We lose power here all the time," I said. "Just a warning. But it usually comes back on quickly."

"Noted." Dax's foot pressed the pedals under the instrument. "Do you mind if I play?"

"Please do." Grinning, I took a seat on one of the rock-hard couches facing the piano, tucking my cold, bare feet underneath me, ready for my private concert. I had no idea if Dax was any good, but he had to at least be better than I was—I could basically only plunk out "Twinkle Twinkle Little Star," which was the same tune as the alphabet song, so, bonus—two for the price of one.

He cracked his knuckles, took a deep breath, and played a chord that made Joanne howl all the way down in the basement. Still, the guy could play, apparently. Dax lifted his hands as if he'd just been shocked, then tried playing a scale. "This is horribly out of tune," he said with a crooked grin.

I winced. "Yeah, I'm not surprised."

"You have to take care of an instrument like this." He wiped a hand across the dusty music rack.

"I know." It was another one of the things the piano salesman guy had lectured me about. But I figured, I never played the thing. How out of tune could it get?

"When was the last time you had it serviced?"

"Um…well, I bought it about three years ago."

"Three years?" he said. "Annie."

"I'm sorry."

"It's all right." He gingerly covered the keys, stood, and tucked the bench back under the piano. "Do you mind if I get it tuned? I know a guy."

"You know a guy?" I said, smiling. "Who knows a piano guy?"

"Pianists," Dax said.

I let that hang there for a moment, Dax suddenly coming in to focus for me, just a bit. "You're a pianist? Why are you a bartender?"

He laughed. "For money?" He paused. "You know the whole 'starving artist' trope?" He leaned toward me and whispered. "It's real."

"Is that why you were staying with your sister?"

"That's part of it." He stepped over to the mantel and peered at the pictures of my mom and dad and my brother's family.

I hesitated to say anything more, to ruin this little moment by going too far and sending Dax back inside his shell. "My dad went to college for music."

"Really?" Dax picked up one of the frames and turned it to show me. "This him?"

"Yeah." I bit my lip. "He'd been in a band of some kind…I don't know, but then my mom got pregnant with me…" I shrugged. "Long story short, he became a banker."

"Well, that's good, too."

"You still play?" I asked.

"Yeah." He shrugged, grinning. "I'm in a band of some kind."

I smiled back at him, my insides warming. "Keep going with it," I said. "Don't give up."

He turned away and set the frame back on the mantel.

I stood and stretched, an idea occurring to me—a way to help this guy, who I was starting to feel an odd affection for. "And, in the meantime, you and I are going to crush the trivia competition for pride, and also so you can have the prize money to keep—" I mimed playing a piano.

He laughed. "Very good technique. But half that money will be yours. I can't take it all."

"Please," I said. "It'd mean much more to me knowing that it was going to help a talented musician keep his dream alive."

He wrinkled his nose. "You don't know that I'm talented."

"I can tell."

We stood there for a moment in awkward silence. We'd reached the point in the evening where we, as roommates, would have to decide—hang out or go our separate ways? Even for Kelly and me, it was kind of a tough dance. We had incompatible tastes in TV, and, really, we each needed our space at different times and in our own way.

"I was going to watch *The Crown*..." I said.

"Good," he said as a smile of relief spread across his lips. "That's...yeah. I want to get changed, and...I'm pretty tired."

"Okay." I stood and fluffed the pillow I'd crushed on the couch as Dax made his way toward the basement stairs.

"But"—he turned around—"if you ever feel like watching a movie sometime, some other night—"

I waggled my eyebrows. "Like a Katherine Heigl rom-com…?"

His face lit up in a crooked smile. "I'm not *not* saying a Katherine Heigl rom-com."

I chuckled, and he started to make his way down the steps. "Hey, Dax!"

He ran back up to the first floor. "Yeah?"

"What's your last name, anyway?"

"Logan." Then he waved goodnight and finally headed down to bed.

CHAPTER TWENTY-TWO

The Brains, the Athletes, the Basket Cases, the Princesses, and the Criminals

Back when I was a kid, I knew my classmates' domiciles by description ("Meg lives in the big, white house") or placement ("Katie's house is third from the corner"). The address where I was about to meet Rob was one of several nondescript Georgians on the north side of Touhy, utterly forgettable to anyone else but me, since this house had served as the setting for one of my biggest and most formative mortifications.

Even though I was probably the only one who remembered the incident, just thinking about it sent shivers up and down my spine.

I supposed these little jolts of nostalgia, if you could call them that, came with the territory of dating Rob. Though maybe, if we stayed together long enough, we'd start to make new memories, and the recurring nightmare of me getting my period and, instead of helping me, Ellen Miller making sure the entire sleepover knew I had bled through my white

Gap shorts would fade away.

Nope. I could be on my death bed at ninety and that one would still hurt.

I grabbed the tray of Tony's macaroni salad from the passenger's seat, made sure I had nothing stuck in my teeth, and left the safety of my vehicle.

My black-and-white sundress flapped around my legs in the warm wind, which carried sounds from several different Fourth of July parties on the block. "Everybody Dance Now" pumped from one backyard, the sounds of kids splashing in a pool emanated from another, and then I caught gusts of laughter coming from behind the Millers' house.

I pushed open the back gate and headed into the yard, eyes sweeping the place, looking for Rob. He'd asked me to meet him at the party because he'd been here all night helping his friend smoke brisket or something like that. Apparently it was a task that required constant vigilance and about fifteen hours.

"Oh my god, Annie Kyle!"

My head swung to the right, and a woman who looked like a slightly aged-up version of herself from twenty-five years ago—same long, thick dirty blond hair in a ponytail, tank top, and cutoffs—dashed over and wrapped me in a hug.

"Hi...Ellen," I said.

Ellen and I never would've hugged back in grade school. Or no, that wasn't completely true. Back then, she would've hugged me while pretending to be my best friend for two days before dumping me like a bad habit after the weekend, which was something that had actually happened.

But that was more than twenty-five years ago. We were

grown-ups now. Ellen had no doubt matured, just like I had.

"It's so good to see you." She held me at arm's length for a moment. "God, you look great." And then walked me up the steps to the deck, where several unfamiliar women were sitting around the patio table, drinking and eating foods in chip-and-dip form.

I felt like I was moving underwater, a little off balance, a little stressed about my breathing. I was used to my friends, to Yessi and Kelly. As a workaholic almost-forty-year-old, I didn't get out much to socialize. But, no, that wasn't true. In the past few weeks, I'd gone out on two successful dates with guys I barely knew, and I'd broken through (at least momentarily) the gruff exterior of my new roommate. I could do this.

"Everybody," Ellen said, "this is Rob's next-door neighbor, Annie."

"Hi," I said brightly, waving to the crowd of women. "Nice to meet you all." I glanced around. "Have you seen Rob?"

One of the women, a blonde who'd obviously been working on her tan, pointed toward the back fence. "Garage."

"Thanks." I grabbed a beer from a nearby cooler—when in Rome—and walked down the steps and through the yard to the garage. The side door was closed, but I could hear a bunch of male voices wafting through the aluminum. I took a deep breath and opened it. All eyes snapped to me. "Hi, I'm…" I gave a timid wave. *Shit*. Rob and these guys were super close. I wondered how much he'd told them about our… situation.

We probably should've had this conversation beforehand.

"Hey, Annie!" Rob set his beer down and rushed over. He

kissed me quick on the cheek, took my elbow, and hurried me over to say hi to his friends. "You probably know all these guys already," he said, smiling. "This is T.J. Collins. He's married to Ellen now, and the two of them bought this house from her parents. These jerks are Jim and Pete and Jack—they were my year in grade school. And of course you know Eric Mendoza." He ushered me over to a bearded hulk of a man with a thatch of thick, black hair on top of his head. Kind brown eyes smiled at me.

"*Ann* Kyle," Eric said jokingly, offering a fist to bump. I obliged him.

Eric and I had been in school together from kindergarten through eighth grade. We were always in competition academically and used to make fun of each other all the time, teasingly, benignly. I even let him call me "Ann," because I knew it came from a place of mutual respect.

"You grew," I acknowledged, smiling. "And you kept your hair. Didn't see that one coming."

He ran his fingers through the thick locks. "Yes, I did."

"I mean," I said, "assuming all that's real."

The other guys laughed. One of them—Jack, I think— grabbed me another beer. I straightened up. This wasn't so bad at all. They were being nice to me. I'd been accepted into this group.

Rob stood near me, our arms touching, just barely. "How are things out there?" He nodded toward the door, smiling nervously.

"Good," I said, grinning. "Everyone was very welcoming."

"Glad to hear it. They can be a tough crowd." He picked up his own beer from a nearby table and started walking toward the main garage door, leading out to the alley. "Come on out here a second."

I nodded in deference to the other guys and followed Rob out of the garage. He led me over to one side, where they had set up the smoker. Tufts of gray smog contrasted the bright blue midday sky. I left the beer Jack had given me on the ground nearby. I knew someone in this crowd would grab it eventually.

"I'm sorry you had to come alone," Rob said. "That wasn't my plan, but T.J. needed my help."

"No problem at all. How's the brisket coming?"

Rob laughed. "It's taking a hell of a lot longer than we thought it would. Should be ready by next Fourth of July, at this rate."

I smiled. There was something sexy about a guy in an apron, poking at meat on a grill. "Do Ellen and T.J. have a nice pantry for you to use, Mr. Cook Guy?"

He laughed. "No!" He ran a hand through his blond hair, squinting in the sun. "I keep begging them to let me work on their house, but no dice." He motioned for me to follow him. "Oh, but check this out."

I followed him a few doors down, taking the opportunity to peek through fences and into the backyards. When I lived with my parents, I liked to walk down the alleys sometimes to get an entirely different perspective on the neighborhood. There were so many hidden treasures to spy—old cars, aboveground pools, the odd shrine—whether to Mary or to the Bears.

Rob stopped near a tall wooden fence. "This will be tough to see, but—shoot, no. We're going in."

"What?" I glanced back toward the Millers' house.

"Trust me." Rob looked around as if trying to figure out what to do. A moment later, a lightbulb went on in his head. "Stay there." Then he jumped the chain-link fence behind the house next door. A few seconds later, he was letting me in the back gate of the house with the very tall fence.

"What are we doing?" I ducked my head and entered the yard, like I was heading into the Secret Garden or something. "This is breaking and entering."

"We didn't break anything."

"Well, we entered."

I followed him into the yard, down a cement walk, and past the garage. This house had a massive addition along the back, with floor-to-ceiling windows.

"Did you do this?" I asked.

"I did." He waggled his eyebrows, then continued to skulk all the way up and onto the deck.

"People have guns in this neighborhood, Rob."

He waved away my concern. "They know me."

"Okay…" I hung back, ready to call 911 and perform CPR—whatever was necessary.

"No one's home," he said. "Come here."

I tiptoed up to the window where Rob had pressed his face to the glass.

"Look in here. This kitchen is one of my masterpieces."

I gazed around at the gleaming counters and cabinets. He'd even installed a mosaic on the backsplash behind the stove. Rob had real talent and passion for his work. I grinned, thinking of the slacker kid I knew back in the day, who never wanted to be anything except "good at video games."

Yet another "pro" for Rob: having a guy around who could fix things in the house. Though I already knew about his business, it didn't hurt to see actual evidence of his prowess in this area.

"See the door there?"

I squinted into the house. "Yeah."

"It leads to a big-ass pantry," he said with a gleam in his eye.

"That's the dream," I said.

"That is the dream." He leaned in and touched his lips to mine, on the deck of some stranger's house. His lips tasted pleasantly malty and sweet, but I could barely enjoy the kiss because I kept expecting some security personnel to show up and bust us for trespassing or Ellen to come zipping around the corner to make fun of me for kissing Rob Casey.

Old wounds persisted.

After a moment, Rob pulled away, patted me on the arm, and said, "I'd better get back to that brisket."

In a fog, I followed him out of the yard and back to the Millers' house.

CHAPTER TWENTY-THREE

Teenage Mutant Ninja Trivia

Very early the next morning, I kept replaying the events of the Fourth of July in my mind, relaying my thoughts as they occurred to me to Joanne as I walked her through the neighborhood.

"It was an odd day, Joanne," I told her as she stopped to pee on someone's parkway.

She glanced back at me as if to say, *Don't bother me when I'm doing my business.*

"Sorry," I said, "but you're the only person I can talk to about this."

Joanne and I continued on her walk. She had let me take her as far as four blocks yesterday. I was determined to hit five today.

"Rob *kissed* me."

Joanne didn't care.

"And I kissed him back, I think. I don't remember. It all happened so fast." I'd been distracted, too. Some people's libido went *zoom* in dangerous situations, like breaking and entering, but I guessed I wasn't one of those people. I liked safe and private. I preferred a venue in which I wasn't breaking any laws. "I think that's why it was a little lackluster."

She sniffed a tree.

And then, after the kiss, Rob went back to the brisket, and I returned to the women in the backyard. "It honestly wasn't bad," I told Joanne. "Everyone was very nice to me. It's just going to take some time for me to learn their language."

Joanne looked back at me.

I chuckled. "They spoke English, Joanne. But they've known one another for so long, they have a shorthand. And they all know the same people, and they talk about them like I should know them, too, even though I haven't lived in that neighborhood for twenty years, and even back then I wasn't really part of the crowd."

I clamped my mouth shut as a car headed my way. The driver did not need to witness me chatting about my love life with a dog. Though, honestly, with all the tiny earphones and whatnots, people could really get away with muttering to themselves all day long. It was the same philosophy I used when I was belting out some old Gwen Stefani songs in the car.

But back to Rob. I thought I got him now—understood where he was coming from. Later on in the evening, after dinner had been served, we were sitting together in a couple lawn chairs, under a tree, and one of his friends showed up drunk and angry. Rob had pulled the guy aside to talk him through what was going on.

"He's obviously a great friend," I told Joanne. "He'd do anything for the people he cares about."

He'd dropped everything—including me—to help his

friend for two whole hours.

"But his friend needed him in that moment. He would've done the same for me, if I'd been in trouble, and I would've done the same for Kelly or Yessi."

Still, even though I knew he was being a good pal, something bugged me. Eric and the other guys had gone to help Rob with the drunk dude, too, but they all came back quickly to hang out with their wives.

Only Rob had gone long-haul with the friend. And he hadn't come back to check on me once, not even to tell me it'd be a bit longer. He never even texted.

During sophomore year of high school, a new girl moved to town from New York (I couldn't help comparing her to Stacey McGill from *The Baby-Sitters Club*), and the two of us got along great. We liked the same music and were in most of the same classes. By the end of the first trimester, I was ready to declare it: she was my best friend. But she'd always talk about her own, real best friend back home, and I got the sense that I was a placeholder—a stopgap friend until she could get back to New York and her real BFF.

That was how I felt with Rob last night. He had his real friends, and then there was me. I'd never truly measure up, and he'd always set me aside for them.

"Eventually I just...left...because I was all alone and I had no idea where Rob had gone."

Joanne paused, ignoring me, her back ramrod straight, as she sniffed the air. The leash tightened in my hand.

"What is it?" I asked.

A second later, she let out one low warning growl and made a mad dash toward the house nearest to us, nearly pulling my arm out of its socket. Along the side of the house, she barked again and then froze. I almost fell over my own feet.

"Come on, Joanne." I tried to pull her away from her quarry, but she ignored me, staring deep into the bushes, at two glowing eyes reflected against the streetlights.

My heart beat faster, and I opened my mouth to say, "Let's go," but then a small black-and-white animal stalked out from the hedge, and the next thing I knew, Joanne and I were covered in skunk skank.

Perfect.

CHAPTER TWENTY-FOUR

Smells Like Team Spirit

"Shit, shit, shit," I kept saying as I dragged Joanne the four blocks back to our house. On the way, still holding on tight to her leash, I pulled out my phone and furiously googled "what the hell do I do if my dog and I get sprayed by a fucking skunk?"

The answer came back: *don't bring your clothes or the dog inside and mix up a concoction of hydrogen peroxide, baking soda, and dish detergent.*

"Well," I told Joanne, who appeared fazed not at all by her now-overwhelming stench, "this is going to be a DIY de-skunking."

I led her into my small backyard and shut the gate behind us. It was only just now six o'clock in the morning, and the street around us was still quiet and dark. "At least it's July," I told her. "Trying to give you a bath outdoors would be an even bigger disaster if you'd pulled this nonsense in October or March." I tied her leash around the pole at the base of my back deck. "You're not going anywhere, my friend. I don't want you getting covered in dirt, too."

She didn't fight it. Joanne sat serenely in the flower bed, the picture of innocence.

Though the ingredients for the anti-skunk funk solution were inside my house, I went into the garage first to see if I could find anything to use as a tub. Right away, I spotted an old baby pool I'd bought a few years ago when my brother came up from Texas with my niece. I dragged the plastic Dora the Explorer tub out onto the grass and set the nozzle of the garden hose inside it.

"Now for the other stuff." I peered into my neighbors' yards. Dark. Quiet.

Joanne watched me as I slipped out of my clothes, down to my underwear, dropping my shirt and shorts in a puddle on the sidewalk. I smelled my bra. Not too bad. My T-shirt had taken the brunt of the spray. I scurried up the steps to the sliding glass door on the deck. Locked.

Crud.

I'd have to go in the front door. I saluted Joanne, slipped out the front gate, locked it, and made a mad dash around the side of the house and up the front steps. A light hit me, and I turned to see a cab idling in front of my house. He honked and flashed his lights at me. I flipped off the driver and yanked open my front door.

Panting hard, I shut the door behind me (and locked it to keep out the lecherous cabbie) and tiptoed upstairs, trying not to wake Dax. Up in my room, I changed into my bathing suit—a navy blue bikini covered in a neon feather pattern—and chucked my underwear out the back window and down onto the deck. I checked on Joanne—still just hanging out. She'd given up on sitting and had curled up in my hostas.

I grabbed a few towels and the ingredients for the shampoo. After I'd mixed up the concoction in an old pitcher, I let myself out the back door onto the deck. "Joanne, what the heck are you doing?" She was on her back, happily wriggling in the dirt and, no doubt, rabbit feces.

"Let's get you cleaned up." I turned on the hose and then untied Joanne, leading her on her leash over to the pool. Once she figured out where I was taking her, she froze. I yanked her leash. "Come on, girl. There's no way out of this."

She would not budge.

"Joanne," I told her. "You smell like ass, and you're not going inside again until we rectify that."

She flopped down in the grass, growing limp.

"Okay, then."

I was a medical doctor. I had gone through years and years of school and training, but nothing had prepared me for trying to bathe a stubborn ninety-pound beast made of solid muscle.

I tried reasoning with her. "We'll get this over with so quickly you won't even know it's happening, and then I'll give you a treat."

Her ears perked up at that momentarily, until she realized I didn't actually have said treat on me.

Damn it. She was too smart for her own good.

"Joanne." I stood firm, hands on hips. "Get in the pool."

She licked her undercarriage.

"Fine." One hand still holding the leash, I pulled the hose toward me. "We'll have to do this the hard way."

She jumped up and attempted to drag me up the back steps.

"Joanne, no! Relax!"

"What's going on?" Dax, in a T-shirt and athletic shorts, appeared along the side of the house, just beyond the back basement steps. He scratched the top of his head, making his bedhead more pronounced.

"We got sprayed by a skunk."

"Oh no." He rushed over, reaching for his dog's leash. "Damn it, Joanne. Are you okay, Annie?"

"It just got on my clothes, I think," I said. "Joanne took the brunt of it. Have you ever dealt with this before?"

He shook his head.

"Google says we have to bathe her with that concoction over there." I gestured toward the pitcher I'd set near the pool.

"Joanne's terrified of water." Dax wrinkled his nose as he caught a whiff of his dog's current eau de parfum.

"So I gathered." I paused. This was his pet, after all. I should let him take the lead. "What do we do?"

"She'll just have to bear through it." He appraised his dog. "I can't remember the last time I gave her a bath on my own. Usually I just trick her into going to the groomer at the pet store once in a while." After a moment, he turned to me, eyes determined. "I'll hold her down. You scrub."

I got to work prepping our instruments—the shampoo, a big sponge, a few towels—as Dax carried his beast over to the pool. Joanne seemed calmer in his arms. She even gave him a quick lick on the cheek, as if to say all was forgiven.

"Okay," Dax said. "Here we go." His grip tight around her torso, he stepped over the lip of the pool and then lowered her into the water. She squirmed as soon as her feet hit the cold bath, but Dax held her there. "Try to avoid her face as much as possible."

"But she probably got sprayed there."

He leaned in and sniffed her head, wrinkling up his nose. "Yup. Definitely did." He turned his nose away from his malodorous dog. "Let's save that for last, then; start with something less traumatic. Get the rest of her body first."

I gingerly hit Joanne's back with the hose. She flinched, and Dax grabbed on tighter.

"That's it," he said calmly. "Nice and easy."

After I'd wetted most of her body, I grabbed the pitcher and poured the concoction over her back. Smiling sheepishly, I knelt down next to Dax and started scrubbing Joanne's fur with the sponge.

"Good girl," he kept whispering in her ear as her body tightened, ready to flee. I couldn't help smiling, watching him soothe his dog with such tenderness.

Like playing a stinky game of Twister, I tried to wash every bit of Joanne's body without invading Dax's personal space and without falling over. "Sorry," I said as my arm grazed his.

"It's okay," he said softly. I wasn't sure if he was talking to me or if that was meant for Joanne.

When I moved around to Joanne's front, Dax and I were suddenly face-to-face. I softly and gently soaped up Joanne's head. "Good," he said, "easy." His warm breath hit my cheek, sending waves of heat to my core. Carried away by my body's response to his calming whispers, I kept rubbing and rubbing and rubbing the top of her head.

"I think you got it," Dax said.

I straightened up. "Right. Yup. I think that's it." I pressed my legs together in an attempt to stanch the flow of blood to that area.

"You need to rinse her off first."

"Of course." A task. I grabbed the hose, trying to ignore the flush rising up the back of my neck. I aimed the hose at Joanne, and she flinched again, now struggling harder against Dax's grip.

"Get closer," he said. "Make sure you wash off all that peroxide."

I aimed the stream at her back, and Dax wiped away the soap as much as he could. Joanne bucked hard against him, finally breaking loose and sending him flying, onto his back, into the pool. His feet kicked my legs out from underneath me, and I landed flat on top of him, my palms pressed into his chest. The two of us burst out laughing.

"Sorry." The top of my bare foot rubbed against his, and I realized quickly that his hands were gripping my hips and his eyes were locked on mine. The laughter had stopped as quickly as it began.

"Um, Joanne," I said breathily.

"Shit, you're right. She probably just undid all our hard work." He struggled under me, so I rolled off him and stood. I offered him a hand to help him up.

"Thanks." He grabbed his dog's leash and led her away from the bushes where she was now hiding. "Maybe I'll just try rinsing her off in the shower with me. If that's okay."

"It's fine."

I watched him, tight white T-shirt, see-through and clinging to his back muscles, walking his dog down the basement steps and out of sight.

CHAPTER TWENTY-FIVE

Gryffindorks

approached the guard at the security desk. "Hi," I said. "I'm here to see Darius Carver."

"ID?"

I showed her my driver's license, and she handed me a clipboard. "Sign your name on there, and someone will be down soon to get you."

"Thank you." I stepped away from the desk and over to a wall of black-and-white photographs of practically every famous person who ever lived in Chicago—Oprah Winfrey, President Obama, Harry Caray, Svengoolie...

A door opened to my left, and out came Darius, grinning big. He waved a hand down his body. "Perks of doing radio: relaxed dress code." And sure enough, for the first time since I met him, he was not wearing a suit. He'd paired perfect, pristine blue jeans with a button-down shirt and a sweater tied across his shoulders. He looked like a J.Crew ad.

Darius took my hand and pulled me in for a quick kiss on the cheek, sending a shiver of excitement through my body. He smelled woody and masculine and clean. I couldn't hide my giddy grin. Darius Carver just kissed me in public.

He led me through the door he'd just come out of and pressed an elevator button going up. "I'm so sorry about this," he said.

"It's no problem. I'm breezy." We'd planned on getting dinner together tonight, but the Cubs game got canceled, and the radio station needed someone to jump on and do a show. For some reason not completely clear to me yet, that person was Darius.

"Well, thank you for being so understanding about changing our date's venue tonight." We stepped on the elevator, and he hit the button for nine. "When duty calls, I have to answer."

"But you're a TV newsperson?" I said.

"That's my main job, yes, but I also fill in on WTS Radio when they need me. It's a sweet gig, really." He flashed his smile. "I'm hoping, if I play my cards right, to get my own permanent slot—late in the evenings or on the weekends, at least to start. It'd get me closer to my next career goal."

"Which is?"

"To be the premier entertainment voice in Chicago."

"Wow," I said.

He counted on his fingers. "Food, music, theater, TV, movies—you name it." He sighed. "But in order to do that, I have to be like a shark and keep swimming. It's always about the hustle. You get it. You have your own business."

"Yeah," I said, "I suppose I do."

"And you'll see even more when your big segment airs on the news this week!" He made an excited face. "Your name is about to become synonymous with 'concierge doctor.'

These days, you can't just do your job and expect to get anywhere. It's all about branding and carving out your own space, making yourself indispensable. That's what I'm trying to do. When a Chicagoan wonders, 'Should I see that play or eat in that restaurant?' I want them to immediately think, 'Let's see what Darius has to say about it.'"

The elevator door opened, and Darius and I stepped off. "I ordered food from the same restaurant we'd planned to visit tonight." He motioned for me to follow him. A bag of takeout sat on his desk. He handed me one of the cartons.

"This is fun," I said, fully prepared to ride the changing waves of our second date. How many people got to hang out at a radio station? This was cool. On our first two dates, Darius had already showed me parts of the city I'd never seen before. "Dining together in a—"

"Oh, we won't be dining together. I'm on the air in"—he checked his watch—"well, very soon, but you have a few options. You're welcome to hang out here." He turned on a TV. "They show a closed-circuit broadcast of the show throughout the building. Or you can sit in the green room with my illustrious guests—at least the ones who were able to come downtown to be interviewed in person. Or you can really see how the sausage is made and sit in the producer's booth."

"Wow," I said, feeling a little overwhelmed. A few hours ago, I'd been anticipating a quiet VIP dinner with Darius at a fancy Italian place, but now I was at the WTS recording studio, about to eat dinner alone…somewhere…in a strange building. "I'll check out the producer's booth." At least that seemed like it'd be close to Darius. "You got to see me at work. It's only fair that I get to see you on the job, too."

His eyes lit up. "That's a fantastic way of looking at it."

I followed him out of his office and down the hall. He peeked his head into a room on the way and shook the hand of a man inside. "We'll come and get you soon."

"That's Steve Pumpernickel," Darius told me as we continued down the hall. "He owns a bakery on the West Side, and he's my first guest tonight." He nodded back toward the green room. "I think he brought samples, if you're interested."

"Free bread? No wonder you like this job," I said.

"Now you get it." Darius finally pulled open another door at the end of the hallway, ushering me into a large studio filled with TV monitors, microphones, and wires everywhere. "News is on now, so we don't have to be quiet." He pointed to a TV screen on which a newswoman was reading today's headlines. Darius walked me into the producer's booth. "Cody, this is Annie. She's going to sit in today."

Cody, a young guy who really took the "dress down" directive to heart in black sweats and a trucker cap pulled down over his face, wordlessly pointed to a chair in the back corner.

"He's not going to be the chattiest," Darius whispered.

"Okay." Maybe I should've stayed back in the office, but we made so many twists and turns getting here, I had no confidence I'd be able to find my way back. I set my container of food on my lap and sat quietly.

Darius went into the studio, and I watched him get geared up with his headphones, microphone, and water bottle. A few moments later, Cody was counting him in. "You're on in three...two...one."

"Good evening," Darius said, launching into his intro, talking about his various guests tonight.

Cody sank into his chair and took a swig from a massive fountain drink. "You guys close?" He nodded toward the picture window in front of him.

"We're getting to know each other," I said.

He spun around, facing me, eyes narrowed. "You're nothing like his last girlfriend." He laughed. "But who is, right?"

I hesitated. "Right."

Cody turned back around, focusing again on monitoring the show and answering calls.

I took out my phone and googled "Darius Carver girlfriend." A picture popped up of him with a gorgeous, young, ethereal woman. *Monica Feathers.* I clicked on her name. Apparently she was a pop star, and a popular one, though I'd never heard of her. Not that my lack of knowledge in this area would surprise anyone. My music tastes stalled back when JT was still with NSYNC.

Monica and Darius looked so happy together in the pictures. He gazed down at her with a look of pure adoration. His carefully curated sheen and poise seemed to disappear in her presence. In the photos, he looked like the rest of us real-world goobers—purely and pathetically in love.

I glanced up at Darius, who was currently chatting up the bread man. I could see it now, the difference. He looked at Mr. Pumpernickel the same way he looked at me—with detached, professional interest.

He reserved his real smile for Monica Feathers.

But they were no longer together.

I opened my dinner container and tucked in. He'd gotten me an order of delicious four-cheese ravioli, because, while maybe he didn't know me and I didn't know him, he knew food. He was a hard worker, and so was I. The two of us had that in common. We hadn't signed on for love and passion. We'd promised each other commitment and nothing more. There was a reason he was no longer with the woman he'd been passionately in love with, just like there was a reason I wasn't planning on jumping into bed with my hot, young roommate. Darius and I were mature, experienced adults, and we were looking for pragmatism.

I noticed him looking at me through the glass partition, so I held up my fork and grinned, making "yummy!" circles with my hand over my stomach. He clutched his hands to his chest and sent me back one of his best made-for-TV smiles.

CHAPTER TWENTY-SIX

Here Comes Treble

Late Sunday morning, I pulled into my mom's driveway and texted her to come out. My mother, carrying a huge lavender gift bag adorned with an obscenely large silver bow, slid into the passenger's seat of my car.

"You can put that in the back," I told her as she balanced the present on her lap.

"I'll hold it," she said. "It might break."

"Well, put it on the floor between your legs, then," I said. "It's blocking my side-view mirror."

My mom reached down, pointedly picked up a grimy gym towel from my floor, and tossed it into the backseat before setting her gift down.

"How's my celebrity baby?" Her hand reached over and squeezed my knee.

"Your celebrity baby is wiped out." I reached for my massive coffee and took a swig before backing out of the driveway. Ever since Darius aired his segment on my practice Tuesday night, right after the second round of the trivia tournament (Dorothy and the Tin Man were currently in a four-way tie for first; we were gonna get Dax that money), Tina and I had been fielding requests from potential patients and answering notes of congratulations from other people in my life.

Darius had been right. People in Chicago now saw me as *the* concierge doctor, and they wanted in. It was an uptown problem, for sure, but I hated to turn people down or tell them no, which was the position I now found myself in. I had planned to take on a few more patients at some nebulous point in the future, but things were getting out of hand. I had an actual waiting list now, and I had to carefully consider how much new work I was prepared to take on, meaning how much of my already paltry personal life I was willing to give up.

"It was a great segment," my mom said. "The knitting ladies were talking about it all week. They came over to Regina's to watch it again with us on Friday morning."

"Mmm-hmm."

"We kept going on and on about how Regina's son is in love with a celebrity."

Serenity now. "Mom, Rob and I have been on two dates together. Let's cool it with the love talk." And we kissed, sure, but I was a thirty-nine-year-old woman in the twenty-first century. I could kiss people without it bringing scandal upon the *ton.*

"Rob has very nice things to say about you."

I drew in a deep breath and flipped on my blinker, focusing on merging onto 294. "I have nice things to say about him, too, but we're just getting to know each other." I left out the part about how I was also getting to know Darius, because I wanted to avoid the emotional baggage that would come with causing my mother's head to explode. "Besides, you should watch what you say around Mrs. Casey."

"Regina? Why?"

I veered right toward I-90. "Because she needs to focus on her health, not pipe dreams about me and Rob getting married."

"It's not a pipe dream, though. Not according to Rob, anyway."

My chest tightened. "What?"

She patted my knee. "Honey, you can drop the charade. Rob told us all about how you guys are 'getting to know each other' with the ultimate goal of settling down."

I rubbed my temple. "Rob told you that."

"Yes."

I focused hard on the cars in front of me as I chewed my lip and willed away a headache I could feel coming on. Rob knew about Darius. He knew that I'd wanted to keep our situation quiet, especially from our mothers, yet he'd gone and burst our circle of trust.

Because the truth was, I honestly wasn't sure yet who I'd pick. I liked the familiarity and the security of being with Rob. I could marry Rob, and my life would stay pretty much the same.

But Darius offered something completely different— excitement and adventure. And, judging by how things were going after his segment aired, a lot of money and career success.

I was choosing between two very disparate options, and both appealed to me equally. In the back of my mind, Dax's warning to marry for the right reasons tried to wiggle in, but I ignored it. Who decided "love" was the one right reason to get married anyway?

"How's Mrs. Casey doing?" I asked my mom, changing the subject away from my romantic life.

"She's been feeling pretty bad because of the chemo," Mom said. "We had to bring knitting to her on Friday."

I carefully changed lanes.

"She's waiting on some tests now, to get a better sense of how far the cancer has spread."

"I'm sure she'll be fine," I said. "She's doing everything she's supposed to do, and her doctors are great." I'd done some research into Dr. Stucco, and he was legit. He'd take good care of Mrs. Casey.

"You're probably right."

I glanced over. My mom was staring out the window, pensive. "You okay, Mom?"

After a few beats, she said, "I lost your dad, and now I'm about to lose my best friend."

I reached over and squeezed her hand. "You have me."

"I know, sweetie. And your brother and the kids… But you all have your own lives." She turned toward me, tears in her eyes. "I'm sorry for bugging you so much about Rob. It's just that…the two of you together gives me hope. Maybe you'll get married and move next door, and maybe I won't be alone."

"Mom," I said, a lump in my throat. "You can't count on that. I mean, it could happen—really, it could; I promise—but don't dwell on it."

My mom had never really had to get out there and meet

people. She never spent much time alone. After my dad died, she threw all her focus to her friends, doing knitting and playing Bunco and volunteering at the church. And she'd done it all with Mrs. Casey by her side.

"I know you're sad about Mrs. Casey, but you can't wait around hoping nothing changes or that folks will come to you. You've got to get out there and try new things, get to know new people, for yourself."

That was what I was doing with Rob and Darius: being proactive, finding someone with a similar worldview with whom I could build a life. I could no longer count on Kelly and Yessi to be there for me, so I had to put myself out there and live the way I saw fit.

"That's good advice," she said.

"Well, I am a very famous doctor."

CHAPTER TWENTY-SEVEN

Iran-Contra with Konami Code

By the time we got to Huntley for Kelly's bridal shower, my headache had become a real, almost corporeal thing. It felt like a tiny-but-strong monster running through my brain. I popped a few ibuprofens as soon as I parked the car.

My mom, thankfully, after our little emotional detour, had quickly turned the conversation over to my cousin who had just gotten engaged to her ex-husband's sister. Thank goodness for relatives with drama.

The banquet hall in Huntley was packed with people, most of them unfamiliar, even to me. My mom, who didn't know anyone, hovered at my side as I glanced around the room, looking for somewhere to go. I finally spotted Yessi, Polly, and their baby, Olivia, in the back corner. "There are our people."

I led my mom over there, and we all did our hugs and hellos. Polly asked me about work, and I asked her how the veterinarian business was going. Yessi, who was holding Olivia, gave me a one-armed hug. "Be forewarned," she whispered in my ear, "Kelly is in full bridezilla mode."

"Well, it's her shower," I said.

"I know, but, dude, I made one little joke about the signature drink, and, well…" She gestured toward our table. "I thought it'd be prudent to sit in the back."

"What's the signature drink?"

Biting her lip to keep from laughing, she handed me a champagne flute filled with bubblegum pink liquid and garnished with gold leaf. "True Love's Kiss," she managed to blurt out.

Wrinkling my nose, I sipped it and immediately started coughing. "Oh my god! What's in this? My lips are burning." I grabbed a glass of water from the table, even though I knew that would only exacerbate the problem.

"It's basically a vodka cranberry, but with liquid smoke and a hint of Scotch bonnet pepper." Yessi waggled her eyebrows. "Apparently Mark likes things spicy."

"Oh shit." I waved my hand in front of my mouth. "I was not expecting that."

Yessi took her seat. "All I'm saying is, tread lightly."

"Unlike this drink." I grabbed a roll from the bread basket. Maybe that would help smother the fire raging in my mouth.

"Yessi," my mom said, "did you see Annie's little video?"

I groaned. "Mom…"

"I sure did," Yessi said. "I thought it was great—especially the part where it looked like you were using a stethoscope for the first time."

"Yessi," Polly said in a warning tone.

"I'm kidding." Yessi patted my hand. "Annie knows I'm just busting her balls."

"I do," I said. "And I'm not used to being on camera, so

forgive me for looking a little wooden."

"A lot wooden," Yessi said, struggling with a squirming Olivia. "But we still love you." She blew me a kiss.

"What do you think about her and Rob Casey?" my mom asked.

I shot daggers across the table at my mother.

"Rob who?" Yessi said.

"My neighbor," my mom said. "He and Annie are getting pretty serious."

Yessi's eyes, usually flashing and laughing, darkened in confusion.

My mom passed Yessi her phone. "Here he is."

Yessi, quiet for once, peered down at Rob. "Wow," she said. "Looks like everybody's got their secrets."

I turned toward my friend. "Yessi, my mom is fully overstating it. I've gone out a couple times with this guy, and we've talked about how we're both up for settling down, but it's nothing more than that."

Yessi stood, hoisting Olivia onto her hip. "I'm gonna go feed her."

"Hon," Polly said, "you don't have to go. No one minds if you nurse her."

"I do," she said. "I need a minute."

I watched Yessi, my last remaining best friend, walk away. Shit. I turned to Polly. "I really haven't been keeping anything from Yessi. I barely know what this thing is with Rob myself."

Polly nodded toward the bathrooms. "You should go talk to her. She's feeling a little insecure with all the Kelly drama. I'm sure it will blow over quickly."

"Yeah. I should." I grabbed my purse and headed purposefully in the direction of the ladies' room to talk to Yessi, but then I heard my name as I passed a table. "Is that Annie?"

Sighing, I turned around and found Kelly's mom and her aunts.

I clutched Kelly's mom's hand, leaned down, and hugged her. "Hi, Mrs. Stafford."

"Glad you could make it, honey!" She kissed me on the cheek.

"Good to see you! Let's talk later." I pointed to the bathroom and kept going. I just had to talk to Yessi. I had to apologize and tell her that I really wasn't trying to hide anything, I just didn't know what to—

"Oof!"

I turned a corner and ran right into Kelly. My hand instinctively grabbed her arm to keep her upright. "Sorry! Are you okay?"

She rubbed her nose. "Man, you have a bony chest."

The two of us burst out laughing, and she automatically, hopefully opened her arms for a hug. Relief flooded my body. Choked up, I leaned in for the clutch. I held on for a few beats too long before letting her go.

She wore a beige A-line dress under a white cardigan. "You look like a bride," I said.

"What do you mean?" She, still giggling, wiped her eyes.

"I mean where are your usual bright colors and shimmery fabrics?" I flashed a smile so she'd know I was just teasing. "You're wearing brown. I distinctly remember you saying you'd never wear brown." I cursed myself inwardly. Yessi had warned me about this, and I'd gone and inadvertently poked the bear.

She glanced down at her dress. "It's caramel latte."

"It's brown." I chuckled.

She frowned. "Well, anyway." She turned to walk away. "I'm glad you're here."

"Kelly, wait." I reached for her elbow. "I'm sorry. I was kidding. You know I was kidding."

She turned toward me, but her mouth was set in a line. "I saw your segment on the news." She didn't come off as impressed as other people.

"Yeah," I said brightly. "I've been getting a lot of calls ever since it aired."

"I'm sure you are." Her voice was flat.

"What's that supposed to mean?" She seemed...pissy?... that my business was doing well?

Kelly shook her head, her blond curls bopping around her shoulders. She forced her own grin now. "It's nothing," she said, shrugging. "Sorry. Bride stuff. I'm too on edge."

"It's fine. I get it." I glanced around at the room full of middle-aged women in beige dresses. I stuck out in my bright pink shirt and gray skirt. "Remember how we used to be the ones sitting in the back together bitching about showers?"

Kelly and I used to have this running bit about how every friend who used to be at the back table with us complaining, promising that when it was her turn to be the bride, she'd never, ever make her friends and family sit through a boring wedding shower, eventually made her friends and family sit through a boring wedding shower.

Kelly sneered and folded her arms across her chest. "And

now I'm one of those hypocritical women."

"No," I said, exasperated. "I meant nothing by it." I shrugged. "It's just…this is life, isn't it? What goes around comes around. The hero lives long enough to see himself become the villain."

"So, I'm the villain now." Her nostrils flared like a bull's. I really thought she was going to hit me.

I felt eyes on us. The women at the two tables nearby were hanging on every word of our exchange.

I backed away, holding my hands up in surrender. "I'm clearly incapable of saying the right thing at the moment, so I'm just going to say I'm sorry, and I hope we can talk later, maybe after the shower. You, me, and Yessi." That was what we needed: a good, old-fashioned chat, just the three of us— no phones, no Mark, no my mother. We could be grown-ups, really hash it out.

Kelly's cold eyes stared me down. "Oh, you can hang around?"

"Yeah," I said. "I'm here for you. All messages are going to Tina. She's not allowed to call me unless it's a certified emergency." I flashed a smile. "Those don't happen that often."

Kelly raised an eyebrow. "And she understands that doesn't mean 'text 911 to Annie if a Bears linebacker gets a splinter'?"

"Yes, Kelly." A headache was starting to take shape in my brain. "I'm all yours."

"Well, that'd be a first." She bit her bottom lip.

"Are you ladies okay?" asked a woman at the table behind us.

"Yes," Kelly and I barked in unison.

"What are you even talking about?" I asked. "I'm always there for you."

"You're there, and you're not. I can't even count how many of our conversations have been ended by your phone," she said, rushed. Tension colored her tone.

"Kelly, you know how demanding my job is."

"Yes." Her shoulders dropped dramatically in faux exhaustion. She pressed the back of her hand to her forehead. "Dr. Annie is so important that she gets featured on the *news*."

"That's not fair." My brow furrowed. "You know how tough things have been for me since Katherine retired." I paused, weighing whether or not to go in for the kill. The anger boiling in my gut pushed me to go for it. "Or maybe you don't. Maybe you were too busy getting engaged without telling me you were even dating someone."

"I tried to tell you, Annie, but you could never give me your undivided attention."

Yessi rushed over, eyes concerned. "Guys, stop it." She pressed Olivia's head to her chest, shielding her ears.

I racked my brain, trying to recall if I could remember her attempting to tell me about it. I supposed it was possible. My shoulders dropped. "Kelly, I'm sorry."

"So sorry that you gave my room to some random bartender and his dog?"

"Wait, what?" Yessi said.

"You were gone," I said. "You were getting married and moving to Galena, and I saw an opportunity to help someone who needed it."

"How *magnanimous* of you," Kelly said.

"And I...I was lonely."

"You were lonely?" Yessi said. "What about *Rob*?"

"Rob?" Kelly said. "Boob Honker Rob?"

My phone buzzed in my purse. Shit. I froze. Maybe it was nothing—just a sales call or a reminder to call the dentist. The phone kept buzzing. "I'm sorry." I turned away, reached into my purse, and fetched my phone. "Tina?" I said when I saw who was calling.

"I thought Tina was taking care of everything today," Kelly said in a sing-song voice.

"Kelly, shut up," Yessi said.

"What?" I said as the reality of Tina's words registered in my mind. "Okay. I'll be right there." I hung up, suddenly emotionally numb and ready for action. "I'm so, so sorry, Kelly, but I really do have to go."

Ignoring her pout, I rushed to grab my mother, take her back home, and then head to the hospital. Gayle Gale had had a stroke.

CHAPTER TWENTY-EIGHT

Long Quiz Goodnight

By the time I got home that night, it was almost eleven, and I was beat. Gayle Gale's husband had noticed she was acting off earlier in the day. He'd called Tina, who told him to get her to the emergency room. It turned out she did have a stroke, but it wasn't clear yet if there'd be any lasting damage.

I technically didn't have to be there—the specialists were in charge of the situation—but I always showed up for my patients if something serious happened, to advocate on their behalf and to make sure everyone was on the same page and aware of medical histories and medications, and besides, when I initially joined the practice, Gayle had been the first of Katherine's patients to call asking specifically for me. Everyone else would agree to see me reluctantly, if they had to, but Gayle believed in me from the start. I would not let her down.

Tonight, I left Gayle at the hospital in good hands, and I'd go back in the morning to check on her.

As I dragged myself up the front steps of the house, I

checked my phone. Still no messages from Yessi or Kelly. My mom, however, had let me know that my nephew had lost his first tooth. Grinning at that bit of good news in a full-on shit day, I opened the door and tossed my phone on the table in the hallway. Joanne, who'd obviously been sleeping, padded over to greet me. I gave her a quick pat on the head.

A low piano note cut through the house, and I followed the sound into the front room. Dax sat at the piano, bathed in the moonlight from the big bay window, his left hand playing the low notes while his elbow rested on the high keys, his hand supporting his head.

"You had it tuned," I said. "That sounds like actual music."

He looked up. His eyes were puffy.

"What's wrong?" I stepped over, my heart thumping. This day had been full of bombshells—what was one more?

Dax reached for a stack of papers on the music rack and handed them to me wordlessly. His eyes turned back to the piano, and he played a gloomy tune with his left hand.

I glanced down at the pages. "Divorce papers?" My eyes snapped to him. "Wait. You're married?"

"Not anymore." He sat up straighter and started playing something beautiful and melodic and sad.

"What happened?" I asked.

He shook his head.

I perched next to him on the bench and placed my hand on his right one, stopping his song. My fingers melted between his until our hands were interlaced.

He didn't pull away, and neither did I. "Hey, talk to me."

He glanced over at me, his usually intense blue eyes pink and puffy. "Not much to say—"

"Don't do that." My fingers squeezed his. "You're obviously sad, and I'm here for you, if you want to talk about it." And I would be here for him, especially after that nonsense Kelly had said about me at the shower today. Yes, I'd had a rough day, but it wasn't as rough as the one Dax had. No one had served me with divorce papers. "How long were you married?"

"We got married when we were twenty and still in college," he said, playing a few quick notes. "So…seven? But we've been separated for two. We agreed to stay together for logistical purposes, like insurance, but I guess that's over."

"What's her name?"

"Muriel." His left fingers alternated between one black key and one white key. Dax didn't normally talk this much, but I got the sense that the piano was like a security blanket, giving him the guts to unload. Or maybe he'd simply realized who he was talking to—the woman who never failed to spill all her beans to him, even about her embarrassing proposal text—and decided, what the hell, why not go for it. "She was going to be a famous opera singer."

"And you were going to be a famous pianist," I said, smiling. "*Are.*" I checked myself. "You *are* going to be famous."

He turned his head slightly and glanced over at me. "After a few years of rejection and disappointment, she took a quote-unquote real job and gave up on her dream."

"And you didn't."

He pressed the lowest note on the piano. "It was really kind of messed up. I was so broke when she ended things, I had to keep living with her because it was too expensive for me to move out, which was something she held over my head for a while." Sighing, he repeated the low note. "And then, when the lease was up, I had the privilege of getting to feel even more pathetic—subletting rooms from my bandmates, moving in with my sister, and now..." He played a chord.

"And now you're here, totally welcome and appreciated in this house." I paused, waiting for him to say something else. "Dax, I'm so sorry."

He, smiling sadly, turned his head toward me. "It's all right, really." He sighed. "I knew this was coming. I just didn't expect it to arrive today."

"Well, she's a fool," I told him.

"She's not," he said. "She has a point." He pressed one of the keys. "I mean, I'm twenty-seven. How long do I keep doing this before it becomes pathetic?"

"First of all, twenty-seven is not the 'I should panic and pack it all in' age. You do it as long as you want," I said. "As long as it makes you happy."

"Says the doctor with the big, fancy house."

"Says the daughter of a banker who never gave his dream a shot," I said. "You're welcome to stay here as long as you want."

"One of the guys you're promising to marry might have a problem with that." He raised his eyebrows.

I chuckled. "Yeah, they might."

Dax stood and stretched, revealing a toned bit of tummy under his T-shirt. "But seriously, Annie, I cannot possibly thank you enough for giving Joanne and me a place to stay."

My stomach soured, remembering Kelly's comments earlier today. She'd moved on with her life. I had every right to do the same with mine, including renting out the basement area where she used to live. "I have the room. I'm happy to help."

He opened his arms, and I fell in for a hug, resting my cheek against his strong, hard chest. I took in his pure, soapy scent as our bodies breathed in unison. This was nice.

Too nice.

I pulled away and smiled sheepishly up at him as he peered down at me with sad eyes. "This day's kind of sucked, hasn't it?"

"What happened to you?"

"Eh," I said, waving my hand. "Friend drama and—" A lump formed in my throat. "One of my favorite patients had a stroke."

"Annie, I'm sorry." He cupped my cheek in his hand, and my face melted into his palm.

I sighed. Even though I'd recently kissed Rob, this still felt like the most intimate thing I'd done in a while. I gazed up at Dax, whose eyes changed, darkened, and intensifed.

He felt it, too.

My body ached in a way normally reserved for Timothy Olyphant. Right, wrong, or foolish, I needed his hands on me tonight.

"I want you to kiss me." There—I said it.

His thumb traced my lower lip, and my groin sent out an SOS signal to the rest of my body. "You don't want that."

"Yes, I do."

"If I kiss you, then what?" His eyes focused on my lips.

"Then...we high five and go our separate ways."

A smirk flashed across his face. "That's not what would

happen, and you know it."

I stepped closer to him, our eyes locked. "You really want to know what we'd do?"

Good lord, what was I doing? I didn't talk like this. But the pull I felt toward Dax tonight—the need inside me for connection, for someone to find me good and desirable and interesting, not just because I was an eligible doctor looking to settle down but because I was an attractive, sexy woman—overpowered the normally dominant rational part of my brain. Rob saw me as an acquaintance, Darius saw me as a business partner of sorts, but Dax was watching me tonight like I was the only woman in the world.

He smirked. "I want to find out if you'll go through with telling me what you'd want me to do."

A dare. Aha. This guy didn't know who he was dealing with. Dr. Annie Kyle didn't back down from a challenge.

A sly smile on my face, I kept my eyes locked on his. "Okay…I think we would kiss…and then…purely hypothetically…you'd lead me back over to the piano bench."

His eyes lit up in surprise, like he couldn't believe I'd actually said it. "The piano bench? Really?"

I'd been too embarrassed to kiss Rob in his neighbor's backyard, but now I was talking about doing it in front of the huge window facing my own street. Eh, it was just talking. We weren't actually doing anything…

"Okay, but I'm having trouble picturing this." His top teeth pressed into his lower lip. "Go sit on the bench."

"What?"

"Unless you don't want to."

Oh, I wanted to. I slowly, what I hoped was seductively,

made my way over to the bench and sat.

"Now what?" He was watching me, amused, like he knew I'd give up and end this game soon, that he'd win our little round of sex chicken by default.

He underestimated me.

"Then you'd...unbutton my shirt slowly...methodically..." I reached for my own shirt and undid the top button...and the next. Dax's eyes focused hard on my hands. When I'd unbuttoned my shirt to the waist, I slid my arms out and sat there in my bra, hands clasped around the edge of the bench.

His eyes didn't—or couldn't—leave my chest. "You just took off your shirt."

I glanced at the large bay window off to the side, checking out my reflection. I didn't look like me anymore. I'd changed. I was wild and free and shirtless and...happy.

I looked right at him. "Yeah, and?"

His eyes focused hard on mine. His brow flickered. "Then what?"

"Then you'd unhook my bra." I reached behind me, hunting for the clasp.

He rushed over. "Let me."

I nodded.

He knelt down in front of me, ran his hands up the length of my body, and undid my bra. He pushed the straps off my shoulders, freeing my breasts. The cold, air-conditioned atmosphere hardened my nipples immediately.

I swallowed. "Then—"

"I think I've got it from here." Eyes firmly on mine, as if waiting for me to stop him, his lips made their way toward my chest. Finally he took my nipple into his mouth, and the sensation hit me everywhere. I moaned. With one final lick, he gazed up at me again. "Then?"

My entire body ached for him. I hadn't felt this way in… I couldn't remember the last time I'd felt this way. Right now, I had this guy in my house ready and willing to do whatever I asked. I would not waste it. "You'd run your hands all the way up my legs."

Dax's large, strong hands made their way up my calves and my knees. He paused. "Keep going?"

I looked right at him. "I said, 'All the way up.'"

His hands ascended up my thighs, toward my core. "Keep going?"

My chest heaved, and again I glanced over at us in the window's reflection—me, a half-naked woman with a man kneeling between her legs, ready to ravish her. My body ached at the idea that someone might see us. I'd been wrong. My libido *could* go *zoom* in risky situations. "Yes. Keep going."

Feathery fingers touched the outside of my underwear. "More?"

My heart thumped loudly in my chest, and waves of heat pulsed across my skin. I'd lost all sense of right and wrong. The only things that mattered now was Dax's hands on me. "Yes, more."

He pushed my underwear aside, and one finger ran the length of me, wet, wanting. I quivered, throwing my head back.

A buzzing sound cut through the moment, taking me out of it for a second. Was that my phone?

"More?"

"Yes."

One of Dax's long digits penetrated me, filling me, completing me, and I moaned.

Buzzing. Again.

I thought of what Kelly had said earlier—how nothing else mattered if my patients needed me, if the job needed me.

Buzz.

I tried to ignore it—it was probably nothing—and I tried to focus on the beautiful man with his hands on me and in me, his lips trailing kisses up, up, up my inner thigh—

Buzz!

"Shit!" I jumped up, shutting my legs tight. "Sorry," I said. "I'm sorry. It's the—you know, my patient had a stroke."

"It's okay." Dax stood and dusted off his knees. "I get it." As I located my bra and buttoned up my shirt, he took my place on the piano bench and folded his hands in his lap.

"This was..." I couldn't find the words.

He winced. "Weird."

I flashed him a smile. "Yes, very weird. But also very fun. Maybe we can..." What? Do this again? I didn't mean that. I never should've let it get as far as it did. I had two guys who were serious about settling down with me—

My phone buzzed again.

"Shit," I said.

"Go." He pressed a few keys on the piano.

I hesitated for one moment, waiting for him to say something else—something to bring meaning or closure to what had just happened. When he didn't, I grabbed my purse and ran.

CHAPTER TWENTY-NINE

I Thought This Was Speed Dating

"Fuck." Every other minute or so, as I drove out to Rob's house on the far Northwest Side, I'd smash the steering wheel with my palm as the scene between Dax and me played out in my head. "Fuck."

I turned up the sound on my Spotify playlist—the one that was just bands and artists I'd listened to back in high school and college, because my musical tastes hadn't really evolved since then. "Closer to Fine" came on, a song my senior year Kairos retreat had introduced to me. I tried to belt out the high harmony with Emily of Indigo Girls, but I kept getting choked up.

Good lord, I could not be further from "fine" right now if I tried.

What had I been thinking—kissing Dax, sitting there on the piano bench half-naked for all the world to see, then jumping up to leave with his finger still inside me. *Who does that?*

I smashed the steering wheel again. "Fuck."

By the time I got to Rob's house, I'd decided that I was

an awful, unlovable person who did not deserve happiness. So, in other words, it was a very productive drive.

I texted Rob just outside his front door to let him know I was there, to avoid ringing the doorbell in case his mom was sleeping. Rob was the one who'd texted me while I was… indisposed…with Dax. He said his mom had gotten some bad health news, and he wanted to talk about it. Instead of calling him, I responded immediately that I'd be right there.

A few moments later, he opened the door and let me inside. I glanced around the Caseys' house, noting a sense of familiarity. I hadn't been in here since high school, probably, but it looked and smelled just like it had back then. I knew for certain that if I opened up the cabinet over the fridge, the one too high to reach without a step stool, I'd find a half-empty box of Little Debbie Swiss Rolls.

I plastered on my reassuring "concerned doctor" smile. "How's your mom?"

"She's sleeping." He shook his head. "You really didn't have to come over tonight. This could've waited 'til tomorrow." He glanced at the clock on the mantel. "Did I wake you?"

I shuddered. *Fuck.* "No," I said brightly. "You didn't wake me." I squeezed his forearm. "And it's no problem. I told you to call me with any questions or concerns about your mom's health. I'm here for you both. What's the bad news?"

Rob led me over to the bulky blue sofa in their front window—the one I viscerally remembered spilling Capri Sun on back when I was in fourth grade, just after Mr. and Mrs. Casey had bought it. I sat gingerly next to Rob.

He leaned forward and folded his hands in his lap, just like Dax had when I walked out tonight. I dug my fingernails into my thigh.

"Do you want me to look at any test results?" I asked.

He shook his head, then glanced over at me with red, watery eyes—the second time tonight a man was looking at me like he had been crying or might cry.

I blew out a long, shaky breath.

"It's not good, Annie," Rob said. "The cancer has spread." Biting his lip, he shook his head. "I knew this would happen. I should've made her go to the doctor more often and eat better—"

I squeezed his hand and held on. He laced his fingers in mine, just like Dax had. But the moment was different; the sensations were different, almost fraternal. We were joined in solidarity and support, not lust stemming from hopelessness. Rob and I were two people with a long history; I knew his family almost as well as I knew my own. Holding Rob's hand was like physically linking myself to my roots—grounding, not distracting.

"Rob, you've taken such good care of your mom. You've been there for her every step of the way, for your entire adult life. You should have no regrets."

He nodded, though I could tell he'd immediately dismissed my words.

"What's the prognosis?"

"A few months." He set his lips in a line. "Maybe."

"This was one doctor's opinion. I can make some calls—"

He shook his head. "It's her," he said. "She doesn't want to fight it anymore." He let go of my hand and leaned back against the couch, running his hands through his thick blond hair. "The chemo has been rough on her, and she doesn't want to spend the rest of her...time...too sick to live."

I sat back, too, our arms touching, moving up and down together as we breathed. My mind went to my own mom, wondering if she knew about this yet, imagining how I would feel if Kelly was the one who'd gotten this diagnosis. Then I remembered my fight with Kelly this afternoon and wondered if I was even on her emergency contact list anymore. Probably not. It wouldn't make sense to have a person three hours away as your in-case-of-crisis person.

I wiped away a tear.

Now Rob was the one squeezing my hand. "Are you okay?"

I furiously rubbed my eyes. This was not about me. None of this was happening to me. Rob was the one with the dying mother. Mine was next door and totally fine. I was feeling off after a row with my friends and a near-boink with my roommate.

"I'm okay," I said, straightening up. "Just tired, probably." I smiled at him. "Rob, please know that I'm still here for you and your mom, whatever you need—help with medical questions, navigating the paperwork. I'd say I'd make dinner for you, but you know I can't cook."

I chuckled, and suddenly Rob's lips were on mine.

I pulled away instinctively, like I'd been burned.

"Sorry," he said, eyes wide.

"No." My hand brushed my lips. *Fuck*. "It's okay." I smiled reassuringly. "You just surprised me."

Rob hesitated a moment, then stood, straight and tall, determined. "Wait here." He left the room.

I rested my head against the back of the couch, listening

to the intermittent traffic roll by down Touhy. I was spiraling. Everything I did today, except when it came to my job, was a hot mess. Maybe I'd been right to focus my attention solely on my work for so long. When I opened myself up to more interpersonal relationships, it only ended in disaster.

Rob came in a moment later, carrying a bottle of wine and two of his mom's ornate wineglasses. I sat up straight, grinning, cheerfully overcompensating for the twisted-up knots in my head. He set the beverages on the coffee table and sat down on the couch at an angle, facing me. "Want some?" he asked.

"I'll have a little bit. I'm driving."

He opened the wine bottle, poured a smidge in one glass, and handed it to me. I took a sip.

"I was thinking." Rob's own pour went right to the brim. "Today has been really hard."

"I'm sure it has been," I said, frowning. "I'm so sorry for what you're going through."

With both hands, he carefully lifted the glass to his mouth and sipped it. I immediately worried about him spilling—like I'd spilled the Capri Sun all those many years ago, though I supposed Mrs. Casey probably couldn't care less about the state of the couch fabric after thirty years. "After we got the results today, I called my friends, T.J. and George, to tell them what was going on. They were sympathetic, but they have their own lives, and I get that." Rob's brow furrowed. "They wrote back something to the extent of, 'I'm really sorry, man, but I'm on my way to tee-ball.'"

I nodded.

He sipped his wine again. "But when I texted you, you

showed up. You didn't have to, but you came right away." His eyes softened.

"It's the doctor thing." I played with the octagonal stem of my wineglass, pushing thoughts of Dax—his hands, his mouth, his eyes—out of my head. "I have a hard time saying no when someone's in trouble. Especially when it's someone I care about." Or when I wanted to escape a situation that was quickly spiraling out of my control.

He scooted closer to me, and my stomach knotted up. "I'm glad to know you care about me."

I had meant his mother, but…yes…I also cared about Rob. We were, in many ways, extended family. I pasted on a smile, wishing he'd just say what he wanted to say.

"I care about you, too," he said finally.

"Well," I said, flashing a happy grin, relieved that the extent of this conversation appeared to be a rehashing of our mutual fondness for each other, "we've been neighbors forever, and I'm closer to your family than most of my aunts, uncles, and cousins." Changing the subject, I said, "Did you hear my cousin is marrying her ex-husband's sister?"

Rob set down his wineglass and reached for my hand. I let him, even as my skin grew cold, and he examined my fingers, turning my hand over in his. "I know we talked before about taking things slow and waiting to see what develops, but I realized today life is too short and we're not guaranteed time." He glanced up at me.

My mouth dried into a desert, and I nodded. "Mmm-hmm."

He shot me a warm smile. "Well…since I believe we were headed this way anyway, and because you and I both know it'd make my mom so happy in the last weeks of her life"—he let go of my hand, knelt on the floor in front of me, and pulled a ring out of his pocket—"Annie Kyle, will you marry me?"

My hand flew to my mouth as my eyes nearly bulged out of my head and my stomach plummeted all the way to my feet. Less than an hour ago, I'd been rounding third base with my hot young roommate, and now the first guy who'd touched my breasts back in junior year of high school was holding an antique diamond ring in front of me.

Was this really my life?

I jumped up, ready to bolt. "Rob, I don't know what to say."

"Say yes." He stood, beaming, as if he'd mistaken my nervous energy for enthusiasm.

I swallowed, taking a few beats to collect myself and my thoughts. "This is all just...very sudden."

"I know," he said, "and I'm sorry about that, but the whole point of us even going out in the first place was to end up here." He showed me the ring, which glinted in the lamp light. "Right?"

My heart pounded against my chest. I supposed he had a point. "Right."

"I don't want to be alone, and I know you don't, either."

My skin crawled on the back of my neck. I could hardly recall the last big, huge life decision I'd had to make. Maybe buying the house? Now a guy I barely knew as an adult was standing in front of me, asking me to be his wife...and I had brought this on myself.

It was too much for a Sunday night.

"So, please," he said. "Please say you'll marry me."

I glanced at the windows behind the couch and caught our reflections there. For some reason, it worried me more that someone might catch me and Rob in this position than the one I'd been in earlier tonight, sitting half-naked on a piano bench, with Dax.

And my reflection now didn't look free and happy, as it had with Dax earlier. My face appeared pinched and scared.

I turned to Rob. "I can't say yes *yet*," I said, "but I'm not saying no, either."

He stood still.

"It's a big decision," I said. "*The* biggest, and I don't want either of us to rush into something we might regret." I racked my brain for a way to delay. "I think we need a little time to let this breathe. Give me to the end of the month," I said. It was mid-July, and August seemed far enough away right now.

"July thirty-first," he said, putting the ring back in his pocket.

I stepped over and kissed him lightly on the cheek, relieved that I wouldn't have to make any decisions tonight. "Okay. July thirty-first."

CHAPTER THIRTY

The Small Wonders

"I'm Darius Carver," he told the bouncer, flashing his press pass. He pointed a thumb back at me. "And she's with me." The bouncer shrugged, letting us both inside.

I glanced around the loud, crowded club. I'd called Darius this morning to set up a date to talk at my house (Dax was going to be out—otherwise, yikes!). Darius had agreed to the tête-à-tête at my house before changing venues on me. There was a band he wanted to hear that was doing "really revolutionary stuff—new wave meets jazz meets big band." Apparently I, the woman who still thought the Talking Heads were cutting-edge, was going to "love it."

Eh, who knew? Maybe I would. I was just pissy because I was about to attempt a very difficult conversation in a noisy bar.

"I know the manager here," Darius said, neck craning. "Oh! There he is. Joe!" Grabbing my hand, Darius led me over to one of the only people about our age in the whole building. "Joe!"

Joe shook Darius's hand. "Great to see you."

Darius gestured to me. "This is Annie. We were hoping you could get us a good spot tonight."

Joe looked me up and down, and I squirmed under his lecherous gaze. There was a reason I stopped going to clubs like these when I hit thirty. "Oh, absolutely." He pushed through the crowd, leading Darius and me up to the front, to a roped-off section of tables marked *VIP* just to the left of the stage.

As we took our seats, Darius leaned in and whispered, "You didn't think I'd make us stand the whole night, did you?"

I laughed. "I kind of did, yeah."

He perused the drink menu. "My *bumping around in a crowd of young strangers* days are over."

"Yeah. Mine, too." I respected that Darius was mature enough to recognize that sitting during a concert was an underrated thing. We could be cutting-edge *and* old at the same time.

"I wanted to talk to you about something!" I yelled over the thumping bass of the DJ.

Darius didn't hear me. The waitress came by, and he pointed at the menu to place our order. I couldn't hear what he picked for me.

I opened my mouth to try again, but Darius jumped in first. "How's Gayle doing?" he shouted.

"Gayle?"

He nodded.

"She's doing well!" I yelled. The music cut out at just that moment. "She's doing well," I repeated more quietly.

He frowned. "I went to visit her yesterday, and she

looked so frail. Her husband said they gave her a...throm... something?"

"Thrombolytic," I said. "Her husband's the real hero. He noticed the symptoms early and was able to get her to the hospital fast, which is excellent because it increases her chance of a full recovery. Still, it's possible she has a long rehab ahead of her. We just don't know yet."

"But she's going to make it," he said, his eyes watery.

I squeezed his forearm. "She's going to make it."

He blew out a long breath. "Good."

"I didn't realize you two were that close."

A guy came out and closed the stage curtain.

"Oh, yeah," he said. "She's my mentor. She found me when I was doing man on the street spots in Dubuque."

"Iowa?" I accepted my drink from the waitress. Darius had ordered me a glass of red wine. Not my first choice for my one drink of the night, but not the absolute worst pick he could have made. Kelly's True Love's Kiss probably would've fit that bill. I tamped down the wave of sadness washing through me. Kelly and I no longer had anything in common. It was time to start getting over that.

"Iowa," he repeated.

I took a sip of my wine. "I can't picture you in Iowa."

He chuckled. "You couldn't picture me on the farm, either."

"Still can't." Okay, now was the time to bring up Rob's proposal. I opened my mouth.

"So, hey..." Darius leaned across the table. "I have an important dinner coming up. It's a Wednesday, the thirty-first—"

My stomach dropped at the mention of that date. "Oh yeah? The thirty-first?" I shrugged, casually scratching the back of my neck.

"The head of the news department is organizing a magnificent summer bash at the Brookfield Zoo." He laughed. "We'll be dining near the giraffes."

I focused hard on swirling the wine in my glass. "That sounds like fun."

"So, you'd like to attend?"

"To watch a giraffe steal my dinner roll? Who wouldn't?" I glanced up, and my eyes met his wide, hopeful ones. My chest tightened in advance of having to deliver this bizarre bit of information. "But I, um...well...I have to tell you something."

At that moment, the curtain onstage opened, revealing a cache of shiny instruments from guitar to drums to keyboard to saxophone.

"Here we go!" Darius jumped up, the crowd enthusiastically cheering for the band, for this group apparently called Farouche, who were making their way out onto the stage.

I shifted around the table so I was next to Darius. The roar of the crowd resonated in my chest cavity, and I could barely hear myself think. "I wanted to tell you," I shouted, "I saw Rob last night—you know, the other guy?"

I could feel Darius's eyes on me.

The band all wore the same silver jumpsuits and white New Balance sneakers. They kind of resembled a cult, actually. The lead singer, a guy with chin-length bleached blond hair, leaned into the microphone and said, "We're Farouche."

The crowd roared.

"Rob proposed to me last night!"

Then the drummer counted the band off, and they launched into a song that was, yes, somehow new wave and house and big band. It was actually really amazing.

"He proposed to you?" Darius asked.

"Yeah!"

I took a moment to scan the various members of the group—the small woman on bass, the very tall, bearded man on lead guitar, and the hot guy with the dark hair and stubble on the keyboard.

"He proposed to you?" Darius said again. "What did you say?"

Suddenly, I barely heard him. I was too busy leaning forward, squinting, peering up at the dour and serious keyboardist tapping his foot in time to the music.

Yes, it was him. It was Dax.

CHAPTER THIRTY-ONE

Victorious Secret

Back in college, sophomore year, there was this one guy, Greg, who lived down the hall from Kelly, Yessi, and me. Somewhere around November, he started asking me out. I kept saying no because he wasn't my type—too goofy, too short next to my five-ten frame, too persistent. Not interested.

Once he finally took the hint, I started seeing him around campus making out with a gorgeous, tall girl who was on the basketball team and had done some modeling. I pointed them out to Yessi and said, "That's really nice. He found someone who likes him."

Yessi, who was a voice major, said, "*Maybe* she really likes him; I don't know. But this thing only started because she came to an orchestra concert and saw him with his upright bass."

I laughed. "What are you talking about?"

She just said, deadly serious, "Come to a concert. You'll see."

To prove my own point, that I would not be tricked into finding Goofy Greg attractive, I went with Yessi to the next available performance—a selection of holiday music. We sat in the front row, on the right side, directly in front of the string section. Greg, who had previously been the absolute bane of my existence, stood there with his arm around his double bass like it was a person—a woman—and he played her with the careful intensity of a skilled lover.

Somewhere around the second movement, Yessi reached over and closed my gaping mouth.

At the Farouche concert, I similarly could not take my eyes off Dax—his furrowed brow, his long, nimble fingers—that had been inside me, oh my god—dancing across the keys, the beads of hot sweat rolling down his cheeks. I realized somewhere around the third song that I'd nearly chewed a hole in my bottom lip.

Musician lust was real.

And this was so far from Dax being "in a band of some kind." This was legit. Farouche was "pre-order their next album, buy all the T-shirts" *good.*

"So, you told the other guy 'maybe,'" Darius said as Farouche left the stage to resounding applause. "Do you have a drop-dead date in mind for this proposal?"

"He's given me until July thirty-first."

Darius nodded. "Okay...okay." A slow smile spread across his face. "I'll just have to up my own game, then."

My stomach sank. For some reason I expected that this news would make Darius bow out, easing the decision for me, but instead he was doubling down.

"For my first act," he said, winking, as he pushed his chair under the table. "I'll take you backstage to meet the band."

An icy chill surged up my back. My head went foggy.

I'd managed to avoid Dax since the...finger incident the other night, but now Darius, one of the guys I was seriously considering settling down with, was taking me backstage for a meet-and-greet with my near-hookup.

"You okay?" Darius asked.

"I'm a little woozy..."

"You just need some water. They'll have that in the dressing room. Come on." Darius waved to Joe the owner and started walking toward the restricted backstage area. I stood rooted to the ground for a moment but quickly relented. He was my date, and I'd come here with him. I'd be a huge jerk if I ran out now.

I jogged to catch up, and the bouncer at the backstage door let us in right away, no questions asked. I suddenly really resented Darius's sway in this town. Why couldn't one little bouncer not know who he was?

Farouche, in various stages of undress, drank water and other assorted beverages while chatting with their guests. Dax sat on the makeup counter across the room, his jumpsuit down around his waist, exposing an expanse of bare, tattooed torso. He took a pull on an icy bottle of Evian, a few beads dripping onto his chest, making him look like he was in a sexy, slow-motion water commercial.

I realized then that he wasn't alone. He hung on every word pouring from the ample lips of a gorgeous woman with long, shiny hair, nearly the same color as her luminous bronzed skin, who was about fifteen years younger than I was. My body immediately replaced lust with jealousy.

He wanted her.

As well he should, Annie. Get it together. I was here with my own date, after all.

Darius motioned me over to the bassist, a woman in her thirties, named Kat. "You were awesome," I told her, trying to sound perky.

"Kat studied music at the Boston Conservatory," Darius said before launching into an earnest, interviewer-type conversation, digging deep into Kat's life and motivation. I could barely take in any of it. I kept thinking about Dax and that perfect, younger woman, wondering where I fit in—if that thing with us the other night had just been a lark, something to cross off his bucket list: finger bang a cougar.

Soon I felt a hand on my shoulder.

"Annie?"

I spun around to find Dax, eyes searching and intense, looking down at me. My heart leaped to my throat, and my cheeks burned.

"What are you doing here?" He stepped closer, eyeing me intently.

I forced a grin, hoping it looked more relaxed than it felt. "I came here with Darius." I tapped my date on the shoulder.

As Darius turned around, Dax, probably realizing he was standing there half-naked in the presence of Chicago media royalty, pulled his jumpsuit back over his arms and zipped it up.

"Annie, who's this?" Darius, TV smile flashing, offered his hand to Dax.

"Darius," I said, "this is Dax. Dax, Darius."

Darius looked curiously from Dax to me. "Do you two know each other?"

I chuckled, half-wishing an earthquake would crack open

the floor of this club and swallow me, entombing me forever under the rubble. But that'd mean Dax and Darius would end up in the hole with me, the three of us buried alive together, and I'd still have to have this conversation. "It's funny, actually. He lives in my basement...?" I shrugged.

Darius dropped his smooth, TV-man persona for a moment. "Wait. What?"

"Long story." I laughed it off.

Darius held up his hand. "I want to hear it. Why does he live in your basement?"

"Because Annie's awesome," Dax said, looking right at Darius with wide, honest eyes. "My dog and I needed a place to stay, and, even though she barely knew me, she took me in. Who does that?"

His gaze shifted to mine, and a wave of heat pulsed through me. I sensed Dax could feel it, too, because he quickly looked away and glanced around the room.

"I should go—"

"Wait a minute!" Darius reached into his coat pocket. "I'm going to need to know more about the whole 'you living in the basement' story." He made a note with a pen on his business card, which he waved in the air to dry the ink. "I'm not sure if you know, but I do the Man on Main Street segment for WTS."

Dax looked at the card. "Of course I know that. Everyone does."

"Talking to you about Farouche could be a great follow-up to Annie's story," Darius said, chin jutted out confidently. "The doctor and the..." He squinted at Dax. "Too bad you don't play the drums." He snapped. "Wait! I've got it! The physician and the musician!" He clapped Dax on the shoulder.

Again I imagined the floor swallowing me whole.

"That sounds amazing," Dax said. "I will definitely call you."

"Excellent." Darius put an awkward arm around my waist, and I immediately felt my body tighten. Before I could relax, Darius had gotten the hint and had removed his grip. "I think it's time to take Cinderella home."

When I reached the door, I took one more glance back at Dax, who'd returned to the shiny-haired girl again. The universe back in its proper order, I followed Darius out to his car.

CHAPTER THIRTY-TWO

Quiz Me Baby One More Time

On the way back to my house, Darius kept asking about Dax.

"You barely knew him, and you asked him to move in with you?"

"I knew *nothing* about him." I laughed, watching the streetlights as we zoomed past. It was one o'clock in the morning, basically the only time of day traffic in Chicago moved quickly. "It was a right place/right time situation. My friend Kelly had just moved out of my basement apartment, and I was there when Dax found out he and his dog no longer had a place to stay." I shrugged. "I offered." I turned to Darius. "Also, I needed a teammate for the citywide trivia tournament, so this was my way of forcing him to play with me."

Darius frowned. Something had shifted in him since we spoke to Dax, but I couldn't put my finger on it. Was he jealous? Could he tell there was something going on with us? He knew about Rob's existence, but Darius had never pressed me for more information on him.

"He's kind of like a—" I almost said "younger brother," but that sure as hell wasn't right. "He's just a guy who lives in my basement."

Guilt crept in. Though I usually thought through every ramification of every move before taking it, I'd behaved recklessly with Dax. I'd allowed my libido to lead me instead of my head. I'd been so, so foolish, and in the process I may have hurt Darius and—though he had no idea Dax even existed—Rob.

The truth was, my little flirtation with Dax didn't matter. It wasn't real. This thing with Darius—or the other thing with Rob—held actual possibility for a future. I reached for Darius's hand, to show him some affection, to prove that I was fully invested in this potential relationship with him, but he picked that moment to clutch the steering wheel with both hands.

Oh, shit. I'd really blown it.

When we pulled up in front of my house, Darius put the car in park. "Annie, it's not my place..."

My heart pounded in my chest.

He turned to me, eyes serious. "First of all, I'm not accusing you of anything." He shook his head. "That's not what this is. Tonight, I'm speaking as a friend."

"Okay..." Panic settled inside me. I wished he'd hurry up and say whatever it was he wanted to say. Call me out, tell me we were over. Whatever it was, I could handle it. It was his calm tone that unnerved me.

"You and I have gotten to know each other a little bit, and we've discussed it—we want the same things."

"Right. We do."

"Dax can't give you that."

I opened my mouth to protest, to tell him that Dax wasn't even truly on my radar, to reiterate that he was and would only ever be just my roommate.

He wiped an invisible spot off the dashboard. "Again, as a friend, I've been there. I know what it's like to have feelings for someone who's never going to be able to give you that commitment or put you before their artistic career."

I didn't have feelings for Dax, but I wasn't about to argue that point with Darius. "Monica Feathers," I said.

"You know about her?"

I shrugged. "Google does."

Darius sighed. "Monica is an amazing woman, and we cared deeply about each other. But to stay together, one of us was going to have to give up on their dream, and neither of us was willing to do that."

"I'm really sorry, Darius," I said, "and I understand where you're coming from, but Dax and I...there's nothing even going on there." I pushed away the memory of his eyes staring intently up at mine as he knelt before me at the piano bench. "It's like I said. He just lives in my basement."

Darius patted my knee. "Please know that if you're questioning anything, if you're having second thoughts about what we're doing"—he pointed to himself and to me—"trust that you're making the right choice. Rob or me, whomever you choose, you won't regret it. The other way lies heartbreak." He leaned over and kissed me on the cheek.

"I appreciate that," I said. "Thanks. And whatever you thought you saw, don't worry about it. I'm clearheaded about what we're doing. I want commitment, and I'm not someone who acts without thinking or makes foolish choices based on lust or id or whatever you want to call it."

Darius gave me a quick hug and said he'd call me soon, and I left the car.

I dragged my body up the front steps and yanked off my shoes as soon as I entered the house. Joanne ran to greet me, and I wrapped my arms around her. "Hi, friend." I sighed. I was beat. This having-to-take-care-of-a-dog thing was nice until it wasn't. "I bet you need to go out."

I changed into my pajamas, washed my face, and took Joanne for a very quick stroll around the block. I kept thinking about what Darius had said. I should probably listen to him. He spoke from experience. I'd seen his face in those pictures with Monica Feathers—it looked a lot like my expression as I'd caught my reflection in the window when I was with Dax.

But that was just a goofy crush, my silly body reacting to Dax in a way that made my very responsible mind howl with laughter. Him being a musician aside, he was way too young for me, and he was going through a divorce. He was just a nice distraction for me, as I probably was for him. I knew that. Nothing was actually going to happen—at least beyond what had happened already.

We'd had our little fun, and now it was over.

By the time Joanne and I got back from our walk, it was after one thirty—way past my bedtime for a Monday night. Dax still wasn't home, meaning he was probably out with that shiny-haired girl. Good for him. He could do what he wanted.

And I would do what I wanted. I settled onto the couch with Joanne and turned on *The Great British Baking Show*.

"You're really going to like this, Joanne," I said, wrapping one arm around her big, furry body. "It's very soothing."

This was nice. This was a mature, reasonable way for a woman my age to end her evening—on the couch with a dog and Paul Hollywood.

I yawned and tried to let the calming British accents wash over me, but I kept finding myself glancing toward the front hallway every so often, thinking I heard a key in the door.

"This show is making me hungry. We've got to get ourselves some doughnuts tomorrow," I told Joanne.

I wondered if Dax would be here tomorrow for the doughnuts. Or...if he'd be alone. Again I glanced toward the door.

Stop it. Dax was a young, single guy who was allowed to go off with a cute girl he met backstage and do the kind of stuff we'd attempted to do on the piano bench the other night. He had his life, and I had mine. He had sexy girls with shiny hair. I had twelve Brits trying to make scones. Not to mention, I'd committed myself to a mature, pragmatic relationship with either Rob or Darius. They were in the same place I was. Dax, divorced at twenty-seven, was smack in the middle of his prime mistake-making years.

I hugged Joanne and wiped my eye. "Maybe I'm allergic to you." A lone tear splashed against her back.

A few minutes later, the front door finally opened, and Joanne jumped, barking, from the couch. I cautiously stood and stepped toward the door, bracing myself for what I'd find there. Dax had crouched down and was rubbing Joanne behind the ears, nuzzling his nose against hers. He was alone.

"Hey," I said, standing there with my arms folded behind

my back. He was home, and he hadn't brought anyone with him.

My body immediately flooded with relief and then immediate annoyance that I'd feel any sort of way about Dax coming home alone.

He looked up, surprised. "What are you still doing awake?"

"Couldn't sleep." I paused. I should just say good night and go to bed. Instead I said, "You're alone."

He stood. "What are you talking about?"

I shrugged, my shoulders staying up near my ears. "That shiny-haired girl you were talking to…"

"Michelle?" He laughed heartily. "That's Kat the bassist's girlfriend."

"Oh." My insides warmed. The shiny-haired girl had just been a friend.

He stepped closer to me. "Were you jealous?"

"No." I shook my head, chuckling. "Just curious."

"Mmm-hmm." He took another step toward me, and suddenly the hallway felt way too small. I could practically feel the heat emanating from his body a few feet away. "And what about you and the Man on Main Street?"

"He went home." I paused. "Are *you* jealous?" My chest heaved, and suddenly I became acutely aware of my lips.

"Fuck yeah, I'm jealous." He crossed to me in two strides and cupped his hands on my cheeks. His lips crashed against mine, claiming me. My legs turned to jelly as I melted into him. My brain kept screaming at me to stop, while my body arched into him.

Finally, my mind won out. I pulled away, pressing my

fingers to my lips. I needed a moment to figure out what this was.

"I'm sorry," he said. "I shouldn't have—"

"No." I shook my head.

He frowned, his eyes watching me intently.

Damn it. I wanted this. I wanted him. I was seriously considering settling down—forever—with two very nice, very respectable men, and it hit me that I still had an oat or two to sow. I had been nothing but utterly responsible my entire life. Darius could warn me against Dax as a serious potential partner, but not as a fling. "If—*if*—we do…anything…it's just for tonight," I said. "You understand my situation, and I know you just got out of a marriage. This would be you and me finishing what we started the other night and nothing more than that, okay?"

"Okay."

"We'll have our fun"—I wiped my hands together, easy-peasy, ignoring the flush creeping up my back—"and then we'll go our separate ways, to our own bedrooms, no muss, no fuss."

"Well, maybe a little muss." He flashed me a crooked grin that nearly sent me into a tailspin. I was a goner.

Enough talking. All the lusty sensations I'd felt while watching him up on stage tonight had returned. "Are we going to do this on the piano?"

"I just had it tuned." He hesitated a moment, as if weighing his options. Then he stepped close, lifted me effortlessly into his arms, and carried me up to my bedroom. He set me on the edge of the bed and stepped back.

"You want me to tell you what to do?" I asked, my body

suddenly missing his warmth.

"No. I'm going to tell you this time."

A spark of excitement hit me. I was in charge of so many aspects of my life. I had to be the thoughtful one, the tactful one (at least professionally), the accountable one. I made responsible decisions all day about business and medicine and health. The very idea of this hot, twenty-seven-year-old pianist/bartender ordering me around thrilled me in a way I hadn't expected it to.

"Okay," I said, leaning back on my hands.

"First of all, where's your phone?"

"Downstairs."

"Leave it there."

My mouth dried up a bit at that. I was rarely more than an arm's length away from my phone. Even in yoga class, I broke the rules and kept it tucked under a towel.

Dax sensed my hesitation. "Did any of your patients have a stroke today?"

I shook my head.

"Do you think they can manage without you for the next twenty minutes?"

"Twenty minutes?"

Dax squinted. "I'm not sure if you're thinking that's long… or short…?" He shook his head. "Anyway, it's been a little while for me, and I haven't been able to get you out of my head for two days, and probably a lot longer than that. So I just want to set expectations at a manageable level."

I grinned. Damn it, he looked so cute standing there bossing me around. "Okay."

"Okay." His shoulders relaxed. "So, stand up."

I stood.

"Take off your pajamas."

I lifted my T-shirt over my head and let my soft pants pool in a puddle around my feet, leaving me standing in front of him in just a strapless bra and pink panties. Dax's intense eyes fixed on my midsection sent the butterflies in my stomach soaring. "Next?" I said, chuckling.

"Did you just laugh at me?" He stepped toward me, eyes mirthful. "I don't think you realize. I'm the captain now."

"Aye, captain. What are my orders?"

He touched my chin and tilted my face toward him. His lips touched mine softly, sending rippling waves of pleasure right through me. This just got serious. "I played a concert for two long, hot, sweaty hours tonight. Get in the shower," his lips told mine.

CHAPTER THIRTY-THREE

Trivia Facts of Life

The next morning, I woke up in my underwear, the little spoon to Dax's big spoon in my bed. He pulled me closer, his lips tickling the outside of my ear.

"Hey." I flipped over and kissed his lips, slowly, luxuriously, not at all concerned about morning breath, since the two of us had just had sex for the second time—I squinted at my bedside clock—about two-and-a-half hours ago. My breath was his breath.

Something cold and wet nudged my arm, shocking me from the moment. Joanne. She was in my bed, too.

Dax and Joanne had spent the night with me in my room, a place where no one but me had slept in...a very long time.

Though we'd agreed to have sex once and go our separate ways, that hadn't exactly panned out. After we did it in the shower—reaffirming my decision to build a massive walk-in spa with seating and *lots* of showerheads—Dax cuddled up with me in my bed, and we watched *The Proposal* on my tablet until we were kissing and pawing at each other again. And then he fell asleep next to me, and I, despite my best intentions, didn't kick him out.

He kissed my collarbone. "Let's stay here all day."

That comment and the sliver of daylight hitting my eye simultaneously set off an alarm bell in my mind, and the urge to look at my phone overcame me. It was still downstairs. How many messages did I have waiting for me? I sat up. I didn't live the kind of existence that allowed for much more than eight hours in bed. I wasn't twenty-seven, like some people.

Dax propped himself up next to me, resting his back against the headboard. "You okay?"

"Yeah." I forced a smile. "Just thinking about work."

He winced. "Ugh. That's not a ringing endorsement for my sexual prowess."

"It is, though." I kissed his lips quickly. "This is the first time I've even thought about work in way too many hours. I don't think you appreciate how remarkable that fact is."

He smiled. "So you're saying we can't stay in bed all day?"

"We?" I said. "No. *You* can feel free…to stay in *your* bed all day." I didn't want him sticking around in here, looking through my personal stuff. He already lived in my house; we needed *some* boundaries. I reached over him, fumbling for my glasses, and then rolled myself across his body and off the bed. I shrugged my arms into a robe.

He rested his hands behind his head, highlighting the tattoos across his broad, muscular chest and on his arms. I learned somewhere around four a.m. that the flower on his wrist was for Muriel, since her last name was Rose. That was why he planned to cover it up.

"I know we said this was a one-time thing," he started,

"but since we've already technically broken that rule…maybe we can do this again sometime?"

My responsibility gene kicked in. One…well, *two*…times was one thing. Any more than that and we'd be forming a pattern. I'd gotten Dax out of my system, which had been my plan going in, and now it was time to get back to reality—i.e., Darius and Rob. "I don't know if that's a good idea." And I was dead right about that, because just looking at him lying there all stretched out, petting his dog, made me want to shed my robe and join them for the rest of the day.

"You're right," he said. "We agreed to one time. Plus, you've got your current romantic situation, and I'm not looking for anything complicated…" He raised his bisected eyebrow. He'd gotten the scar at age eight when he was hit in the eye playing a very dangerous game of rock baseball, which was something he told me while he was kneeling in front of me in the shower.

My breath quickened, remembering that little moment. The two of us spent, he rested his head on my thigh while I ran my fingers through his soft, dark hair, the warm water sluicing over us.

The now-familiar warmth coursed through my body at that memory. He was like a roller-coaster ride. Now that I'd had a taste, I kept wanting to get back in line for more every time I got off.

I straightened my shoulders. "I've got to get to work."

Smiling, Dax scratched Joanne's head. "Good."

"You should…" I nodded toward the door.

"Of course." He lifted the covers and rolled out of bed, revealing his toned, tattooed, and fully naked body.

My mouth watered as he scanned the floor, hunting for his clothes.

"They're in the bathroom."

"Right." He grinned, standing and stretching.

Fuck it. Resistance was futile. One more time, and then *that's* it. Full stop. End of story. Time to leave the amusement park for good.

I shed my robe.

"What are you doing?"

I shrugged. "I have to take a shower. If anyone is interested in joining me...to save water, then that's their decision."

I headed toward the bathroom, and seconds later I heard Dax's footsteps padding behind me.

What the hell is going on with me? I kept asking myself as I drove out to the hospital later that morning.

I had to chalk it up to pure, basic, pathetic lust. I'd never been someone who *had* to have it. Kelly had always been the one, when we were out together, who'd spot a guy at the bar and immediately announce, "I want him." For me, it took a little more time, a little more knowledge, and a little more context than a hot body and an engaging scent. Even my thing for Timothy Olyphant was really more of a ha-ha joke. He was very attractive, but it wasn't like I'd immediately jump his bones if the real deal showed up on my doorstep.

Restraint and decorum had always been my middle names, and they had served me well.

With Dax, for some reason, all that flew out the window. It had to be circumstantial. The fact that he lived in my house plus the musician effect, coupled with the fact that I had one proposal on the table and suspected there might be a second in the offing, all added up to me needing to sow those final oats—one last ride—before I settled down for good.

That had to be it.

And nothing against Dax. He was charming and sweet and talented and serious and sexy, and he knew tons of useless trivia. But he was twenty-seven, barely old enough for me to respectfully screw, and he was a musician who could pick up and leave at any moment. He was not the one.

I banished all the personal drama from my mind as I headed up to Gayle's hospital room. I'd gotten all the frivolousness out last night, and it was time to be Dr. Responsibility again.

"How are you?" I said, shaking her hand. She was sitting up and had replaced her hospital gown with a silky blue pajama set from home. "You look strong and healthy." I checked her chart. Everything seemed to be going well so far.

"I got out of bed today." She spoke slowly, methodically. Her smile looked a bit lopsided.

"I'm very glad to hear that. How'd it go?"

"Made it to the bathroom, but my—" Her right hand hit her left leg.

"Your left side is weak?"

She nodded.

I proceeded to check her out, listening to her heart and lungs, checking her reflexes. After I'd convinced myself she was doing as well as the chart said she was, I wrapped my stethoscope around my neck and pulled the visitor's chair up next to her bed.

"Has the doctor given you a timeline on rehab?" I asked.

"Nothing…concrete," she said. "But that's…okay. I have time."

I squeezed her hand. "The news broadcast is suffering without you."

She laughed. "I don't know about that. They're trying on some new…for size." She skipped over the word "anchors."

I patted her leg. "You have nothing to worry about. They can't hold a candle to the great Gayle Gale."

Gayle shook her head. "I hope…they find someone…"

I frowned. "What are you… You're going back to work, right?"

A hint of a smile played on her lips. "Husband and I discussed it. Time to"—her right hand mimed taking off in flight—"retire."

"This"—I mimicked her flight action—"are you saying you're leaving Chicago?"

"Probably. Time for new sights, better weather."

I'd always admired and looked incredulously at people who could take off and leave like that—move to a new state or country, up and go to a completely foreign environment. My brother did it when he moved to Texas after college. Heck, Kelly's parents had done it when they moved out to Galena, and now she was picking up her entire career and transplanting it to the other side of the state. I couldn't imagine doing any of that, even for a little while, even for a weekend. I had too many responsibilities here. What would my mom do without me around? How would my practice survive?

"I'll miss you," I told Gayle.

"You'll forget all about me."

"Not possible." Gayle had never displayed anything less than full confidence in my abilities. She was the patient who made me believe I could actually do the job.

She reached for my hand. "What about you...Annie?"

Even when she was in the hospital recovering from a stroke, she still thought to ask me how I was doing. Gayle Gale was a straight-up legend—professionally and personally. "What about me?"

"You need to remember...work isn't everything."

"I know that." I squeezed her hand and set it back on her leg.

"Did you know Jim—husband—and I were high school sweethearts?"

"I didn't." Grinning, I leaned back in my chair. "Tell me about it."

Her eyes moistened. "He stayed in our town. Couldn't go to college because...family."

"He had to help them out?"

She nodded, and a tear trickled down her cheek. I grabbed a tissue from the bedside table and wiped it away. "We lost touch. I married once...I married twice...then I saw Jim on Facebook." Her lips curled into an awkward grin. "I slid into his DMs."

I cracked up at this sixty-something woman knowing the lingo. But that was Gayle Gale. She stayed on top of everything.

"We've only been together five years."

"And you'll be together a whole lot more." I patted her shin.

"Don't waste time. All…they say is true." She looked me right in the eye. "I wish I'd had more time with Jim."

I forced a smile. I remembered my grandfather talking like this when he got older, too, waxing nostalgic about everything. It was one thing for a woman in her sixties to make the broad pronouncement that she was going to retire and go off on some great adventure with her love, but my career was just getting off the ground. I was finally starting to see the fruits of so many years of school and training. For the first time, I was my own boss. This was what I'd worked my entire life for. It was my passion.

When I tried to envision myself at seventy, looking back on my own life, I knew I'd regret not giving my all to my career. That was what mattered to me. It was what I had built. Yes, it had cost me things—possibly even my friendship with Kelly—but it was my baby.

"I'm glad you're feeling better, Gayle." I stood.

"I mean it, Annie," she said. "Don't—"

I reached for my phone, pretending to check it. She meant well, but I'd heard it all before. For my entire childhood, people—my parents, teachers, whoever—told me to work hard and be the best. And now, right when I could see the pinnacle of success in front of me, they were telling me to slow down and smell the roses? I didn't think so. I smiled at her. "I will check back in on you soon. Take care, Gayle."

CHAPTER THIRTY-FOUR

Let's Get Quizzical

"I should be the Tin Man," Yessi said, dipping a cheese curd in some kind of sauce. "You know I don't have a heart."

"That's not true, and you know it. Besides, Dax is the Tin Man," I told her, writing our team name across the top of the answer sheet. I'd brought Yessi along for trivia tonight. The idea had occurred to me a few hours ago. Dax and I needed a sex buffer, and there was no better buffer than my very opinionated, very dynamic best friend. "He's been my trivia partner for the entire tournament so far."

"Yeah, well, I've been your best friend for twenty years." She grabbed the pen from me. "At least give me a name. Let me feel like less of a third wheel." She wrote "plus the Mother of Dragons" at the top with a flourish.

My cheeks flushed, even though I knew she hadn't meant "third wheel" like "third wheel on a date."

"You have someone new on your team." Brad the Very Stable Genius sidled up to us.

"This is my friend Yessi."

He looked her up and down. "Is this legal? The

tournament is already in its third week. I don't think it's right to be bringing in new talent."

"You know it's legal, Brad." I looked at Yessi. "He's full of crap. His team swaps out members all the time. The rules state each team may have up to eight players on any given week."

Yessi shrugged. "If the rules state it, Brad."

He backed away. "I've got my eye on you."

"What a wiener," Yessi said when he was out of earshot.

"He's not that bad. He's one of your people, actually."

"A hottie with a body and an ass that won't quit?" She made a muscle and kissed her biceps.

"A lawyer."

She dropped her arm. "Then I stand by my original assessment." Yessi glanced around. "Where is this Dax?"

"He'll be here," I said, suppressing the automatic smile at the mention of my recent bang buddy. I changed the subject. "Have you talked to Kelly lately?"

She shook her head. "I've called her a bunch, and she hasn't called me back."

"I'm worried about her," I said. "She obviously has reasons to be annoyed with me, but I can't believe she's 'cut you out of my life' pissed off."

Yessi and I had cleared the air quickly after the shower incident. She'd been a little hurt by my not telling her about certain things in my life, but we both realized that we needed to do more to prioritize our friendship, even when it wasn't convenient. That was part of the reason she agreed to come tonight. Kelly, however, seemed determined to keep pushing us both away.

"It has to be wedding stress," Yessi said.

"I don't know. I think there must be more going on."

"More what going on?" I glanced up to find Dax—dark jeans, black tee, scruffy beard, and messy hair—standing next to me. My heart skipped a beat.

"Hey…" I beamed at him, resisting the urge to jump up and hug him. Instead I shot him a little wave, which he acknowledged with a quick wink that sent the butterflies in my gut soaring. "Dax, this is my friend Yessi. Yessi, this is Dax."

"Nice to meet you officially." Dax shook Yessi's hand. "I'm gonna grab a drink. Can I get you both anything?" His eyes narrowed at Yessi. "You're…Green Line?"

"Good memory. Yeah, I can have one." She waited until Dax was up at the bar. "I like him."

"What?" My ears burned.

She tapped her head. "Good recall. He must be solid at trivia."

"Oh." I sipped my water. "Yeah." I watched him at the bar, his elbows on the counter and his gaze on one of the TVs, while a trio of young women nearby giggled and gawked at him. He didn't give them a first or a second glance. I couldn't help smiling.

"How are things with you and Rob?" Yessi asked.

She snapped me out of my little daydream about what had…gone down…between Dax and me earlier this morning. "Oh," I said. "Fine. Whatever."

Dax set Yessi's beer in front of her.

She sipped the foam off her Green Line. "Dax, what do you think about this whole Rob thing?"

He took a seat adjacent to me and across from Yessi. "Rob is...?"

"The guy Annie's seeing? The one she grew up with?"

"Oh, he's one of those guys." Dax was checking out the score on the TV. "I don't know anything about him."

Yessi's wide eyes snapped to me. "One of what guys?"

"You know," Dax said. "One of the guys she's going to settle down with."

I turned to him. "Thank you," I deadpanned.

His eyes met mine. "What?" Then he looked from me to Yessi. "She didn't know? I just figured. She's your best friend..."

No, I hadn't told either of my best friends about this, only the random dude in my basement with whom I was now hooking up. Why was that so hard to fathom?

Yessi rested her chin on her hand. "Tell me more, Dax."

I shrugged. "Go ahead."

"You should tell her," Dax said.

He was right. I probably should. Yessi and I had vowed to keep each other in the loop better, hadn't we?

I swung around to face Yessi, who I knew would not approve of any of this, but we were trying to be more open and honest with each other. I would trust her not to eviscerate me tonight in a bar full of people, one of whom I had just had sex with three times this morning. "Okay...the night I found out about Mark, I got a little drunk—"

"Wait wait wait wait wait wait wait." Yessi held up a hand to stop me. "*You* got drunk?"

"Yes, I got drunk, and I sent a text to several—"

"Thirty-nine—"

I shifted my narrow gaze to Dax for a moment. *What the heck, man?* "Sure. Thirty-nine." And then I was back to Yessi. "I sent a text to thirty-nine men that I was ready to settle down and...in the light of day, I realized I truly was. *In vino veritas*, right? So, I contacted Rob and"—before Dax could drop another truth bomb, I got out ahead of the story—"Darius Carver—"

"The Man on Main Street?" she squealed.

"Shhh! Yes, the Man on Main Street," I said. "The two of them are both serious about getting out of the dating rat race and...getting married." I whispered those last two words.

Yessi's inscrutable eyes watched me for a few moments before turning to Dax. "What do you think about this?"

I opened my mouth to stop him from answering but quickly closed it. I actually wanted to hear this answer. I glanced over at him.

He'd fixed his eyes on Yessi. "I think it's a terrible fucking idea," he said. "I think marriage, if that's truly what she wants, should be for love, and I think she's selling herself short thinking that she'll never find that."

My mind bounced between the idea that Dax could be talking about himself and the reality that I knew he'd never be able to give me what I wanted. He was a young musician, and he'd just gotten divorced. He wasn't ready for the kind of commitment I needed. I'd be knee-deep in my Bunco phase by the time Dax was ready to settle down.

Yessi sat quietly for a few seconds. "I agree with Dax." She reached over and patted my hand. "Hon, we both know people who stayed together out of convenience. It never works out. I don't know, maybe you could love Rob or Darius, but if you don't and you go through with a marriage, it's going to end in disaster."

Everything was always black and white with Yessi. She was as analytical as I was, but she always saw things as right or wrong, good or bad. There was no gray area. She just so happened to fall in love with someone who was in the same mental, physical, and emotional space she was, and since it all worked out for her, she had no reason the question the magic of love—no reason not to believe that if it happened for her, it would happen for everyone.

Meanwhile, I was pushing forty, and I'd never even come close to having what she and Polly had. "Forgive me for being a realist," I said. "You've been with Polly for a long time now. You don't know what it's like to be out here, with all your friends pairing off and moving away." My lip trembled. "All I know for sure is that I don't want to be alone." I puffed up my chest. "This is me solving that problem."

Dax reached for my hand and squeezed. "Hey." My eyes met his sad, serious ones. "There is nothing lonelier than a loveless marriage. I speak from experience."

"Time to start the tournament!" Ronald's voice boomed from the stage.

I wrested my hand from Dax's. "Your marriage started with love and passion, and those things faded. I'm talking about doing the opposite: starting from a place of similar goals and mutual respect. Maybe the other stuff will come later."

I positioned my pencil over the answer sheet, visibly ready to crush the competition. But my mind kept flitting to thoughts of Rob's brotherly, passionless kiss, to Darius beaming at Monica Feathers, to Dax holding me this morning like we'd been together for years. I snuck a glance at him, and his eyes were on me. I felt a tug behind my belly button.

Just as Ronald announced question number one, Dax said, "You deserve the other stuff *now*." His bisected eyebrow flickered.

My stomach in knots, I pulled my eyes away from his and wrote the correct answer: Thomas Jefferson and John Adams. "Yeah, well," I said, "we can't have everything, can we?"

CHAPTER THIRTY-FIVE

Can We Use a Lifeline?

On Thursday night, I made microwave popcorn—one of the only foods I was qualified to prepare—and set the bowl on the coffee table in the family room to watch Darius's segment on Dax. I sat on the opposite end of the couch from where he and Joanne were cuddled together.

We hadn't really spoken about anything of substance since trivia on Tuesday. After the initial discussion about my love life, he, Yessi, and I got down to the business of kicking everyone else's butts. And then Yessi invited me back to her condo for a little more friend time.

While she nursed Olivia, I'd sat in the chair opposite her, feeling like I was a witness in one of her trials. "You need to be straight with me. What's going on with you and Dax?"

I grinned, making sure to hold eye contact with Yessi, whose superpower was being able to smell bullshit a mile away. "Nothing. He's living in my basement."

With the disbelieving look she gave me, I half expected her to say, *Ma'am, you're under oath.*

"Seriously," I said. "Basement."

"We promised to be more forthcoming with each other."

She had me there. "Okay," I said, "in the interest of our friendship, you should know we slept together a little."

Yessi raised an eyebrow. "How little is 'little'?"

"Only one night. Three...times."

"Annie." She shifted Olivia's position.

"It's not a big deal," I said. "We discussed it beforehand, and we both agreed it would be a one-time thing." ...Which ended up being a three-time thing, including a sleepover, but shit happens.

"He likes you," she said.

"And I like him," I said in a steady, even tone, "as a human being."

"He likes you more than that," she said. "I can tell. And you like him, too."

She always thought she had the exact right read on every situation. Well, not this time, Yesenia Cortez-Bean, Esquire. "Our feelings are irrelevant in this situation," I said. "We are in completely different places in our lives. We want different things. The timing isn't right."

"The timing is never right." Yessi glanced down at her daughter, who was growing sleepy-eyed. "I think you're under the impression that things were all smiles and rainbows when Polly and I got together."

"Well, weren't they?" I said, chuckling. "I mean, the two of you were both professionals in your thirties with 401(k)s and no car payments."

"It's not that simple," she said. "When we first met, Polly hadn't come out to her family yet, so that was an issue. And I'd just made partner and was suddenly under a whole lot of pressure to perform at work and bring in clients."

"Not to belittle your situation," I said, "but those issues sound surmountable to me."

"Well, maybe they do now," she said, "because we surmounted them. Falling for the cute, smart, single guy who lives in your basement doesn't sound like the worst problem to me, either."

I sighed.

"And look at Kelly," she said. "She's been working her whole life to build her real estate career in Chicago, but she fell for someone who lives all the way across the state. You don't think that seemed insurmountable to her?"

I had no answer for that, mostly because Kelly had stopped talking to me and I had no idea what she might have been thinking when she met Mark.

"That's all I'm saying," Yessi said. "All problems are unsolvable until you solve them."

And now I was back in my house, sitting on the couch with my own unsolvable problem (not to mention his massive pooch), about to watch his interview with one of two guys I'd pledged to possibly marry.

I grabbed a fistful of popcorn and shoved it in my mouth.

"Good evening," said the anchor filling in for Gayle Gale.

I attempted to swallow the wad of popcorn mush. "She's not as good as Gayle," I said, spraying a little popcorn on my shirt. *Classy, Annie.*

"No one is," Dax agreed. His fingers played with Joanne's ears as he stared at the TV. He seemed a little on edge, and I understood why. I'd been the subject of one of these segments recently, and he'd seen firsthand how my professional life blew up afterward.

"You're gonna do great," I told him. "I'm sure the camera loves you."

He flashed me a quick, sweet smile.

Jana Philipps, tonight's anchor, continued, "Tonight our Man on Main Street, Darius Carver, spotlights a hot local band on the verge of making it. Darius?"

The camera cut to a smiling Darius in front of a screen bearing his "Man on Main Street" logo. "Thanks, Jana. Tonight I highlight Farouche, a band making very innovative music in a very interesting way." His eyes twinkled. "And stick around to see if you can spot a link to one of our other recent stories."

The screen cut to Farouche playing a gig at a small bar in town, then Darius talking to other members of the band. I glanced over at Dax, whose eyes were glued to the TV.

"He's making you guys look great," I said.

Dax nodded.

I focused on the TV again. Darius was talking to Kat, the bassist, about her classical training. "But Kat isn't the only one who studied Mozart and Beethoven." The camera cut to Dax on keyboard. "Dax Logan started playing piano at three and never looked back."

Now on-screen Dax was sitting at a diner booth, hands folded on the table. His usually messy hair was combed, and he appeared to have shaved. My heart swelled. He looked so cute, like he'd been trying so hard to make a good impression in his big TV debut. I shook my head. *Stop noticing his looks.*

I straightened up and focused on what he was saying.

"I would play anything," he said. "I started plunking out melodies by ear, and then, once I could read notes, I studied every style of music I could get my hands on."

Darius's voice cut in: "Dax ended up at Yale on a music scholarship."

I turned to him, eyes bugged out. "Yale? You went to fucking *Yale*?"

His cheeks turned pink.

My eyes went back to the TV. We'd discuss this later. I needed the whole story.

"But life isn't easy for these musicians," Darius was saying, his voice taking on a hint of gravitas. "As you know, Man on Main Street likes to give the full story of our subjects, even when it's tough, and though Farouche is highly regarded among music critics and fans, they're still only on the verge of stardom. Everyone in the band has a day job."

"I'm an office temp," Kat said, before the other members rattled through the roster of their jobs.

"I like that he does this," I said. "It's good for people to know the amount of work and sacrifice it takes to make it."

Finally, on-screen Dax said, "I'm a bartender."

"Interestingly enough," Darius was saying, "that job put him in touch with another of our Man on Main Street subjects—concierge doctor Annie Kyle."

My stomached dropped. Here it came. The big link to me. Darius was a professional, and I trusted he wouldn't say anything to embarrass me, but still. I wasn't comfortable being in the spotlight. I did my job and went about my day. I didn't crave attention.

The video returned to the shot of Dax in the diner. "Yeah, Annie showed up one night and ended up performing first aid on my leg after a shard of glass cut me." He laughed.

"And then she started coming in all the time, and we got to talking. She found out that I needed a place to stay, and she, out of the kindness of her heart, told me, a guy she barely knew, that I could move into her basement."

"Did that throw you for a loop?" Darius asked.

"Yeah, it did." Dax laughed. "And for a minute there I did worry I was walking into a *Misery* situation."

I reached over and slapped him playfully on the arm. "I'll *Misery* you."

"But it's been great, actually," on-screen Dax was saying. "Annie and I have gotten to know each other a bit, and she's so supportive of my music." He chuckled, shaking his head. "We've been competing in this big Chicago trivia tournament, and she agreed to give me all our winnings to help me keep following my dream." His eyes turned serious. "I'm not sure she realizes how close I was to quitting the band before she came along."

I hesitated for a second and then reached across Joanne. Dax took my hand, and my entire body relaxed.

As the segment moved on to the future of Farouche, I said, "You're making this whole 'no feelings, just-one-time' thing really difficult."

I felt his eyes shift to me, and I looked over. "Maybe we jumped the gun a little when we agreed to that," he said.

"Dax—"

"I mean it," he said. "I like you, Annie. I like you a lot more than 'one time.'"

I kept thinking about Yessi's advice—that timing was never perfect, that love was never easy. What Dax was proposing would be the epitome of that. It might feel good now, but where would we be in six months? A year? We barely knew each other—*Yale!*—and I couldn't seriously consider giving up two sure things for a guy that could pick up and hit the road with his band at any minute. I was way too practical for that. "Dax, it's not that I don't feel the same way—"

"Great." He gently removed Joanne from his lap and rushed to my side. He took my hands in his. "If you feel the same way, that's all that matters."

My mind ran through all the ways this would end badly. The two of us had never really discussed anything of importance. I didn't even know where he stood on the issue of having kids. I literally just found out where he went to college.

"The rest we can figure out as we go along. Annie, what do you say?"

He moved in closer as my doorbell rang, and Joanne rushed to the door, barking. Grateful for a pause in this conversation, I jumped up. "Sales call, probably," I said.

Dax followed me to the hallway and grabbed his dog's collar, dragging her away from the door. I looked through the peephole.

"It's Darius," I said as I fumbled with the doorknob.

Dax pulled Joanne toward the basement steps. "I'll take her on a walk and keep her out of your hair." He shot me one last look—full of both hope and concern—as he disappeared down the stairwell.

With a deep breath, I pulled open the door. "What are you doing here—?"

My eyes traveled down to the stoop. Darius knelt in front of me on one knee, holding a gargantuan diamond ring. "Dr. Annie Kyle, please say you'll marry me."

CHAPTER THIRTY-SIX

Game of Phones

Glancing down the street to make sure no one had witnessed what just happened—least of all Dax—I motioned for Darius to get up and come inside. "What are you doing here? Aren't you live on TV right now?"

He stood and brushed off his pants. "Oh, I recorded all that earlier in the day." He grinned. "The magic of television. I gather you watched the segment?"

"Yes," I said. "You did a great job highlighting Farouche. I'm sure it will up their profile."

"I'm sure it will." He stepped into my living room and ran his finger across the back of the dusty piano. "What did you think about the last bit?"

"The last bit?"

Darius frowned. "You didn't watch until the end? I sent you a secret message."

I shook my head.

He scrunched up his face a bit, and I could tell he was annoyed. "No matter," he said. "It was just a sly nod to our little arrangement—me telling you that I was about to make good on our promise. No one who wasn't in on it would suspect anything." He winked and handed me the ring box.

I opened it, and the canned lighting above us glinted off the marquise-cut boulder. Darius had impeccable taste, even if the ring was too flashy for me. Kelly would probably give it four drooly-face emojis. I snapped the box shut.

"Darius," I said. "I...this is very fast—"

"Fast is the point, isn't it?" He looked me right in the eye. "Remember when I said it's all about the hustle? This is us hustling. We need to strike while the iron's hot."

"I don't know—"

"Think about it." He waved his hand in the air as if picturing headlines with our names in them as he crossed the room to my kitchen. "You're already on your way to becoming a bona fide Chicago celeb now, like it or not, and the two of us together could be the premier couple in town. Once I finally get my radio show, it could include a recurring segment with my illustrious wife, Dr. Annie Kyle."

"That's a lovely thought, but—"

"Imagine all the people you could reach and help with a segment like that. You told me that part of your frustration with being a concierge doctor was having to keep your client list small." He opened my kitchen cabinets, looking for something. A glass.

He had a point, but no. I shook my head. "Darius, please listen to me. I can't say yes...at least not right now." I had too many things to consider, including two other guys who were in the picture.

"Okay." He poured himself a glass of wine from the bottle I'd left on the counter.

Well, that was easy. "I'm sorry," I said, "and I hope you don't mind waiting—"

"I don't mind because I know you'll eventually say yes." He sipped the wine and made a face.

This guy's confidence was legendary. "Oh, do you?"

"Sure, I do." He pressed his lips together and stepped toward me. "I'm the only answer that makes sense."

"Really."

"The Rob guy, I'm sure he's nice, but he'll end up boring you to tears. And Dax—"

"Dax isn't in the picture."

"Annie." He raised his eyebrows. "You can keep telling yourself that, but believe me. I've been in your shoes."

"Our situation is different." I clamped my mouth shut.

Darius patted me on the shoulder. "Maybe your situation is different, and I hope for your sake you're right. I wouldn't wish the heartbreak I had to endure on anyone, especially not you." He reached for my hand and opened my palm, into which he pressed the ring box.

"I told you—"

"Hold on to this," he said. "Think about it. When you come to your decision, call me." He shook his head. "No judgment, no 'I told you so.' I promise." He closed my fingers over the box. "I believe we will do great, important, impressive things together, Annie." He looked me dead in the eye. "No one is going to understand the demands of your career like I will. No one."

He squeezed my hand and set his half-drunk wineglass on the counter. "We'll be in touch."

I wordlessly watched him walk out my front door as

I heard Joanne's chains jingling in the basement. A few moments later, Dax appeared at the top of the stairs.

"Well, that—" I started to say, but Dax cut me off.

A worried frown clouded his face. "Something scary happened with Joanne."

I shoved the ring box, forgotten, into the bottom of my purse and ran downstairs to check on the dog.

CHAPTER THIRTY-SEVEN

In Dog Beers, We've Only Had One!

Polly managed to fit Joanne in for an early morning appointment. Even though Yessi and Polly had been together for a while, I'd never been inside her vet's office before. It was as expected—lots of dogs barking at one another in the waiting room and birds cowering in their cages. The place smelled like a kennel. Joanne, for her part, took the whole thing like a champ.

Polly only kept us waiting for a few minutes. When she came into the exam room, I gave her a hug, and then she got right down on the floor with Joanne and fed her a treat. "Okay, guys. What seems to be the problem?"

Dax had clammed up, worried about his dog, so I took the lead. "Last night, Dax took her for a walk, and when she stopped to do her business, her back legs kind of gave out." I glanced at Dax to make sure I had that right. He nodded.

Polly examined Joanne's hind legs. "Could she get up?"

"No. I had to physically lift her." Dax mimed that action for her. "She couldn't do it on her own."

Polly nodded and beckoned to Dax and me. "Can one of

you come down here and help?"

Taking charge, I jumped down to the floor, even though I was already dressed for work in nice pants and a button-down shirt. I'd dealt with patient families of all kinds. Some people sprang into action in the face of hard news, and others clammed up. Dax and I represented both ends of that spectrum. We made a good team, at least caretaker-wise.

Polly instructed me, "Just pet her head and try to keep her standing still for a moment."

She lifted Joanne's back leg and set it back down, pushing her toes underneath her paw. "Hmph." She did the same thing with the other leg, and then she gave Joanne a treat.

"Okay," Polly said. "See this?" I craned my neck to watch what she was doing. "Normally a dog's paw will automatically flip back out, the way it's supposed to be, but Joanne's stays like this—tucked under." She pulled herself off the floor and wiped off her pants. I stayed on the cold tile with Joanne.

Then Polly gave us the face I knew too well, the "it's all going to be okay, but it's really not, because I'm about to give you bad news" smile. "It appears Joanne is in the early stages of degenerative myelopathy, which is a disease that affects the spine."

"Can we treat this?" I asked. The word "degenerative" didn't instill me with confidence that this would get better with time.

"There are ways to slow the decline," she said gravely. "We can give her vitamins and supplements that may help. Since we're catching this early, I'll tell you exercise is a good thing—keep her mobile, keep working her muscles." Polly's eyes softened. "I went through this with my lab a few years ago, and it's hard. I wish I could give you more hope. It starts with what you witnessed today, but then she'll have trouble going up and down stairs, she'll become incontinent, and"—she shook her head—"eventually she won't be able to get up on her own. It's a tough road ahead." She looked at Dax. "For all of you."

I glanced back at Dax, who sat statue still, face muscles tight, hands clutched in his lap. I got up and took a seat next to him, resting my arm against his. I was here for him and Joanne—whatever they needed.

"Well," I said brightly, doing my own version of the Dr. Good News Dance, "I've been walking Joanne a lot lately. She started out only wanting to go a block, but now we're making it four or five. She seems really happy about it."

"That's great," Polly said. "Keep that up."

"How long?" Dax said, his voice low and grave. "How long does she have?"

Polly frowned. "Sad to say, by the time we diagnose this, it usually means the dog will be gone within the year." She pressed her lips together.

Dax's head dropped, and he pressed the palms of his hands into his eyes.

"I'll be right back with the information about those prescriptions," Polly said.

I jumped up and gave her a hug. "Thanks, Pol."

She patted me on the back. "I'm happy to help, doc."

I took the seat next to Dax and reached for his hand. He laced his fingers in mine. I held on, even if the action unnerved me. It felt like home. It felt like we were a real couple dealing with bad medical news together. My mind tried to flit to moments in the future when we might have to be there for each other as a couple—funerals, firings, food poisoning—but I wouldn't let it. We sat there for a moment in silence.

"Thank you," he said finally. "You're better at handling this stuff than I am."

"I've had a bit more experience."

He rested his head on my shoulder. Out in the hall, a cat meowed.

This was very real and very nice but also extremely fragile. Yes, we had this thing connecting us now—the care and feeding of Joanne—but beyond that...there was nothing keeping him here with me. He could find a new apartment and pick up and leave at any moment, and I'd be right back where I started.

I let go of his hand and jumped down to the floor to be with Joanne, which seemed like the safer option, my pants be damned. "It's going to be okay," I said, lifting her head into my lap and stroking the soft fur between her ears. "We're going to take good care of Joanne. I'll keep walking her. We'll get her one of those little pill boxes to organize her medicine." I made a box with my hands.

Dax stared hard at Joanne on the floor, who gave her tail a wag. Then he came down to the floor with us. He knelt next to her and scratched the spot just above her tail, which she loved. He laughed as she squirmed with glee.

"Seriously," I said. "Polly said one year, but that's just an average. You and I are overachievers, Mr. *Yale*." I raised my eyebrows at him, and he laughed.

"A year from now, she'll probably still be playing ball in

the park." He grinned at me.

My face slipped into a frown.

He came around to my side of the dog. "What?" Smiling, he tried to look me in the eye. "I'm supposed to be the weepy one in the vet's office."

I focused on Joanne's ears. "A year is a long time."

"Not that long."

"A lot can happen... You're talking about playing in the park with Joanne, and I'm wondering if I'm still in the picture."

"Are you saying you want to be in the picture?"

"I don't know, Dax." I turned toward him, both of us kneeling next to his dog, who, based on the cacophony outside the room, appeared to be the most relaxed creature ever to set foot in this vet's office. "Darius...proposed to me last night."

His mouth opened wordlessly.

"I didn't say yes," I said, "or no." I looked him right in the eye. "He senses that there's something brewing between you and me, but he says he's been in a similar situation, and what we have"—I pointed to Dax and me—"will flame out because we're in such different places in our lives."

"That's..." He shook his head. "Anything can flame out. Let's say you and Darius get married and your plus-one gambit works for a while. But then he—or you—meets someone new and falls in love. *Boom*. Flame out." He reached for my hand, and I gave it to him. "Muriel and me? Totally same page. We were so in love and secure in our relationship that we didn't even wait to graduate to get married. But time passed, and we changed, individually, apart from each other.

Boom. Flame out."

I let out a slow, shaky breath. Suddenly, with the vet out of the room, Dax had become the take-charge person. "Being left behind—being alone—scares me."

He wiped a tear from my cheek. "Like I told you before, there are worse things than being alone. You don't think you're going to feel alone when Darius chooses one night to go out on the town without you or when Rob spends every Friday night with his buddies?"

"But—"

"This isn't about them...or me, really. It's about you, Annie. People change, they leave, and they die. You can't control any of that. You can only control your reaction to it."

I patted Joanne's head. "Says the guy who was a blubbering mess worrying about his dog."

"Yeah." He tilted my chin toward him with a finger. "I will be devastated when Joanne is gone. It will rip me to shreds, but I know I'll be okay, eventually." He touched his lips lightly to mine. "Look, Annie, I'm not planning on going anywhere in the immediate future. I've been working for years to make Farouche a success, and it hasn't happened yet."

"Yet," I said. "You still haven't experienced the Man on Main Street effect."

"No, but I'm used to disappointment. In all honesty, you'll probably be begging to get me out of the house in a year."

Polly came in at that moment with the prescription information. She looked at the two of us kneeling together, holding hands, with pity, probably assuming all of this emotion was Joanne-related. "You can check out at the front desk," she said solemnly. "Take all the time you need."

After the door had closed behind her, Dax said, "Annie, I'm falling for you, and I think you feel the same way."

There was no more denying it, even if the idea still scared the crud out of me. "But you're so much younger than I am, and you're not looking for anything permanent."

He shook his head. "But also not about to deny myself happiness when I think I've found it."

My eyes stung with tears. I couldn't fathom going to either of the other guys and vowing to marry one of them while Dax still existed in my world. He'd always be in the back of my mind. And the front. And the sides. "I'm scared of what might happen—"

He cupped my cheek. "Don't think too far ahead. Focus on you, me, and Joanne: our little dysfunctional family. We'll take it one day at a time, no sweeping proclamations, no premature engagements. Yeah, it's scary, and maybe it will flame out spectacularly..."

I hesitated, trying to ignore the feeling of doom settling inside me and Darius's words echoing in my ears. This was what I wanted, and I couldn't deny that anymore, no matter the outcome. I reached for Dax, pulling him toward my lips. "Or maybe we'll live happily ever after by accident."

CHAPTER THIRTY-EIGHT

E=MC Hammer

After the vet, I had to get to work, so Dax and I said goodbye in the car outside the house. "I have to bartend tonight," he said after kissing me for a good minute plus, "but that's probably a good thing. If we're going to do this, you need to let the other guys off the hook before we go any further."

"You're right," I told him. "And I need to do it in person." I had to give Darius his ring back, for one thing. "I'm going out to my mom's for lunch on Saturday. I'll talk to Rob then."

I showed up at my mom's house at one o'clock sharp that weekend, ready to rip off the Rob bandage. It wasn't fair to him to string him along. He deserved to move on, as I was doing with Dax. I'd get him alone and break the news, neat and clean. He'd be fine. We'd both gone into this potential relationship with eyes wide open, and he'd understand why I needed to move on.

But when I got to Rob's house, he wasn't there. I'd knocked softly, so as not to disturb his mother. Instead of ringing the doorbell, I sent him a text. *Hey, are you home?*

He sent back, *I'm at your mom's house :)*

Great. Super. A new kind of dread settling in my chest and shoulders, I tramped across his front lawn and into my mom's backyard. There I found Mom, Rob, and Mrs. Casey all seated around the patio table.

I smiled, pretending everything was fine and normal and wonderful. "Hi, everyone."

"Annie," my mom said brightly, glancing at her watch. "You made it."

"It's one-oh-two," I grumbled. "I'm two minutes late." I glanced at Rob, who was smiling hard, his teeth bared in determination.

Rob jumped from his seat and took my hand. He kissed my cheek and led me over to the table, pulling out a chair for me next to him. I moved as if in a dream, taking in the spread of food my mom had laid out—bread and lemonade and lasagna and salad. I'd gone through the looking glass. I was at the Mad Hatter's tea party.

I glanced at Rob's mom. "Mrs. Casey—"

"Regina," she said.

"—you look great." I wasn't just blowing smoke. She did look great. She wore a fashionable sunhat and big glasses and had wrapped herself in a colorful muumuu, but I could still tell that her color had improved since the last time I'd seen her. And she'd filled out a bit. Her plate was crammed with food, and she was eating it.

"Thank you, dear." She reached for Rob's hand. "I feel so much better these days. Thanks to Robbie...and you." She winked.

My stomach churned as my eyes swung to Rob, who was

staring hard at the table, focused on the large pepper grinder in front of him.

I straightened up, starting to get a sense of what might be going on here. "What do you mean?" I said through clenched teeth.

Regina chuckled. "Why, your engagement, silly."

"Your what?" My mother squealed, her hand flying to her lips.

"Did she not tell you yet?" Regina said. "She and Robbie are getting married."

Shrieking, my mom jumped up and wrapped her arms around my back, bouncing up and down, squeezing me tight. "Annie, why didn't you say anything?"

Seething, I glanced at Rob and spoke through a plastered-on smile. "I thought we agreed we weren't going to tell anybody until things were official."

"What do you mean?" Regina's nervous eyes swung between Rob and me. "I thought this was official? You said, Robbie…"

Rob glanced over at me, pleading, concern draining his face of color. He nodded slightly toward his mother, and I got it. He'd told her about us, and now she was sitting here looking healthy and happy. He was asking me not to ruin it.

I cleared my throat. "I meant—I thought we were going to wait until I actually had the ring." I looked my mom straight in the eye. "I'm sorry I didn't tell you about it sooner. We're having it resized."

"Understandable." My mom scooted her chair right next to Regina now, and the two of them started squawking about showers and timelines and guest lists.

This had gotten out of hand. I stood and motioned for Rob to follow me out to the front.

"Look at the two lovebirds stealing some time alone!" my mom cooed.

My heart in my throat, I opened the gate and headed silently to the front of the house. When we were out of earshot, I hissed at him, "What the hell, Rob?"

He gestured toward the backyard. "You saw her. A day or two after I…proposed…she started going downhill quickly." He ran a hand through his blond hair. "I really thought she was going to—" He cut himself off, blinking, his jaw working to hide a trembling lip. "I told her we were engaged, so she could die knowing I would be okay. I honestly thought that was it. I didn't think she'd get better."

I closed my eyes for a moment, calming myself. My own jaw was starting to hurt from all the tension of the past few days. "I understand why you told her, Rob; I do." I wasn't mad about that—not really. He was desperate, and I just happened to get wrapped up in it. He only thought he was jumping the gun. "But what happens now? We're not engaged."

"Yet." His face lit up hopefully.

I blew out a long, shaky breath. "I have to tell you something."

His brow furrowed. I took my time searching for the words, pacing along the front sidewalk until I came and stopped right in front of him.

I waited a few beats. "Darius proposed to me."

He exhaled. "Shit." Then he frowned. "And what was your response?"

"I told him I'd think about it, but Rob…" I paused. "I'm

going to turn him down."

He grinned, his shoulders relaxing with relief. "Good."

I held up a hand. "But that's not all."

"It's not?"

"There's...someone else..." Me of two years ago—heck, me of two months ago—would not recognize the soap opera my life had become.

He shook his head in disbelief. "Someone else you texted."

"No. Someone I met more recently and who I have very real feelings for."

His lips parted for a moment in surprise, but he quickly morphed that into a tight smile. "Okay."

"I slept with him."

"You slept with this guy you have feelings for." His voice came out measured and calm. Too calm.

"Yes," I said, "and we want to continue seeing each other. We're serious about giving this thing between us a real shot. I'm so sorry, Rob. I had no idea this would happen." I chuckled. "I mean, I'd barely had a second date in years."

Rob set his jaw, and now it was his turn to pace. I waited until he returned to me. "That's...fine," he said finally, his shoulders squared and strong.

"What do you mean, 'that's fine'?"

He stood straight, chin up. "I mean, you and I are an unconventional couple."

I resisted the urge to remind him that we weren't even actually a couple.

He kept looking off to the side, and I could practically see the wheels turning in his head. "These are the kinds of things that we'll have to work out between us before we're married."

"You do know we're not actually engaged," I muttered.

His eyes snapped to me, but he caught himself quickly and lowered the temperature of his reaction. A wan smile on his face, he said, "Who's this guy? This third guy?"

"He's"—I shook my head, shrugging—"he's a musician."

Rob laughed. "A musician."

"He's wonderful, really," I told him. "So smart and kind and funny—"

"You know." Rob spoke in a slow, even voice. "A musician isn't going to give you what you want."

"And what's that?" I folded my arms. I'd barely spent time with Rob since high school, and now he was an expert on what I wanted? All he thought he knew about me he got from one drunken text and two dates.

"You want stability, companionship, and commitment." He waved his hand. "Isn't that why we're here right now?"

"Yes, and I think Dax—I think *he* will be able to give me those things." At least I hoped he would, or that they'd magically no longer matter to me someday. Either way, we were going to try to make this work. I doubled down. "I'm *sure* he will."

"Okay, Annie," Rob said. "Maybe it will work out; maybe it won't. But I've been married before, and I'm older than you."

"One year," I reminded him, holding up an index finger. "One."

"My prediction is that eventually you'll find yourself alone again and you'll wish you'd picked stability over passion."

"I won't, but thanks." This conversation took me right back to my childhood when Rob and I would play board games together and he *always* knew the rules better than anyone. You couldn't tell Rob Casey anything he didn't already know. He had that one year on me, and he still wouldn't let me forget it. "Tell our moms I'm sorry but I had a medical emergency." I couldn't go back in the yard and listen to the wedding plans, but I wouldn't bust up Regina's healthy glow, either.

"Annie." He placed a hand on my shoulder. "I'm sorry. I'm not trying to be an ass. I'm very clumsily trying to tell you that I'll be here for you, if and when you come to the decision that you still want stability."

"Fine," I said. "Thanks." I couldn't wait to get back home to Dax, where I wouldn't have to think about these other two guys anymore.

Ugh, but I still had to get through one more of these conversations. That was the problem with juggling two guys— double the breakups.

"One thing." Rob reached into his jeans pocket and grabbed something. "Here. Take this. In case your mom or my mom or whoever asks to see it." He placed his engagement ring in my palm. "Just until she…"

I stared at it for a moment, like it was a toad or a hideous spider or something. Still, I'd stick to my promise. I wouldn't do anything to jeopardize Mrs. Casey's health and well-being. I clamped my hand around the ring and shoved it down into the bottom of my purse. "Okay. Sure. Goodbye, Rob."

CHAPTER THIRTY-NINE

N'THINK

I finally got a hold of Darius late Saturday afternoon, and he gave me more of the same rigamarole: Dax and I would never last; I was welcome to call him when my little flight of fancy finally ended; and only he, Darius, could give me the commitment I craved.

"Noted," I told him. "When can we meet up so I can give you the ring back?"

"I'm swamped at the moment," he told me, "so hold on to it for now. Just in case."

"There is no 'just in case,'" I told him. "I will give you the ring back the next time I see you."

I pressed the "end call" button hard, wishing landlines were still a thing. Hanging up on someone used to be much more satisfying.

Feeling lighter and a bit relieved, I went downstairs to the basement, where Dax and Joanne were cuddled up on the couch. He glanced up when I came down. "Done?" he asked.

"Done." I flopped onto a chair across from him. "I don't like admitting anyone else was right—"

He raised an eyebrow.

"But…maybe you were right. Trying to force relationships with two guys I barely know, and…it turns out…maybe I don't even really like, might not have been my best idea ever."

"Ouch to them," he said.

"No." I rolled my eyes to the ceiling. "I like them. They're nice. It's just…they're not for me. Let other people have them."

"Who is for you, then?" He shot me a crooked smile.

I grinned back. "Well, that's a really good question. I like to think I've learned a lot about myself these past several weeks." I scrunched up my face. "I think I'm looking for someone who knows a lot of useless trivia."

"Check." He rose from the couch.

"Maybe…plays an instrument?"

"Check." He took a step toward me, eyes darkening with each moment.

My insides warmed. "Went to…Yale?"

"Yup." His toes touched mine.

I sucked my lower lip under my top teeth and gazed up at him. "I want someone who's…over thirty-five."

"No you fucking don't." He grabbed my hand and helped me up from the couch, pulling me toward him into a tight, warm embrace.

We spent the rest of the afternoon, until Dax had to go into work, cuddling in his bed, watching rom-coms and not watching rom-coms. When he finally left me alone, my arm draped around Joanne, I realized I felt like a huge weight had been lifted from me. I was—dare I say it?—happy.

I kissed the dog on top of her head. Maybe this could actually work.

. . .

On Tuesday night, I showed up for trivia at almost the last minute. "Sorry," I said after kissing Dax hello. "Long day at work."

He pushed an old-fashioned toward me, and I beamed in thanks. He could be so thoughtful. I sank into my chair, suddenly relaxing for the first time all day.

"Tell me all about it," he said.

I shook my head and sipped my drink. "Oh, nothing huge, just some bug going around—fevers, chills, cough. Almost like a summer flu. Everyone thinks they have it."

"Do they?"

"Nope."

He laughed. This was lovely. Being with Dax, competing in this tournament with him, snuggling with him in bed watching movies, having him—and one of his old-fashioneds—to come home to at night after a long day. I couldn't imagine doing all those things with either Rob or Darius. If I'd stuck with one of them, I'd probably be watching sports right now, being forced to make small talk with Ellen Miller, or I'd be getting dressed up for a fancy night out when all I wanted to do was relax and unwind after a hellish workday.

Not that those things were bad. They just weren't for me. I knew that now.

"I'm sorry you had a bad day," he said, "but I had a great one."

"I can't wait to hear about it," I said.

But then Ronald got the trivia started—famous Nickelodeon actors, LOL—and we had to put our conversation on hold for a moment. Dax positively crushed the round.

I stirred my drink after he returned from submitting our answer sheet. "I never considered that one of the perks of dating a twenty-seven-year-old might be him knowing way too much about the cast of *iCarly*." I raised my eyebrows. "Now I know what got you into Yale."

He chuckled.

"Tell me about your amazing day."

He leaned forward, resting his hands on the table. "Well, the *thing* is paying off." After the Man on Main Street segment aired, we started calling it "the *thing*" to avoid talking about the Darius of it all. "This weekend, Saturday night, five short little days from now, Farouche is invited to open for..." He drummed his hands on the table. "Monica Feathers."

My stomach dropped. "Wow, I've actually heard of her."

"Now *that*"—he sipped his beer and waggled his eyebrows—"is truly amazing."

I forced a smile. "I haven't listened to her music, but I hear she's good." She was the kind of woman who brought a legitimate, goofy smile to Darius Carver's face. And now my cute, young boyfriend was going to be working in her presence. Cool. Cool cool cool. So very cool.

Stop it, brain. We're having a lovely night. Stop imagining it all imploding.

"Monica's awesome," he said. "The band met with her earlier today, and I think we really jibed. She's a total pro and takes her work seriously, which always impresses me."

"Good." I reached across the table and squeezed his hand. "I'm so happy for you." And I was. Or, at least, I really, really wanted to be. Maybe I could convince myself this sinking feeling that the other shoe was about to drop was nothing more than joy and excitement.

"Round two!" Ronald announced.

I pulled the answer key toward me. "Let's do this thing." I held the pencil poised, ready to go. "Hopefully the next round is something I know about, like *30 Rock* or the movies of Paul Thomas Anderson. I'd like to at least have a shot at impressing my young Yale-alumnus boyfriend."

"He's already impressed," Dax said.

On Saturday afternoon, I put on my most churchy little black dress and kissed Dax goodbye. "Have fun," he said.

"What's more fun than a baby's christening?" I held up the very nondescript yellow gift bag I'd picked out for Olivia. My mom, who was taking my role as godmother very seriously, had urged me to get the baby a Bible or a rosary or something else equally religious. Instead I, as her appointed spiritual guide, bought her my favorite books from when I was a kid and wrote a personal message about why I loved them on each of the inside covers. Let someone else do the Bible thing.

"You'll be back in time to walk Joanne?" Dax's brow furrowed.

"I'll make sure I am." I double checked that I had my phone. "And then I'll head right over to the concert." He had to be at the venue soon to prepare for the show.

"Before you go," he said, handing me a thumb drive. "For your ride."

I looked at the device in my hand. "What's this?"

"Music," he said. "My music."

How sweet that he'd made me a mix. "How do I play this in the car?"

He shrugged. "Don't you have one of those high-tech vehicles that can do anything? My car still has crank windows, so I don't know how any of this works."

"I'll try to play it." I kissed him again and dropped the drive into the bottomless pit that was my purse. "Thank you very much for the thoughtful gift, and good luck at the concert."

He recoiled in horror. "You don't say good luck."

"I'm sorry." I winced. "Break a leg?"

"We'll pretend this conversation never happened."

A little while later, Yessi met me outside the church in Schaumburg, near where she grew up.

"What are you doing out here?" I squinted into the sunlight. "Shouldn't you be doing the whole schmoozing-with-your-relatives thing?"

"I threw Polly to the wolves for a few minutes. My mom is insisting that I put my brother in as Olivia's godfather instead of having two godmothers." She shook her head. "She didn't say it this rudely, to be fair, but she said something to the effect of, 'Olivia needs at least one male role model.'" Her lip quivered.

I pulled her in for a hug, squeezing her tight.

When she pulled away, she wiped her eyes hard. "I mean, she's really going to hold up Miggy as the paragon of male virtue? He's thirty, and she still does his laundry."

I laughed. "Who's the other godmother?" I asked. "Your sister?"

"Nope." Yessi waved past me, and I turned around to find Kelly coming toward us, Mark next to her.

"Hey…" I said cautiously, pulling her in for a hug, which she accepted. "How's it going? Hi, Mark." I hugged him, too.

"Good to see you again."

Kelly stared at the entrance to the church. "I'm sorry about our interaction at my bridal shower. I hope your patient is doing okay."

Mark patted her supportively on the shoulder.

"Thank you, and she is," I said, frowning a little. Chatting with Kelly used to be so easy, so fun. We used to belt out show tunes in our kitchen, and now she could barely look at me. "How's wedding stuff going?"

"Good," she said stiffly. "Everything's coming along." She glanced at her watch. "We should probably head inside."

Kelly and Yessi walked toward the door, but Mark hung back. "Hey, Annie. Can we talk a second?"

I watched my friends disappear behind the heavy doors. "Sure."

"Not my place," he said, "but since Kelly appears to be in one of her stubborn moods—"

I laughed. "So you're already well aware of those?"

"Yes." He grinned. "You should know: Kelly's mom's eyesight has gotten much worse over the past six months or so, and the doctors think she won't get it back."

My stomach dropped. "Oh no. That's awful." That was part of the reason Kelly had to go out to Galena in the first place—because her dad needed to get to and from rehab appointments, and her mom couldn't drive him. "She should've called me. I could've gotten her in touch with a specialist." I pulled out my phone. "I still can. My friend from med school—"

Mark held up a hand to stop me. "I already told her to do that, and she refused. She didn't want to bother you, especially since things have been so tense between you two lately."

My shoulders sank. I would do anything for Kelly—she had to know that. "I don't care about any of that. I only want to help, if I can."

He leaned in a little closer. "I think it's a pride thing."

"Right." Kelly could be the most fun and bubbly person, but she also had a bit of a temper lurking underneath. She once put a friend of ours in college on the "dead to me" list because she drunkenly kissed Kelly's crush at a bar one night—a guy who, to be fair, had no clue Kelly actually existed. I just never thought she'd actually cut *me* out of her life. "I'll try to talk to her," I told Mark. "Thanks for keeping me in the loop. I really appreciate it."

"When we first met," he said, "she used to talk about you and Yessi all the time and with such admiration." He smiled. "I hope you all can work it out."

"Me too."

After the ceremony, during which I held a screaming and squirming Olivia while a priest dumped water on her head, we all went over to the Cortezes' house for a backyard reception. I stayed in the car for a few minutes to answer some questions that had come in during the baptism. I had three messages, on a Saturday. My patients were really nervous about this flu.

I checked the clock before heading back to the party. It was three thirty now. The ceremony at the church had gone long. I had to be on the road by four to get back to walk Joanne and then order a ride to the concert. On my way in, I grabbed a bottle of water and a corner piece of cake covered in fluffy white buttercream. Kelly and Mark were at one of the back tables. I joined them.

"Hey, guys," I said, setting down my stuff. "They lucked out. This weather is amazing."

Kelly mumbled in what I assumed was agreement.

I snuck a glance at Mark. "So, Kel...how are your mom and dad doing?"

"They're fine," she said.

"Your dad's knee?"

"Good as new."

"And your mom?"

"She's fine."

I was fighting a losing battle. Mark shot me a sympathetic smile.

My phone buzzed just as I'd shoved a mound of cake in my mouth. "My goodness. This is getting..." I swallowed and sent a quick message back, telling my patient I'd call in a few minutes. "Have you guys heard about this virus going around?"

"A little bit," Mark said.

"As far as we know, it hasn't actually made its way to the United States yet, and, as far as I know, it's not super transmissible," I said, "but all my patients think they're going to be the first case."

"Maybe they will be," Kelly said. "I suppose it's possible."

Okay, that was a tiny, little opening. I'd take it.

"How's everything else going, you guys?" I said. "The wine shop, the real estate…?"

"Good," Kelly said.

"Kelly just made her first big sale," Mark said.

"Awesome! Congratulations! I knew you'd jump right in and be as badass in Galena as you were in Chicago."

She shot me a smile. "Thanks. How about you? How's… your love life?"

I laughed. "Actually, there has been a bit of a development on that front," I said, shrugging. "Dax and I are together."

Kelly laughed. "What? Really?"

That was…? Was she making fun of me? I could no longer tell. We were so out of sync, I'd lost my ability to read her. "Is that so hard to believe?"

"No…" Kelly looked right at Mark. "Dax lives in Annie's basement. He was that bartender from the trivia night…"

"Oh yeah." Mark smiled kindly, which was more than I could say for his fiancée. "He seemed very nice."

"He is." I frowned at Kelly.

"I'm sorry." She shook her head. "I mean it. I'm sorry. I'm just confused. I thought you were looking to settle down. I'm surprised you're dating a twenty-five-year-old bartender."

"He's twenty-seven."

She took a swig of water. "I actually love this for you," she said, turning to Mark. "Annie's never really dated much—"

"Yes, I have." My jaw tightened. I was getting really tired of people feeling like they had license to comment on my love life.

"Well, first dates. Annie has gone on a lot of first dates." She paused. "It's nice to see you're having fun. That's all."

"It's more than fun," I said. "Dax and I are serious."

Kelly smiled. "Of course you are. You're so scared of being alone that you invited a random dude to live in your basement, and now you've convinced yourself dating him is a good idea in an attempt to keep him there."

"Whoa. That escalated quickly. It's not like that," I said. "You make me sound like a—"

"Like the kind of person who'd pursue a relationship with her mom's next-door neighbor even though she's not even attracted to him?"

My mouth opened and closed like a fish. "You were one of the ones telling me to go for it with Rob!"

Mark, apparently trying and failing to redirect the conversation, said, "Isn't Dax trying to be an actor or something?"

"He's a musician," I said. "And the band is doing really well." I stood, grabbing my cake plate. I couldn't take this anymore. "I have to get going, actually, because he has a big concert tonight."

Kelly laughed. "Okay. Have fun in the mosh pit, Annie!"

I rushed toward the gate, shooting Yessi an "I'm sorry" look on the way, tears streaming down my face. I didn't know if Polly's theory that Kelly was trying to push me away held any water, but, regardless, that's what she had done. It was official. I'd lost my best friend.

CHAPTER FORTY

Thundercat Hoes

That night, without the benefit of Darius's VIP status, I ordered a car and headed to Dax's concert, which was in some neighborhood I hadn't been to since my twenties, Kelly's mosh pit comment ringing in my ears. Well, she could suck it up. I, Dr. Annie Kyle, was going to a concert to watch my hot young boyfriend play keyboard in his band, and I was proud of it.

And I was so not in this with Dax because I was scared of being alone. If that were the case, I would've already married Rob at City Hall or something. She had no idea what she was talking about.

I showed my ticket at the door and went in to try and find a good seat. But there were no seats. This venue was standing room only.

Fine. No big deal. I didn't mind standing. I stood practically all day at work. I was here to see Dax perform in the biggest concert of his life—so far. There would be many big concerts in his future, I was sure. And I was here to enjoy myself.

I went up to the bar to order a drink, and I smiled at the woman next to me—who was much closer to Dax's age than mine. "You like Farouche?" I asked.

"They're hot." She turned her attention to her phone.

Okay then. I grabbed my drink and made my way through the crowd of people all dressed up like they were going to, well, a show. I'd put on jeans, my black Converse, and a Lilith Fair T-shirt I still had from my freshman year of high school. The way I looked, I could be going to the grocery store.

One of those sinking feelings started to creep in. Dax would someday realize—possibly sooner rather than later— that I didn't fit in here. No, I couldn't think that way. Dax and I were doing great. We were very happy together, and it wasn't as if he didn't already know what a huge old nerd I was. Sipping my drink, I tried to blend in near a pole and watched the stage as some guys in black tested the sound.

I texted Dax. *Hey! I'm here!* I sent him a smiley face to show him how excited I was. And I *was* excited for him and to see his band play again.

He wrote back, *You should come backstage.*

He'd told me right from the start that I should come with him, to hang out with him and the band before the concert, but I didn't want to get in the way. This was their night—their big moment—and I wanted Dax to enjoy it with the people who got him here. We'd celebrate in our own way later.

You guys have fun and break all *your legs. I'm going to stay out here with the real Farouche fans.*

He clicked the love button on that text.

Next to me, a group of fans was talking about the band. I, pretending to find an article about the mating rituals of gophers fascinating, listened in.

"The lead singer is hot, but the keyboardist is hotter."

This guy and I were in agreement on that.

"I don't think any of them are *hot*," said another. *Boo! Hiss!* "But Farouche are, like, serious musicians. I have to respect that." Okay, this girl wasn't so bad.

Maybe dating a musician would be fun. Yes, it was something totally out of my comfort zone, but that was a good thing. I was thirty-nine, not dead, and should be willing to give new things a try. I just had to relax into it, enjoy the show, tolerate the crowds, and be a little less forty.

Easier said than done, my brain was helpful to remind me. I had a good decade on everyone in this club.

Still, I would fake it till I made it. For Dax. For us.

One patient text and two articles about this annoying new virus later, Farouche finally came out onstage. The crowd went wild. I shoved my phone into my back pocket and cheered along with them. "Woo!" I yelled. "Woo!" When in Rome, *woo*.

Like the last Farouche concert I attended, the drummer counted the band off, and they launched into a song that had since become familiar. I sang along and shimmied in time to the tune. Okay, maybe this would be fun. The group next to me, the ones who'd been talking about Farouche earlier, beckoned me to join them.

"You know all the songs!" one of them shouted.

"I think they sunk in!" I pointed to the stage. "The keyboardist lives in my basement."

The guy's eyes lit up. "What? Really?"

"Yeah!" I bit my lip and scrunched up my nose. "He's my

boyfriend." My cheeks pulled into a big smile. If I looked in a mirror, I knew I'd see an image like Darius when he was with Monica Feathers. I probably looked like a dork.

The guy appraised me, hands on hips. "I love that he's dating an older woman," he said finally.

I shot him a thumbs-up. I'd take that at face value. I was, in fact, an older woman. We were all here having fun tonight, celebrating our mutual admiration for a very talented band. The guy hadn't meant anything by it.

A few songs in, the band slowed things down, and Dax leaned into the microphone. "Tonight, someone's here who's really special to me."

"Ooh!" My new Farouche friends nudged me in the side, and I giggled.

Dax squinted out at the crowd. "Annie, this one's for you."

My phone buzzed in my back pocket. I reached behind me and turned off the ringer. Probably just another question about that virus. I should've created an auto-response earlier that said, *You don't have it.* Anyway, I could get back to them after the concert. I'd ruined my relationship with Kelly partially because half my attention was always on my phone, either answering it or waiting for it to ring. I wouldn't make the same mistake with Dax. Tonight belonged to him, and I would do my part to support him.

The guitarist started playing, and then Dax came in on the keyboard and Kat on bass. Dax, his eyes lowered and dark, sang, *"When you walked into the bar/I wasn't thinking so far/ahead..."*

My hands went instinctively to my chest. I could feel my heart beating, thumping. My eyes watered. I'd never had anyone write anything personal about me, and the fact that it was Dax—beautiful, talented Dax—

"*You shocked me/you surprised me/you truly recognized me!*" And then they launched into the pulsing, soaring chorus. "*Dorothy!*"

I burst out laughing as I swayed in time to the music.

"*You are at the end of my rainbow! Dorothy!*"

I waved my hands in the air like I just did not care.

"I thought your name was Annie," said one of my new friends.

"Yup," I said. "It's also Dorothy." Dax's eyes met mine, and I waved.

He winked at me, and suddenly my stomach hurtled toward the floor. Instead of living in the moment, excited and moved that this gorgeous, talented man had written a song about me, my brain took it to a place of despair and fear, imagining the day, someday soon, when he'd leave me for good. Chills snaked up and down my spine as I pictured myself alone in the house without him, pacing the floor, looking for something to do, anything to distract me from the pain. The image overwhelmed me. I couldn't bear it. Being with Dax would mean hurtling head-first toward my worst nightmare.

Shit. What was I doing?

My phone buzzed again, and I instinctively grabbed it, grateful for the diversion, ready to text the person back with advice about fever reduction and drinking fluids, to deal with some solvable problem I knew I could handle. But it wasn't just a flu question.

Gayle Gale was unconscious.

CHAPTER FORTY-ONE

Geek Tragedy

I dragged myself home from the hospital later that night and walked inside to find Dax waiting for me in the front hallway. "Annie," he said, "where have you been?"

I shook my head, numb, and he pulled me into a hug, rubbing my back. I stiffened, and he pulled away, holding me at arm's length. "What? What's going on?" He let me go.

I set my purse down on the floor and paced the room. My mind was in a fog. This night had been such a rollercoaster. "I was at the concert, dancing and having fun, letting myself go—"

He smiled. "I saw you hanging out with some people in the crowd."

"But when you started singing the 'Annie' song, I could feel my phone buzzing." I patted my back pocket, replaying the incident in my mind. "I thought, 'I'm not going to check it. I'm going to keep dancing, and I'm going to enjoy my night and be here for Dax.'" My eyes felt dry. I'd cried at the hospital and all the way back home in the car, but now... nothing.

"Annie? You're scaring me," Dax said. "What happened?"

"Gayle Gale died."

His hand went to his mouth. "Oh no. I'm so sorry."

He reached for me, but I moved away and pulled my phone from my pocket. I held it in my hand like some unrecognizable object I had no use for. "Her husband texted me to come. I felt the buzzing in my pocket from the message, and I was going to ignore it. I thought it was just some person with a regular question, but it wasn't."

I didn't tell him that the only reason I even checked the text was because I'd been in a panic about eventually losing him. He didn't need to know that.

"What happened?"

I shook my head, playing through what Gayle and Jim had experienced, even though I hadn't been there for most of it. "Another stroke. A blood vessel just burst. I talked to Jim while the paramedics were on their way, but she was already gone by the time they got there."

I'd met them at the hospital, where she'd already been pronounced dead, and I stayed with Jim for a while to help him through the paperwork and everything. We talked about the amazing woman she was as much as the retirement Gayle would never have.

Jim's daughter, who lived out in the suburbs, arrived just as I was leaving. He told her, "I'm glad you're here. I...I don't want to be alone."

God, I felt that in my bones.

"Annie, I'm so sorry. That's awful," Dax said now.

"I wasn't going to check the phone," I added. "I let it buzz a few times before I looked at it; I was going to ignore any calls that came in during the concert."

"I get it, but I never asked you to do that," he said. "And, in this instance, it sounds like there wasn't anything you could have done."

"But what if it had been a different call where my quick response could've made a difference?" I bit my lip.

"You can't play the what-if game," he said. "And here's the thing—I understand how demanding your job is, believe me. I don't want you to ever feel bad about putting your patients first. Take the call if you need to take the call."

"But I do feel bad. I will feel bad. I worry you'll start to resent me—"

"No." He placed his hands on my shoulders. "Annie, no. I want this to work out; I really do."

I smiled at him, pushing through the sadness and that persistent image of me alone. He was right. He hadn't asked me to turn off the phone or ignore my patients for him. That was all me. I'd been feeling insecure since Kelly, and I was starting to question everything. "I'm sorry," I said. "I'm just sad about Gayle." And the demise of one of my oldest friendships and the fact that no matter what, I'd never be able to give 100 percent to a relationship. My job didn't allow for that.

"You want to hear some good news?" he asked.

"Absolutely." I followed him toward the kitchen, where he poured me a glass of white wine and handed it to me.

"The concert went really well tonight."

I grinned. "It really did. You guys crushed it. So many broken legs on that stage."

"It went so well..." He swallowed as if gathering his nerve.

"Monica Feathers wants us to go on tour with her. In Europe. Apparently they really 'get' her there. Another band dropped out, and she needed to replace them quickly." He smiled. "We were in the right place at the right time."

All the blood drained from my face. "Wow," I said as happily as possible. "That's…amazing."

"It's…not forever," he said, clutching my hands in his. "It's a temporary thing. But we're leaving in less than two weeks for at least six months, and she did mention something about recording an album at some chalet in France with her afterward…" He waved his hand. "But I'm sure that was all empty promises. You know how people talk, making plans that will never happen."

I touched my forehead. Holy…this was it. This was the nightmare scenario. Dax and I were just getting started, and now we were ending. Already. My dread had not been premature. "I think I'm getting a headache."

He grabbed the wineglass from my hand and walked me over to the couch. "Here. Come sit down. It's been a rough day, and that was a lot of information I just threw at you. I should've waited. I'm sorry."

I leaned back and closed my eyes, focusing on the black and red colors behind my eyelids.

"I hope you know," he was saying as he rummaged around behind me, "I don't expect this tour to change things. I mean, maybe you can actually take some time off to come see us play, or I can talk to Monica about cutting the tour short or recording the album back here in Chicago instead. I'm all in on us, Annie, and I hope—"

He stopped talking. I sat up and turned around. He was

in the hallway with his hand in my purse. *Oh no. No, no, no.*

I jumped off the couch and rushed to him, my heart pounding in my chest.

He stood. "I was getting you something for your headache. You said you always have ibuprofen." He opened his palm, and there were the two gleaming diamond rings.

"Dax, I can explain. I—"

"What is this?" he asked. "You took their rings."

I shook my head. "I didn't take them. They gave them to me. I was just being polite, you know, giving them the brush-off. Like, 'Sure, fine, I'll hold on to it, if it means you'll leave me alone.'"

"That's…not how engagement rings work." Dax closed his fist. "These are engagement rings. And you have *two* of them."

"I have perfectly good explanations," I said. "The Rob one, I took that because his mom, who's really sick, thinks we're getting married, so to keep her from feeling worse…"

I trailed off as Dax's jaw dropped.

"This dying woman believes you're marrying her son?"

I swallowed. "Yeah."

"And Darius?"

I chuckled. "He was very insistent that I keep the ring so that if things didn't work out between you and me—"

"You were keeping him as a backup."

"No," I said. "I was trying to get rid of him. That's it. I kept the ring to try to get rid of him. I've been trying to give it back, but he's dodging my calls."

Dax tossed the rings back into my purse. "Do you think this is going to work out between us?"

"Dax—"

"Do you think…this can work?"

I hesitated, recalling the image of myself wandering around the house aimlessly, alone. "I want it to."

"That's not what I asked."

I exhaled. "You're so much younger than me," I said. "It's only natural to think that maybe, probably someday, you'll want to move on."

"So as far as you were concerned, this relationship was over before it began."

I reached for him. "No, Dax. Remember? Take things day by day? Accidental happily ever after? That's what I want."

He moved away from me. "Yet, you've been holding on to these rings the whole time, as backup for when this inevitably failed."

"That's not why." I shook my head. "You have to believe me—"

"God, Annie." He slumped onto the couch. "What are we doing?"

I sat next to him and gripped his hand in mine. "We're doing us," I said. "We're doing 'it's not perfect, but let's try until we flame out.'"

"I think we're flaming out." He took his hand back and stood, pacing the floor, running his hands through his hair.

"Dax, I'm so sorry about the rings—"

He turned to me, eyes serious. "I'm leaving," he said, "for at least six months. Maybe more than that."

"I get that," I said, "and if my reaction was anything other than total enthusiasm for you, I regret it. I'm very happy for you. I'm excited for you. I'm only sad you'll be gone."

"That's just it," he said. "This is the bridge we said we'd

cross if we ever came to it. It's here. I'll have the tour, then the album and promotion, and then the cycle will start all over again." He turned his face toward me. "There's no end," he said. "There's no coming back. This is it."

I swallowed. "Those damn rings."

"It's not about the rings," he said. "Or maybe the rings jolted me into thinking. I don't know." His eyes grew slightly watery, and he flared his nostrils as if he were trying to suppress any emotion. "I've tried this kind of relationship before, with Muriel. She sat at home, mad at me, while I performed gig after gig and worked late hours at the bar, trying to make ends meet." He shook his head. "This would be like that times forty. She ended up resenting me." He balled his hands into fists.

"I won't resent you."

"You will, though, because I'll be off living my dream, and you'll be here, grinding it out day after day, when you should be off doing the same."

I laughed. "What are you talking about? I am living my dream. I've been working my entire life to get where I am. If you can't understand that—"

"From where I sit, you're miserable. From here, you're constantly on edge, waiting for the phone to ring. Even if we did agree to stay together while I was on tour, it wouldn't be like you could come visit me. You're tethered to Chicago for the rest of your life."

I pressed my lips together. Goddamnit. Darius was right. Dax didn't understand. He would never understand. "Well, good. You should go on tour, then, because I wouldn't want you to be with someone so *miserable*."

"That's not what I meant."

"Well, it's what you *said*."

His shoulders sank. "I've been trying to get to this point for years—which is something I'm sure you can respect. I'm going on this tour. I wish you could come visit me, but—"

I couldn't do this anymore. Today my favorite patient died and I officially lost my best friend. I could not keep having this argument with Dax about my failures as a person. "I absolutely understand what you're going through right now, having to give up one thing you love for another thing you love," I said. "Welcome to success. It sucks. Maybe you can write a song about it." My eyes, suddenly able to produce tears again, stung. I moved toward the stairs.

Behind me, Dax said, "Annie, don't go. Talk to me. Let's not end things like this, please."

"How did you think this would end, Dax?" As the tears streamed down my cheeks, I stormed upstairs and slammed my bedroom door shut.

CHAPTER FORTY-TWO

The We Were on a Breaks

Dax took Joanne and left.

When I woke up the next morning, every remnant of him was gone, like he'd existed only in my dreams. It was the waking nightmare I'd had at the concert come to life.

I padded downstairs, noting the eerie quiet—no jangling chains coming up from the basement. A lump formed in my throat. I would drown it with coffee.

This was for the best. Dax was going to be leaving on tour anyway, and it could span a years-long cycle, so why prolong the inevitable? I should get used to being alone again, like I always had been and always would be.

I took my coffee into the family room, and instead of reading the newspaper like I usually did, I turned on the TV, putting on an old sitcom I nearly knew by heart. Pop culture comfort food.

Straightening up in my seat, I prepared to feel better immediately. Slipping back into a favorite show always did that for me. In anticipation, I sipped my coffee and stared at the TV. Nothing. No dopamine hit. The scenes and dialogue barely registered in my brain.

I blew out a deep breath and shut off the show. This wasn't working.

I stood and stretched. Maybe I should read or work out. Go for a walk. Instead, I wandered into the front hallway and rummaged in my purse for my phone. No patient calls. I stared hard at the screen, willing it to flash with a new message.

What the hell was I doing? Was I seriously urging the universe to endanger the life and health of one of my patients because I was *bored*?

I tossed the phone onto my purse. This was how it all started, wasn't it? I couldn't be alone. I shouldn't be alone. Everyone kept telling me to wait around for love, not to give up on romance.

Well, romance just gave up on me. Now. Stinking. What?

I shoved my hand back into my purse, grasping around, touching old tissues and loose change, until I found exactly what I was looking for. The solution to all my problems.

The next day, in the late afternoon, I went to Gayle Gale's wake. The line outside the funeral home, naturally, stretched around the block. Gayle had been a legend, and everyone wanted to say goodbye.

I got in the queue, my stomach heavy with nerves, and scanned the crowd, looking for that familiar, bright smile. I knew he wouldn't miss this.

Though, who was I kidding? VIP Darius didn't have to

stand out here in line with us peons. He'd probably been ushered in the moment the doors opened and allowed to grieve in private on the celebrity side of the velvet rope.

As I waited, moving an inch or two every fifteen minutes, I read articles on my phone, scrolled through Twitter, and kept one sharp eye on the funeral home exit. Finally, after about forty-five minutes, a murmur buzzed through the crowd, and I looked up to see Darius Carver, the Man on Main Street, stepping out of the funeral home in a perfect bespoke suit.

As nerves pinged every part of my body, I mentally prepared myself for what to say: *Darius, you were right. We should be pragmatic and join forces to become Chicago's premier dynamic duo. Yes, I will marry you!*

But then he turned to hold the door open for someone else. Monica Feathers—in a dramatic black pantsuit with a veiled fascinator—stepped out. The din from the crowd grew louder.

Darius, along with the rest of the crowd, could not take his eyes off her. He helped Monica, in her five-inch stilettos, down the steps. The two of them walked together past the crowd, ignoring the comments and requests for photos and autographs.

I ducked my head, focusing on a random article about the debt ceiling. I knew a long time ago that he'd never look at me the way he looked at Monica, and now I'd seen the proof live and in person. Even more than that, though, seeing the two of them together brought into sharp focus the fact that I couldn't live my life, day after day, knowing for sure that I was nothing more than someone's backup. I owed myself better. I owed Darius better.

Who knew if the two of them could work things out, but it was up to them to try, if they wanted. I would not stand in the way.

When I sensed them nearing, I took a deep breath and looked up, smiling, putting on my bravest and most sincere face. "Darius," I said softly.

He looked over, and when he saw it was me, he shot me a sad smile. "Annie." He came over and gave me a warm, comforting hug.

"I'm so sorry," I said.

"Me too," he agreed. "She meant a lot to both of us."

I nodded toward the line. "Obviously she meant a lot to everyone."

No one more so than her husband, Jim, who'd been about to set off with his love on an adventure, who didn't want to be alone.

All the more reason to grab on to companionship now, even if that no longer meant Darius.

"Have you met Monica?" He gestured for his ex to step over. She was a tiny woman with shiny black hair and alabaster skin, but her glamorous stature belied her small frame. I probably had a good six inches on her, but it felt like she towered over me. "Mon?" Darius said. "This is Dr. Annie Kyle."

Monica offered me a small, delicate hand. "Oh, hello." Her voice was like a songbird's—sweet and melodic. I could see why Darius fell hard for her.

"I've heard so many wonderful things about you," she said.

I glanced at Darius. "Really?"

"From Dax," Monica added.

My throat closed up. I could only nod.

She squeezed my hand lightly. "I'm so sorry things couldn't work out between you, but I understand." She snuck a quick peek at Darius. "It isn't easy to maintain a relationship with someone who's on the road all the time. Anyway," she said after a pause, "nice to meet you, Annie."

Monica Feathers stepped away, and I said, "Tell Dax—"

She turned around.

A dullness settled in my chest. "Tell him to break a leg."

She shot me a warm smile.

"So…?" Darius watched me, his eyes questioning.

"I can't say yes to you." I reached for his hand and closed his fingers around the ring box. "You've given me a lot of advice and sage words over the past several weeks, so let me return the favor. I don't know if you and Monica can make it work," I said, "but what's the harm in trying?" I leaned in and kissed him on the cheek.

"Thanks, Annie," he said.

I nodded and faced the front of the queue. The line was moving again.

So, Rob it was.

Kind of by default, but not entirely. Rob had been my pick from the start, from right after I'd sent the dreaded text. I had been looking for companionship and stability, and Rob, even more than Darius, could give me that. We had a friendly rapport, and our families loved each other. Rob and

I would be very content together.

After making my way through the wake, which took a whopping two hours, I drove out to Edison Park to give Rob the news: I would accept his proposal.

But when I pulled up in front of his house, I found my mom leaving hers, a big bag over her shoulder.

I got out of the car and waved. "Hey, Mom. Where are you going?"

She glanced up in surprise. "Annie! What are you doing here?"

"I asked you first."

She patted the bag. "Work."

"You have a job now?" Good lord, everything was changing.

"No." She laughed. "WERQ with a Q. It's a hip-hop dance workout class."

My jaw dropped. I was speechless. My mother walked. Not "hiked," despite my encouragement that she get a little more vigorous exercise—*walked*. Strolled. She'd once taken a yoga class and quit halfway through because people kept passing gas. She did not go to "workout classes."

"The class is really fun." She stepped closer to me now, and I could see that she was wearing fitness tights under a long teal tunic that went almost to her knees. A pink headband held her hair back from her forehead.

"How many times have you gone?" I asked.

"This is my second week." Her eyes gleamed. "You should come. I think you'd like it."

"What?" I wrinkled up my nose. I ran and cycled and lifted weights. I didn't do dance classes. I rarely even danced at weddings. She knew this.

"Seriously," she said. "Come on. Don't you keep gym stuff in your car?"

She was right. I did. Damn it.

I snuck a quick glance at Rob's house. He could wait. I had to see my seventy-year-old mother dance hip-hop. This was the kind of opportunity someone like the legendary Gayle Gale would never pass up.

At the wake, Gayle's family had put up pictures of her doing everything from going snorkeling to making focaccia in Italy to driving a race car on a track. Gayle hadn't lived past sixty five, but she had *lived*.

She'd want to know all about this WERQ thing.

I grabbed a bag from my trunk and followed my mom to her car.

Hip-hop dance aerobics wasn't exactly for me, per se, but I did not regret going. The class was a hoot, and I could see quickly why my mom had gone back for a second session. Women of all shapes, sizes, and ages comprised the class. The two instructors, who represented different body types, talked about self-acceptance and the joy of movement.

A little touchy-feely and not exactly my style, but I appreciated the sentiment.

I looked at it anthropologically, as Gayle would have, like a reporter getting to the bottom of the story.

"It doesn't matter how you move," one instructor, Angela,

said during the second song. "It only matters that you are moving."

The crowd cheered.

The words *What Would Gayle Gale Do?* popped into my head.

I cheered along with the crowd, and I, Annie Kyle, who'd never been the first one out on the dance floor at any wedding ever, boogied next to my mother for an entire hour. And we boogied hard.

When we took a quick break in the middle of the class to grab water and wipe off our sweat, I told my mom, "My face hurts."

She slapped me with her towel. "You're smiling."

Shit. I was. When had I done that recently, moments of Dax-based elation excluded? "Well, you look so cute out there!"

She rolled her eyes, but I could tell she was pleased.

Afterward, still on our WERQ high, my mom and I stopped for frozen custard at Culver's.

"I think it's awesome you're going to that class," I told my mom as I hunted around in my Concrete Mixer for a hunk of peanut butter cup. "I just can't believe you ever went in the first place."

"It was because of you." She sipped her chocolate malted.

"Me?" I honestly couldn't fathom how the me of the past few months would've inspired anyone to do anything, except maybe hide their head in the sand and never, ever drink too much.

"What you told me on the ride to Kelly's shower really hit home."

Narrowing my eyes, I shook my head. I couldn't remember much about what had happened that day besides the fight with Kelly and Gayle ending up in the hospital.

"I was sad about possibly losing Regina, and you said something about not living my life for my friends and my needing to get out there and find something I like to do for myself—"

Damn it, Annie. "That sounds like kind of a dickish thing to say, so I'm sure I said it." I shoved more ice cream in my mouth.

"Language," my mom warned. "It wasn't rude the way you said it. Anyway, I started thinking about how I spend my time. I watch the news all day long, and I gossip with my friends at church and at knitting, and I started to question whether or not I was happy doing those things anymore."

My eyes bugged out—what she said struck a chord. "That happened to me the other day. I turned on the TV, and I was bored immediately. That was kind of why I came out here today."

She frowned at me.

I set my spoon down. As far as I knew, my mom still believed Rob and I were engaged. At least I could avoid having to break that bad news. "I came to talk to Rob," I said, "to speed up our timeline and get married sooner. I'm going to marry Rob."

She licked the whipped cream off the bottom of her straw and looked right at me. "No you're not. Don't do that."

CHAPTER FORTY-THREE

Making the Same Mistakes Our Parents Did...But Faster!

"What?" I said. "I thought you wanted me to marry Rob."

"So did I." She chuckled. "But I've been doing some thinking the past few days, since I started coping head-on with my own situation." She paused. "I was responsible for my own loneliness."

I pressed my lips together. Maybe she was, but I wasn't. Kelly had made the decision to move out. Dax chose to take Joanne and go.

"Instead of getting out there and WERQ-ing it—" She snapped her fingers in a sassy Z formation.

"Never do that again," I told her.

"—I'd made the choice to sit home waiting for my friends and my kids to call." She sipped her water. "I realized that I resented if people had their own lives and their own plans, when I could have been out there doing the same thing."

I shoved a scoop of custard into my mouth. Shit. Truth bombs from my mother.

"I started thinking, 'I'm seventy. What have I always wanted to do but claimed I didn't have the time for—because I felt like I had to be available for my friends and family whenever they needed me? Those things were just excuses not to put myself out there.'" She paused. "I know it's not quite the same for you. You have real restrictions on your time, with a demanding job."

I set my custard down. She had a point. I did often claim not to have time for things—relationships, friendships, you name it—and the excuse was always work. "I looked at my phone yesterday and was willing it to ring with a patient question, just because I was looking for something to do."

She nodded. "I get it. I tried to fill my life by meddling in yours and Regina's and your dad's before that, when I should've been focusing on myself."

I frowned. "But the thing is, my job actually does take up most of my time and energy. That's not simply a cop-out. I really don't know how I'd fit in something like WERQ... or the Annie equivalent. I've always said I don't even have time to take care of a plant."

"And you were going to have time for a ready-made marriage with Rob?"

The sugar soured in my mouth. "I know what you can do next," I said, impressed and annoyed with my mother's newfound depth and introspection. "Take psychology classes and write a self-help book."

"I mean it, Annie. How do you see Rob fitting into your life?"

I had no real answer for that. I kind of just assumed that he would somehow fold into my life, easy-peasy. But that wouldn't have been fair to him. "I don't."

She raised her eyebrows.

"I can't marry Rob," I said.

"No, you can't."

When I got back to my mom's house, I went right over to Rob's and texted him to come see me on the porch.

He came right out, an expectant smile on his face. "Hey, Annie." He assessed my wardrobe—red running tights with a pink-and-purple sports bra.

I ran a hand down my body. "I was just at a hip-hop dance class thing…" I shook my head. "Anyway, Rob, I came here to tell you I'm sorry." I handed him the ring.

He stared at the box for a moment before looking at me with panicked eyes. "Annie, no. Please."

I dug in. I was making the right choice, even if it meant me disappointing Rob and having to figure out my own life, on my own, sans a man. "Rob, maybe the two of us could be content together, but I don't think we'd be happy. We come from the same place, but we don't have much in common." I shook my head. "It's not going to work."

He clutched the ring in his fist. "Please. Don't do this. It doesn't have to be forever—just for now. My mom—"

"Your mom will be fine," I said. "She will be. Be honest with her. She can handle it." I softened my voice. "Do you really want her to die believing a lie?"

He shook his head. "I don't."

"Rob, I'm so sorry. About all of this. When I texted you all those weeks ago, I was in a very desperate place. I thought the only thing missing from my life was a committed, stable, drama-free relationship. But I was wrong." I tried to get him to meet my eyes, but he kept glancing away. "The truth is, I was avoiding trying to fix the real problem." I chuckled. "Me."

Now he looked at me.

"For my entire life, I threw myself into work. It became the only thing that mattered, and it cost me people I truly cared about." I paused. "I have to deal with that, in my own way, by myself. Jumping into a relationship for convenience would only be putting a bandage on a wound instead of actually trying to heal it, and it wouldn't be fair to you."

"Okay," he said with a deep sigh. "Okay."

"Okay," I replied.

"I hope we can be friends," he said. "Regardless of how this all ended…it's been nice reconnecting with you."

My chest tightened, not from fear or sadness or stress or any of the other feelings I'd been experiencing lately. My heart felt full. "I'd love that, Rob. Seriously."

"Good." His nose wrinkled. "Because after"—he nodded back toward his house, where his mother was resting—"you and your mom will be the only family I have left."

"You have your friends," I said.

"I do," he agreed. "But they see me one way. You and your mom know me as Regina's son." His voice cracked on that last word.

I pulled him in for a tight hug. "You'll always have us."

"How did you come to this whole enlightened conclusion?" he asked after I let him go.

"Well," I said, recalling the image of my mother twerking, "my mom inspired me, if you can believe it, and a patient who recently died."

Concern flooded his expression. "Oh, Annie. I'm sorry."

My body filled with gratitude for the people I had in my life now—my mom, Rob, Yessi—and those who I might, or would, never connect with again—Kelly, Gayle, Dax. "Thanks, Rob, but I've been thinking about her a lot over the past few days, how she was always subtly—and not so subtly—trying to steer me in the right direction, to start carving out some time for myself." I shrugged. "I'm going to honor her by taking her advice. WWGGD. *What Would Gayle Gale Do?* That's my new motto."

"I like that." He smiled. "So what's first on your agenda?"

I looked him in the eye. "Attack the problem at the root."

CHAPTER FORTY-FOUR

What Willis Was Talking About

For the second time in the month of July, a limo picked me up outside my house, this time on a Saturday.

I grabbed a tiny pink gift bag from the table in the front hallway, left the house, and locked the door on the way out, my stomach gurgling with nerves. Tonight, I'd dressed in yet another of my "going out" black shifts and the same gunmetal Michael Kors pumps I'd worn on my first date with Darius. The limo driver opened the door for me. I reached into my purse and handed him something as I slid in.

Inside the car, I plastered on a smile.

"Hi!" I said nervously, glancing at the other passengers.

Yessi, who was sitting next to Kelly behind the driver's partition, toasted me with her champagne flute. I shot her a quick thumbs-up.

Kelly barely looked at me. I could tell she had no confidence that tonight wouldn't end in a fight.

Well, she had not yet met the new and improved Dr. Annie Kyle.

"This is going to be so fun!" I said, making a quick little

wish for that to come true. I took it as a good sign that Kelly had come at all, even if Mark had encouraged her. It meant she hadn't completely written me off yet. "Just the three of us, out on the town like old times." Yessi poured me some champagne, and I raised my glass to Kelly. "To our lovely and talented bride! I got you something special."

Grinning like the Cheshire cat, I passed her the small bag.

Kelly took a deep breath, probably expecting disappointment, which was all I'd given her for the past several months, then reached into the tissue paper. She pulled out a small, rectangular object. "Is this…your phone?" She turned it over in her hand.

"Yes," I said. "That is my phone. I want you to hold on to it all night. Do not give it to me, no matter how much I beg. You will also notice that it is turned off."

She glanced at the black screen. "It is."

I held up my wrists, shaking them, silver and gold hoops clanking against one another. "And I am wearing fancy, jangling bracelets on my wrists instead of my Apple Watch. I have no connection to the outside world. I am all yours for the next however many hours."

She stared at the phone in disbelief.

"She means it, Kel," Yessi said.

"I do. I've been talking to my friend Kim from med school, who's awesome and has been looking for a change in her career." I paused. "I invited her to join my practice. Tonight is her first night on call."

"Wait…what?"

"I'm bringing in a new doctor," I said. "Someone to share the load so maybe I can take a night off here and there." I shrugged. "Heck, maybe even a whole weekend."

"Really?" Kelly said. "You're bringing in someone new to help?"

"Well, I had to figure out a way to plan lots and lots of Galena trips in the future."

"Oh my god!" Kelly lunged across the car, wrapping me in a big hug. "Thank you," she whispered in my ear. "This is the greatest present ever."

I patted her on the back, choking up, and not just because some of her curly blond hair had landed in my mouth. "I'm so sorry for all the times I wasn't there for you."

Her shoulders relaxed, and she pulled away, looking me right in the eye. "And I'm sorry I've been a monster lately."

"You're stressed about the wedding and your parents and relocating," I said. "We all get it."

She retreated to her seat, eyes glistening with tears. "No," she said. "No excuse." She sighed. "I've been acting like all the women we used to make fun of. I've been a total cliché."

"Well," Yessi said, pouring herself another glass of champagne. "Clichés are clichés for a reason—there's some truth to them." She offered to refill my glass. "What do you say, Annie? Go for more than one drink?"

"Why not?" I held out my glass to her. "I'm actually, for real, one hundred percent free tonight!" Though our friendship wasn't total out of the woods yet, and we still had a lot to discuss, I wouldn't dwell on it now. Baby steps. I passed Kelly a notecard. "Here's what we're doing tonight."

The bachelorette party itinerary that Yessi and I had planned would take us to some of Kelly's best-loved Chicago haunts. I got a little choked up thinking about crossing the threshold into Kinzie Chophouse, one of her favorite restaurants. That place had been the first "real" steakhouse, the first fancy restaurant, the three of us went to after I was out of med school, Yessi had passed the bar, and Kelly was getting started in her real estate career. I'd never felt so grown up in my life as I did ordering a drink here back in my twenties.

Yessi cried into her champagne flute. "I don't know. Tonight feels like a goodbye tour of our friendship."

"No!" I said, touching my glass to hers in celebration. "This is the beginning of our next phase of friendship—our golden years."

"I love that," Kelly said, handing me the index card.

"We're turning forty," Yessi said. "Not eighty."

"Some of the characters on *The Golden Girls* were only supposed to be in their fifties when the show began, so we're not far off. I hate to break it to you," I said. "But what I meant by 'golden' is that we're about to enter the best phase of our lives. I can feel it."

"I don't know," Yessi said. "I just took on a piano student for the first time in years, and she's a real dick." She raised her eyebrows at me.

At first the idea of learning Dax's instrument saddened me, but it was either reframe the piano (i.e., finally learn how to play it) or steer clear of the living room altogether for the rest of my life, simply to avoid conjuring up memories of Dax. I shrugged. "I am what I am."

"What? You?" Kelly squealed.

"I always said I'd learn my dad's instrument."

"What does Yessi get out of this?" Kelly asked.

"Free babysitting," Yessi said. "And I get to tell Annie what to do for, like, an hour a week."

"So, it's really all upside for Yess," I said.

Kelly's eyes turned dreamy.

"What's up, Kel?" I asked.

"Nothing," she said. "Just wondering what I can offer you to get in on this sweet free babysitting deal..."

"Are you...?" I glanced at her half-drunk champagne glass.

"Not yet." She shook her head. "Mark and I have been trying, but no-go so far. That might also be part of the reason I've been a bit quick-tempered lately."

"Wow," I said. "This is amazing news! And you haven't been trying that long," I added, wanting to reassure her.

"Yeah...but I think I'm just anticipating having a hard time getting pregnant. I'm not exactly young."

I reached over and squeezed her hand. "We'll deal with it when we have to deal with it. I know all the best specialists in town—"

"Annie hooked Polly and me up with our doctor when we were doing artificial insemination," Yessi said.

"See? We've got this handled." I scooted over and wrapped my arms around Kelly. "Never feel like you have to go through this alone. You call—anytime—and I will be there for you. I promise."

She kissed my forearm, and I gave her some space. "Wait a minute. Doesn't Dax play piano? Why couldn't he teach you?"

I waved a hand, dismissing the conversation. "That's all over. I am...once again...the sexless and single Dr. Kyle."

"I think it's bullshit," Yessi said.

"It's not. I really mean it. No more guys. I'm focused on me."

Kelly's eyes ping-ponged between the two of us.

"Oh, I *know* you mean it," Yessi said. "What I meant is that I think your whole 'I'm giving up guys forever' thing is bullshit."

"Will someone please tell me what's going on?" Kelly asked.

"I will." Yessi took a pull on her wine. "Annie, a few weeks ago, sent out a text to the guys in her phone that she wanted to get married—"

"What?"

Yessi held up a hand. "Let me finish. She decided to choose between the two guys, Rob and Darius Carver."

"The Man on Main Street?" Kelly squealed.

I ducked my head in embarrassment.

"The very one. Annie eventually turned them both down to 'focus on herself,' but I don't see why she can't focus on both herself *and* Dax. She was her best self with him."

I drank some water. Yessi had been on me about Dax since we broke it off. She thought he was great and that we were great together. "We want different things," I said. "He's a young musician, and he's right in the middle of potentially his big break. I'm not going to begrudge him that."

"He loves her," Yessi told Kelly. "I can tell."

"You're not some all-knowing being," I said with a teasing grin. "Just because you think you know something doesn't mean you actually do."

I do, she mouthed to Kelly. "And Polly agrees."

Kelly frowned. "Polly's seen the two of them together?"

"At the vet's office."

Kelly looked at me. "Do you love him?"

I hadn't thought of it in those terms. The words scared me even more than simply being alone did, because being on my own was one thing, but being alone and without the person I loved was another. I'd never survive that.

"It's complicated. He's a lot younger than I am, and he's going to be on the road for at least a year. It wouldn't work out."

"No relationship is guaranteed to work out," Yessi said.

"That's not what I asked." Kelly's eyes widened. "Do. You. Love him?"

I leaned over and rapped on the partition, getting the limo driver's attention, desperate to focus on something other than me. "Hi," I said when he'd rolled down the window. "Can you play the mix I made?" He rolled the window back up. "You're going to love this," I said. "Basically our freshman year of college in song form."

"You're avoiding the question," Kelly said.

A piano chord cut through our conversation.

"I don't know this song," Yessi said.

"Me neither," Kelly agreed. "Is it...Backstreet Boys?"

But then Dax's voice came in as clear as day. *"When you walked into the bar/I wasn't thinking so far/ahead..."*

"Oh no." I'd given him the wrong flash drive. This was the one Dax had given me, which I'd forgotten about at the bottom of my purse. I knocked on the window again. "Turn it off," I said. His voice was like a vise on my heart.

"You shocked me/you surprised me/you truly recognized me!"

"What is this?" Kelly asked.

He'd already launched into the chorus, wailing *"Dorothy!"* like a primal call, cutting deep into my soul, before the limo driver finally turned off the music.

Kelly and Yessi stared at me, mouths agape.

Tears pooled in my eyes, and I lifted my glass to my mouth with shaking hands. "To answer your question, Kelly, yes." I swallowed. "I love him."

"You love him!" Kelly smacked her palm on her thigh. "Then we need to find him and tell him that."

"No, Kelly," I said. "It doesn't matter. Dax and I have already been through—"

She leaned forward. "Remember when I first came back from Galena and I was a total mess?"

"Yes," I said. That was the first night I met Dax, when he'd called me *ma'am*. I couldn't decide whether to laugh or cry at the memory of that evening.

"That was because I'd just told Mark that we couldn't be together—that it'd be too hard with him in Galena and me in Chicago." She looked me right in the eye. "You know what I realized when you and I went out that night?"

I shook my head.

"Who fucking cares if it's hard? Even harder than that would be life without Mark."

I pressed my lips together.

"So I went home and called him, and he asked me to marry him. I was willing to uproot my life to be with him. You're already halfway there, bringing a new doctor into your practice. You're suddenly going to have all kinds of time to follow him on the road wherever he goes. So let's go find this guy and tell him you're willing to do the work." She paused. "Where is he?"

I shook my head. "I don't know. He left without telling me where he was going, and we haven't talked since."

"Maybe he's still putting in hours at the bar," Yessi said.

Since my tolerance was extremely low, maybe the wine was getting to me. I was starting to believe that this wasn't the worst idea. Dax and I had definitely cared about each other once; maybe we could again. At the very least, I could find him and tell him that I was sorry and that I was wrong, and I'd be willing to give things a shot with him.

I stood and raised my fist in the air. "To O'Leary's Barn!"

CHAPTER FORTY-FIVE

Angry Nerds

"I don't know where he is," Peter the bartender said. "I'm sorry. He's off tonight."

I waved a twenty in front of him. "Can you tell me where his sister's apartment is?"

His eyes followed the bill. "No, I can't."

Yessi flashed another twenty. "Maybe you can run to the manager's office and look in his employment file."

"Yessi!" I said.

"What?" she said. "We just want the address." She looked right at Peter. "You know us, Paul—"

"Peter," I said.

"Peter," Yessi corrected herself.

Kelly slid him yet another twenty. "Peter, you don't know me, but it's my bachelorette party tonight, and Annie is my maid of honor."

"Congratulations."

"Thanks. Annie just wants to tell Dax how much he means to her."

Peter looked at me, frowning. "Really?"

I nodded.

He straightened his shoulders. "Then I'll do it."

"Really?" I said. "Thanks, Peter."

"I'm only doing it because I know how sad Dax has been since you broke up. I hope you two can work things out."

I shot him a grateful smile. Damn, for someone who thought she was doomed to loneliness, I sure had a lot of people who cared for me when I stopped to look. I wouldn't discount them again.

Kelly started to slide her twenty back toward her, and Peter pressed his hand on the bill to stop her.

"But I still want the money."

Dax's sister, Lily, lived only a few blocks from the bar. We took the limo over there and all went up to the door to knock. I could hear a dog barking inside.

A few moments later, Lily answered the door. Surprised, she looked from me to Yessi to Kelly, a questioning expression on her face. Finally, she stopped on me. "Annie?"

"Yes." I smiled. "Hi. We're looking for Dax."

"Oh...he's not here."

I glanced inside, scanning her apartment. Something occurred to me. "Where's Joanne? Why isn't she coming to the door?"

"She has to stay in my room," Lily said, "because of Travis's allergies. She's only allowed out on her way to and from the outside door for her walks."

"Like prison," Yessi muttered.

"Well," Lily said, glowering at Yessi, "this is the situation we're in. What else are we supposed to do with her?"

"Lily," I said, "do you know where Dax is?"

She folded her arms across her chest. "Why do you want to know?"

"I...I just want to talk to him."

She stared me down. "I don't think that's a good idea."

"Well, you don't get to decide that," Yessi said, stepping forward. "Dax is an adult, and he chooses whom he speaks to."

"Maybe," she said, "but I know where he is, and you don't." She glared at me. "You broke his heart," she said. "He's in the middle of the most important time in his music career, and all he can think about is how sad he is now that you're gone." She glared at Yessi. "So, no, I won't be telling you where you can find him."

Behind Lily I heard someone sneeze—probably Travis, the roommate. Lily was right to be upset with me. Because things hadn't worked out between Dax and me, she was now in a very uncomfortable living situation...one I could actually make a little bit better.

"If I promise to take Joanne off your hands, will you tell us where Dax is?"

Lily glanced behind her. Again Travis sneezed.

"Dax doesn't want to be away from her," she said. "He's worried about her."

"I know," I said, "but he trusts me with her. I know all about her walking regimen and her pill schedule."

"I thought you didn't have time for a dog."

"Right, I didn't," I said, "but my circumstances have changed. I've brought in someone to help at work, plus"—I gestured to Yessi—"my best friend's wife is a vet—the one who looked at Joanne recently—so she'll be in good hands."

I straightened up. This was the right thing to do, and, more than that, it was what I *wanted* to do. I felt great about the progress we'd made with our walks, and I'd keep her moving for as long as she could handle it. I liked to take care of people (and animals) who were sick and needed help maintaining their medical regimen. If I were able and had an army of Annie clones at my disposal, I'd move into all my patients' houses and make sure they were taking their meds. In my own home, I could micromanage Joanne's care.

Lily looked me up and down. "Okay," she said, "but just because Travis is about to throw us all out and Dax is leaving on tour soon and still hasn't figured out what to do with her. I'll go get Joanne." Lily padded down the hallway.

"Is she really giving away her brother's dog without asking him?" Kelly said.

"I...think so...?" said Yessi.

"We'll tell him all about it when we see him tonight." I grinned. "Besides, if all goes well, he'll be moving back in, too, at least until he leaves on tour."

Yeah, that was still an issue, and I hadn't figured out in my mind how we'd cross that hurdle. But I wasn't going to do the Annie thing and overthink it. No, tonight was about honesty and telling Dax how I felt. What he chose to do with that information was up to him.

Lily came back with Joanne and handed me the leash. She gave Kelly a box full of food and supplies. "Thank you," she said, "for taking the dog."

"My pleasure," I said. "I'll take good care of Joanne."

She handed me a slip of paper with an address on it. "Here's the club where Dax is playing tonight."

"Great!" I said, reading it over. "Wonderful!" I waved the paper in the air. "Thanks, Lily! Come on, Joanne!"

I carefully led Joanne down the steps and out to the limo. Hopefully the driver wouldn't mind the dog in the car. Eh, we'd give him a big tip at the end of the night and offer to get the car cleaned—

"By the way," Lily shouted from the steps.

I turned around.

She pointed to my hand. "That's a private club, so good luck getting in!" She gave us a big wave.

I followed Yessi and Kelly into the car. Yessi was already convincing the driver that he should let Joanne take a ride. I handed the paper with the address to Kelly. "Well, this is a bust."

She looked at it. "What? Why?"

"Because it's a private club. You probably have to know a password or at least know somebody who knows somebody."

Yessi turned around and slunked back into her seat. "Wait," she said. "You do know somebody who knows somebody." She raised her eyebrows.

"Who?"

"You know somebody who knows *everybody*." She checked out Kelly's and my blank faces. "Come on, you two. The Man on Main Street...?"

"No." Yessi had to be kidding with this.

Kelly squeezed my arm. "Yes! Of course."

"You said Darius could get in anywhere," Yessi said. "Let's see if that's true. Come on, Annie. He's our only hope."

She had me there. "I'll need my phone."

Kelly reached into her purse and handed it to me.

I watched it in my hand as it turned on, worried how Darius would respond to a request like this, if he'd even entertain the idea of getting me in. I'd recently turned down his proposal, he didn't believe Dax and I were a good idea, and then there was the whole unsavory part where I was calling him out of the blue to ask for a favor, which I hated doing even under the best circumstances. "I don't know," I said. "Maybe we should cut our losses. I should probably get Joanne home, anyway."

"Nope." Kelly grabbed my phone. "Uh-uh. This is my bachelorette party, and what I say goes. You're calling Darius, and we're getting into that club." She pressed a few buttons on my phone and handed it to me.

I took it from her like it was a bomb about to explode. The phone rang in my ear. Once…twice…

"Annie?" His rich baritone hit my eardrum.

"Darius?" I squeaked.

"Good lord," Yessi muttered. "This will go well."

My eyes shot her daggers.

"Is anything wrong?" he asked.

"No." I checked my vocal pitch level. "No," I repeated at a lower frequency. I sighed. "I hate to ask this, but I'm with my girlfriends for a bachelorette party, and the bride really wants to get into this club…"

Kelly shot me a thumbs-up and nodded. "Well played."

"Congrats to your friend!" he said cheerfully. "Which club?"

"Um…I only have the address… Wait a second."

Yessi typed it into her phone and showed it to me.

"The club is called…" I squinted at the phone. "…Isolate?"

Darius was silent on the other end.

"Have you heard of that place?" I laughed. "Of course you have. You know all the hot spots in t—"

"Is this really your friend asking?"

I glanced up at Kelly. "Yes?"

"Because that's Monica Feathers's club, and Farouche is playing there tonight."

Shit.

"Annie, I thought you were moving on from him," Darius said. "I thought we agreed that he'd never be able to give you the commitment you wanted."

"Yeah," I said. "We did, and I was." I straightened my shoulders. "But since we talked, I decided that I'm okay without the commitment. I'm focusing on myself and what makes me happy. Dax makes me happy."

Kelly clapped her hands with glee.

"And maybe I'll show up there tonight and find out he doesn't agree, or maybe we get back together and it doesn't last. At least I'll know I put myself out there and gave it a shot." I paused. "Darius, a friend of ours just died. I think we both can see now how life is too short not to even try to be with the person you love. What Would Gayle Gale Do?"

I could hear him breathing on the other end.

"Darius?" My own breath caught in my lungs as I waited for his response.

"I'll meet you there in twenty minutes."

CHAPTER FORTY-SIX

That's So Ravenclaw

Twenty minutes later, we parked outside the club. Yessi, taking one for the team, said she'd stay back in the limo with Joanne.

Darius walked toward us, carrying flowers.

Oh my goodness, he hadn't gotten the hint. He thought What Would Gayle Gale Do meant "propose to Annie again."

"Hey, Darius," I said warily. "Nice flowers."

He shook them a little but did not attempt to hand them to me.

"This is my friend Kelly," I said. "She's the bride."

He flashed her his TV-news-guy smile. "Nice to meet you, and congratulations!"

"Thanks!" She beamed.

"Should we go in?" I said.

"One moment." He gestured for me to join him a few steps away.

I sent SOS eyes to Kelly. This was about to go sideways. Darius was going to try, again, to convince me why Dax and I shouldn't be together, and that he and I should. She just waved.

"This may be premature," he said, "but I want to thank you."

"Thank me?" By offering me this ring...

He smiled. "You convinced me I was wrong about something—a rare feat." He chuckled, but then his eyes turned serious. "For the past several days, ever since Gayle passed"—his voice turned heavy with emotion—"I haven't been myself. I've been moping around, eating cookies, and watching silly TV shows." He shook his head. "Pathetic."

"Not pathetic," I said. "A normal part of the grieving process." *And most of my evenings for the past twenty years.*

"I miss my friend, my mentor, of course," he said, "but I started to realize that the hole inside me was there even before she died." He frowned and glanced down at the flowers. "I thought denying my emotions was the safe way to deal with them. I came to the logical conclusion that even having emotions was weak and pathetic and should be avoided at all costs. But then I saw Monica at the funeral, and I realized the feelings weren't gone. They were just hiding."

I grinned. "I knew it when I saw you two together. The energy bouncing between you." I patted his arm. "She loves you, too, Darius."

He smiled. "We'll see. Even if she does, we'll have a lot of work to do. We're both very ambitious."

"I can see that," I said.

"But it will be worth it."

"Yes, it will be."

He gave me a hug, and I knew he'd be okay.

Darius led Kelly and me into the club and over to the roped-off VIP section. Farouche was onstage and in the middle of their set. Dax, already sweaty, focused hard on his fellow musicians.

He looked serious, obviously, and focused, but there was more to it than that. He had a gleam in his eye. He looked like how I felt at a trivia tournament or my mom when she was doing WERQ. He was in the zone, happy, and complete.

He had a real shot to truly make it—to achieve all his goals.

Kelly nudged me in the side. "Look at Dax go."

"He's talented, right?"

"Amazing."

A lump in my throat, I watched him up there living his dream, performing his heart out. He had worked his entire life for this. His marriage had failed because of it, and suddenly I just knew.

I couldn't put that same amount of pressure on him now. I'd already achieved so much in my own career. I'd been allowed to do that.

I had to let Dax do the same.

"What are you going to say to him when you see him?"

I shrugged, blinking back tears. "I…don't know."

After Farouche finished playing, Darius, with Monica Feathers on his arm, led us backstage. Dax, once again, had unzipped his costume down to the waist and was talking to Kat's girlfriend. I fought my body's urge to bolt.

Finally, as if he sensed me there, he turned toward the door. I gave him a little wave, and he stepped over, zipping up his jumpsuit on the way. "You're here," he said. "What are you doing here?"

I gestured to Kelly. "Remember Kelly? It's her

bachelorette party."

Dax gave her a nod.

"Can we talk a sec?" I asked.

His brow furrowed. "Yeah."

He led me out of the dressing room and down a long hall toward an exit. We stopped right inside the door, the moonlight from outside the door illuminating his eyes. They were so beautiful, and I couldn't do this.

I had to do this.

"I came to tell you something."

He folded his arms, watching me, his bisected eyebrow arched.

"I came to tell you I love you—"

A smile played on his lips.

"But I'm not going to do that."

A grin full-on took over his face. "I think you just did."

"No, I didn't."

"Agree to disagree."

I sighed. "Let me finish, please, Yale, okay?"

He leaned against the wall.

"I came to tell you I love you, but then I decided not to do it, because it wouldn't be fair to you." I paused to let him interject. When he didn't, I kept going. "You're so, so talented, Dax, and I don't want to get in the way of that, even a little bit."

"You won't."

"I will." I shook my head. "You have a great opportunity in front of you, and your entire career has been building to this. Most people don't even get this chance."

He frowned. "No, they don't."

I stepped toward him and reached up to play with the zipper on his jumpsuit. "So, that's why I came to tell you this. Not that I love you, even though I do—"

He tilted my chin up and gazed into my eyes. "I love you, too."

Hiding my watery gaze from him, I focused on the zipper. I had to keep going. I, Dr. Annie Kyle, the queen of pragmatism, had to do what I'd been training my whole life to do—put my feelings aside. Only this time, it was for the good of someone else, not to keep myself from being hurt. "I came to tell you that *because* I love you, I want all the best for you. I want you to go create all the music with Monica Feathers and make a gazillion dollars."

He opened his mouth to say something, but I cut him off.

"I want you to focus on what you have to do, and I don't want you on the road worrying about making sure to call me at the right time every day or whether or not I'm okay at home. I will be okay. I *am* okay." I let go of his zipper and stood up straight.

"You're okay?"

I forced a smile. "I am. I'm bringing in help at work. I have some other irons in the fire. I have your dog—"

"Excuse me?"

"Oh yeah, I stopped by your sister's place and told her I'd take care of Joanne."

"Annie." His eyes watered.

"I'll bring her on lots of walks and make sure she takes her medicine. When you're on tour, I'll send you pictures, and you're welcome to visit her any time you—" A sob escaped my lips.

Dax pulled me into a hug and held me, stroking the back of my head.

After a few moments, I pulled away. I didn't trust myself to hold on any longer. This was for Dax, yes, but it wasn't *only* for Dax. I was doing this for me, too.

"Goodbye, Dax." I ducked my eyes and headed out the exit.

CHAPTER FORTY-SEVEN

A Test of Us for the Rest of Us

Yessi eyed me accusingly. "You didn't practice."

"Yes, I did." I pressed down on what I now knew as "middle C."

"How much?"

I drew in a deep breath. "Fifteen minutes a day?"

"*Bull*shit," Yessi said, waving her hands in front of her. "But I'm not going to harp on you too much today; I know you're sad."

"I'm okay," I lied.

"You told a guy you loved him last night, and it didn't work out."

"I told a guy I loved him and told him it couldn't work out. There's a difference." Though try telling my heart that.

"Still." She closed my beginner's piano book. "Seriously, how are you doing?"

I patted her knee and stood from the bench. "I'm not exactly fine. But I think I will be." I stretched.

Joanne, who had been sleeping in the other room, started barking.

"What is it? A squirrel?" It was usually a squirrel.

But no, this wasn't her squirrel bark, and it wasn't her STRANGER DANGER APPROACHING bark. It was more like her "I see one of my favorite people on the horizon" yelp.

"Um…Annie?" Yessi pointed to the bay window in the living room.

Dax was coming up the steps. My pulsed quickened.

"He's probably coming to see Joanne." I shrugged, brushing it off like it was nothing. "I told him that was fine."

"Sure." Yessi's eyes narrowed.

I went to the door and opened it. Joanne immediately, as best she could, flung herself at Dax.

"Hey, girl." His voice wobbled. He crouched down next to her and hugged her neck.

"I'll…get out of your hair," Yessi said. "Good to see you, Dax."

He glanced up. "You, too, Yessi."

When Yessi left, Dax stood, hands in pockets, and faced me.

"You came to see Joanne?" I asked.

He shook his head.

"Dax…" I tilted my head.

He looked right at me, jaw tight. "I decided I'm not okay."

"You're not."

"No. You said you're okay with the two of us not being together, but I'm not."

A weight of longing settled in my chest, and I motioned for him to follow me into the living room. I wasn't sure what this visit was about, but I feared it would only make his leaving harder on us. He took one end of the couch, and I made sure to take the other. I couldn't be held responsible for my actions if we got too close.

"You think we're going to end up resenting each other if I go on tour and you stay here, but I disagree." His brow furrowed. "We both love each other."

"That's not enough." My eyes stung.

"I think it is."

I turned to face him, pulling my legs up under me on the couch. "We talked about this."

"No, you talked about it," he said. "You came to me last night making a bold statement about love and sacrifice, and now I'm doing the same to you. This is the grand gesture, right? Now we forgive, forget, and make up."

I grinned at him. "That's what happens in a rom-com, Dax. This is real life."

He frowned. "I want it to be a rom-com."

I reached for his hand, my chest tight. "Me too."

"So we're in agreement then."

"But everything I said last night is still true. You weren't wrong about me being unhappy. I need to be happy, and you need to be successful. And I'm not sure both can happen with us together."

He scooted toward me. "So what if we just see what happens and go from there? What if we stop thinking and worrying and jump right to the 'happily ever after?' Like, what would happen if we were Jennifer Garner and Ryan Reynolds at the end of a movie?" His fingers grazed my cheek. "All the problems have been solved. Everything is wonderful. You've just admitted you love me. I love you…"

"I suppose we'd kiss," I said, grinning despite my aching heart, "but there'd also be clapping, because we'd be, like, in a ballroom on the last day of a big corporate retreat."

"Would you settle for the sounds of Joanne over in the corner cleaning herself?" he asked.

I laughed. "I guess that would do."

He scooted even closer, cupped my face in his hands, and kissed me slowly and tenderly, trailing the end of the kiss over to my ear, and my heart went wild. "We've done the kiss. Then what?"

I pulled away slightly, looking him right in the eye. "You know, most rom-coms don't usually show the next part. Sandra Bullock and Hugh Grant kiss...but then what? I think we all know what happens." I waggled my eyebrows. "Bow chicka wow wow."

He laughed. "They never let us see what kind of sex those folks are having. Is it just regular vanilla, or are they throwing in all kinds of toppings?"

I nodded knowingly. "You can bet Sandra and Hugh are going for the full rocky road—nuts, marshmallows, chocolate with a cherry on top—sex."

He took my hand. "Do you want to show me what that looks like?"

"Yes," I said, leaning toward him, "but no. Because this isn't a rom-com, and you're leaving—"

"Tomorrow."

That knocked the wind out of me. I knew he was leaving soon, but I hadn't considered the timeline. Not that I assumed we'd still be competing together, but he was leaving before the end of the trivia tournament. Tomorrow he'd be gone and

Dorothy would be without her Tin Man. "Leaving tomorrow for a big, long tour."

He scooted closer and kissed my neck. I melted into him. "Okay, so I'm leaving on tour. And you're focusing on you. So just say you'll come visit me," he said. "We'll start there, and no promises other than that. You can send me pics of Joanne, and I'll update you on the tour. Once in a while. No timelines. No other expectations. Just you coming to one stop on the tour."

"I don't know, Dax." I closed my eyes as waves of pleasure pulsed through me. "What if I show up and you regret ever inviting me?"

"I won't." He nibbled my earlobe. "But okay, let's say something happens and I'm busy or things don't go as swimmingly between us as we'd like. You'd still get a few days away in an exciting city like Minsk."

I chuckled. "Mmm...hot."

"Or...maybe not Minsk." His lips made their way down my collarbone. "I think we'll be in Prague at Christmas."

"Maybe." He worked his way back up to my ear, and I moaned. "I'm bringing in a partner to the practice—"

He held me at arm's length. "What? Really?"

"Really." I widened my eyes to show him just how serious I was about this. "I'm relaxing my responsibilities at work so I can focus on other things—like taking care of Joanne and learning the piano."

His hand cupped my cheek.

"And I'm sure Yessi and Polly would watch Joanne, so maybe I really *could* take a trip." A trip was what Gayle would do. It'd be something to look forward to, and, like Dax said, it could mean nothing more than the two of us being in the same place at the same time for a few days. No pressure.

I shifted our positions so I now straddled him on the couch. My mind whirled with a million thoughts of what could go wrong—everything from the plane crashing to him meeting someone new in the meantime and me showing up in Prague to find him engaged to his pregnant fiancée. I pushed all of that out of my head and said, "Okay, Prague. Let's do it. I will plan on being there for Christmas."

He pulled me in close, and I leaned down so he could whisper in my ear. "We'll always have Prague." He paused. "Now, rocky road sex? Once? For old time's sake?"

I stood, offering him my hand. He took it, and I pulled him off the couch.

"I prefer cookies and cream," I told him as I led him toward the stairs.

"I have no idea where this metaphor's going," he said, "but I love it, and I can't wait to find out more."

CHAPTER FORTY-EIGHT

Oops...I Quizzed It Again

One year later...

"Welcome, ladies and gentlemen, to the final round of the Second Annual Windy City Trivia Championship tournament!" Ronald held the microphone out toward the crowd, catching the roar of excitement and blasting it through the speakers. "This year, we have four great teams competing for the grand prize, but first let me introduce our illustrious guest emcee—Darius Carver, former Man on Main Street and current evening news anchor!"

Yes, Mr. Man on Main Street got Gayle Gale's old job. Though he still had dreams of being the entertainment guru of Chicago, for the moment, he liked the stability and predictability of being an anchor.

Darius, waving like a monarch and flashing his megawatt grin, stepped onto the stage. I couldn't help smiling. He was in his element. "Good evening!" Darius said. "For the past year or so, I've been confined to the newsroom, but it's delightful to be back on the street again with all you wonderful people." He cupped a hand around his ear. "Now, do you want to meet the teams?"

The crowd erupted in applause. Yessi, at my table, stomped her feet on the floor and whistled with her fingers.

Kelly clamped a hand over her ear. "Yessi. That's enough."

Mark wrapped a protective arm around his wife's shoulders.

Yessi rolled her eyes at Polly, who laughed.

I leaned back in my seat, happy and content and ready to kick some trivia butt.

"We have..." Darius read a name off a cue card. "Last year's second-place team, the Very Stable Geniuses!"

Brad and his buddies paraded around their table, clutching their hands above their heads in premature victory.

"Boo!" I shouted, playfully flashing a thumbs-down signal. My teammates joined me.

Darius shot me a grin, and I waved. "And, of course, we have last year's reigning champions, the first winners of the Windy City Trivia Championship, previously known as Dorothy and the Tin Man, but you know them better this year as Marky Mark and the Trivia Bunch!"

My teammates and I shot up and raised our hands in victory, imitating Brad and the Very Stable Geniuses. I offered my palm for high fives from Rob and Lily, which they returned. With a potential romance no longer on the table, Rob and I really did become good friends after the whole engagement fiasco. He even got me to start watching the Cubs...sometimes. Lily and I bonded initially over Joanne but soon discovered we had a lot in common, like love of TV and movies and, well, her brother.

Once, not long after Dax left on tour, Lily mentioned she

and Travis had a leaky pipe in their bathroom, and I put her in touch with Rob. Now the two of them were engaged to be married. I was more than willing to take full credit for that romance.

"Before we get started..." Darius's eyes twinkled. "I have a little surprise for the founding member of Marky Mark and the Trivia Bunch, Dr. Annie Kyle." He leaned in closer to the mic. "What you may not realize is, it's Annie's birthday today."

"How old is she?" Brad shouted teasingly.

I flipped him the bird. "I'm forty-one!" I fist-bumped Yessi and Kelly.

Darius waited for the crowd to die down a little. "For Annie's birthday surprise, we have a special person here to serenade her—"

My heart skipped a beat. "What the hell?"

"Fresh off the plane from a grueling tour around the world—"

My palms started sweating. I locked eyes with Kelly, who had gritted her teeth in excitement.

"I'd like to present to you..." Darius held out an arm toward the front door of O'Leary's Barn. "My personal favorite musician, my wife and the mother of my future child, Ms. Monica Feathers."

The door pushed open, and in swanned Monica Feathers, a basketball-shaped lump under a tight pink dress. On five-inch heels, she hobbled up onstage, grabbed the mic, and performed a rendition of "Happy Birthday" that would've made Marilyn Monroe blush.

"Oh my god!" As she left the stage, I widened my eyes at

my friends, trying to tamp down any lingering disappointment. "Monica Feathers just sang to me."

"She did!" Kelly squeezed my hand, and the underlying sympathy did not go unnoticed.

"If Monica's back," Yessi said, looking pointedly at Lily. "Does that mean…?"

"Oh!" Lily looked surprised for a moment, then glanced over at me. "Are you wondering about Dax?"

I shrugged, shaking my head and taking a peek at the inactive front door to the bar. "No," I said. "The last time we talked, it sounded like he wasn't sure where he would end up after the tour. I wasn't expecting him."

True to our word, Dax and I hadn't put any pressure on the other person to stay in touch. There were no set conversations and no expectations. He seemed to be doing great on the road, and I was enjoying my new, less pressurized life with my friends, my mom, and Joanne. Dax and I would text once in a while when something funny occurred to us, and we'd share pictures—him of life on the road, and me of Joanne, a short video of my terrible piano playing, or shots of my new, not-quite-dead-yet houseplants.

I had lived up to my promise to meet him in Prague at Christmas, which was wonderful. Dax and I hadn't missed a beat. Even his bandmates, whom I worried would see me as old and out of touch, were lovely to me. When I got back from the trip, I basically spent the next week and a half in bed crying and listening to sad love songs on repeat.

The trip had solidified it for me: I wanted to be with Dax; yet, here we were.

I knew the score, and I was fine with it. I had a very full

life now and wasn't sitting home thinking about him—*much*. I even tried dating other people, and I suspected he did, too, though I didn't ask. For my part, I never met anyone who warranted even a second date.

Though we were careful not to get too serious and emotional in our texts, I could tell Dax felt the same way. After our meetup in Europe, his messages came in faster and more regularly. He'd keep me posted on the little things that happened almost every day, and I'd do the same.

But we never discussed the future, and I held no expectations that he'd be coming home to me anytime soon. I was sad, but I would deal with it. Annie 2.0 was alone, and she was doing great.

I'd come to realize that I couldn't formally tether someone to me with a marriage contract, and even if I could, it wouldn't give me the sense of peace, joy, and satisfaction that came from spending time—however much we could scrape together—with the people who truly mattered to me.

Lily said, "I think my mom talked to Dax last week, and he told her he'd gotten an offer to collaborate with"—she clamped her mouth shut—"I shouldn't say."

"Who?" Polly leaned forward.

Lily shook her head furiously and sought Rob's eyes for help.

"We're not allowed to talk about it yet." Rob patted his fiancée's hand. "But you'll know soon enough."

"I'll give you a clue." Lily's eyes darted from side to side. "Cardigan." She clamped her mouth shut.

Holy frick. I had full faith that Dax would succeed, but working with Taylor Swift would be beyond my—and probably his—wildest dreams. As much as part of me had been holding out hope all this time that maybe, just maybe, after a year of recording and touring, he'd be up for taking at least an extended break back home in Chicago with me, I could not deny that this was a huge, amazing, life-changing development for him.

Not that I wasn't bummed. Of course it'd be nice to have him around, but only if his career allowed.

I reached for my phone, not to check for work messages (Kim was on call Tuesday nights for trivia purposes) but to look in on the security cameras I'd placed inside the house. Joanne was lying peacefully on her dog bed in the family room. I'd put up baby gates to block off the stairs and had closed all the doors to the rest of the house. She was still hanging in there, but steps had gotten tough for her. I had to help her up and down whenever she needed to go outside. She was a trouper, though, and always a sweetheart.

I'd also started taking in foster dogs, which was something Polly had suggested. She was impressed by how diligent I was about caring for Joanne and asked if I'd be willing to look after some needier rescues who came through her office. Right now, I was fostering Boo, who we were nursing back to health after being found abandoned and severely underweight. She and Joanne got along like gangbusters.

In fact, if we ended up winning tonight, the team agreed to give the money to Polly's favorite local canine rescue foundation.

So, we had to win. I couldn't allow myself to be distracted by whatever Dax might or might not be doing now that Monica Feathers was back in town. I had my life here. Maybe one day he'd be back and a part of it, but for now, my focus was on crushing this tournament.

During the breaks between rounds, my teammates and I talked about all the exciting things happening in our lives—Rob sold his mom's place after she passed, and he and Lily were renovating a house in…wait for it…the suburbs, even though he'd long ago vowed never to leave Edison Park.

Kelly and Mark were loving life in Galena and were currently starting their first round of in vitro. I was fielding so many calls from her day and night for medical advice, I jokingly sent her a bill for services rendered. She, in response, sent me a case of wine from Rob's store, which I gladly accepted.

Yessi and Polly had decided, once Olivia turned one, that they really needed to focus more on their own social lives, so they made standing dates each week to hang out with me at trivia and with Polly's friends for Sunday brunch.

Darius and Monica Feathers stopped by after the eighth round. I stood and gave him a hug. "Congratulations, dad-to-be!" I said.

He beamed and pulled out a chair for his extra-famous wife, and she gracefully glided onto it.

The crowd at our table grew silent, unsure how to behave with a certified diva in our midst.

She spoke quietly, barely above a whisper. "Do you mind if I join your team for the next few rounds?"

My mouth dropped open. "Yes," I said. "I mean, no. Of course we don't mind."

"I heard the next round is music," she purred. "I think I know quite a bit about that."

Our team chuckled, and Kelly nudged me hard in the ribs.

She hissed in my ear, "If Monica Feathers thinks the answer is the British Empire, you write down 'British Empire,' got it?"

"Got it." I pecked her on the cheek.

I didn't get to spend much—if any—time with Monica when I was in Prague visiting Dax, as the two of us kept each other a bit busy. I wasn't even sure Monica remembered who I was, but after the ninth round, she looked right at me and said, "Dax spoke about you often."

"Oh really?" I focused on my glass of water, feeling a blush creeping up my neck.

"He said many nice things about you." She frowned. "He and I spoke one night, and I said, 'Dax, when are you going to realize you should be with this woman, as I realized I was meant to be with Darius?'" She rubbed her belly. "But he said, 'I have to go where the music is.'"

"That sounds like him." I flashed a smile at Lily, showing her I held no hard feelings about her brother. We were fine. We just wanted different things. He was becoming a world-famous musician; I was happily becoming a dog lady, and I'd learned how to play "Für Elise" on the piano...in theory.

"I told Dax," Monica continued, "the music can be wherever you want it to be. I said, I'm going back to Chicago to have my child and be with my love. Come home with me, I begged him." She shook her head. "But he said he needed to be free."

Smiling hard, trying to deny the sour feeling in my gut, I tossed my pen to the table. I knew the next round was about to start, but I couldn't sit there and listen to this. I had to get up, move around, and settle my head. God, it was fine if Dax wanted to travel around, pursuing his dreams. It was what he was supposed to do. It was what I wanted him to do, for him, for his career. But did everyone have to rub it in my face?

I marched up to the bar. "Hey," I said to Peter, "can you—"

A head popped up from below the counter. Smiling blue eyes flashed at me, and I nearly fell backward.

"What took you so long to get mad enough to come over here?" he asked. "My sister was supposed to tell you I was planning on traveling around with Taylor Swift, and Monica was supposed to—"

My mouth opened and closed like a fish's. "What are you doing here?" I asked. "Are you—?" My eyes watered.

"I'm back," he said.

"You're back?" My knees wobbled. I didn't dare believe it. "I… What does that mean?"

"It means that when Monica found out she was pregnant, she started talking about moving back here and working on some projects together in our home base, and I thought that sounded like a great idea." He flashed me a hopeful smile. "Annie, I've missed you so much."

I was still stuck on logistics. My brain and my heart wouldn't allow me to fully accept this news. Not yet. "How long have you known about this?"

"Officially, not that long. Unofficially, I started thinking about moving back as soon as you left me in Prague."

Tears welled up behind my eyelids.

"I should've said something," Dax said nervously. "I shouldn't have assumed. You've probably met someone or moved on."

"Oh my god, no." I shook my head. "I'm just wondering what's taking you so long to come over here and kiss me."

He ducked out from under the bar, rushed over, and planted a huge kiss on my mouth. My entire body relaxed into his arms. I had been doing fine without Dax, and I would've continued to happily enjoy my time with my friends and family, but life would be so much sweeter with him around. We'd never be certain we wouldn't eventually—*boom!*—flame out, and there was still a lot we had to discuss, but we'd get to it.

We'd deal with it. Together.

But for now...

"Let's get out of here," I said just as Ronald announced the start of the final round of trivia.

"Don't you want to see this through?" he asked. "You're about to win the Windy City Championship for the second time in a row. It's not like you to leave your trivia fate up to everyone else."

"I trust them." I grabbed Dax's hand and pulled him toward the door, imagining the two of us back at home together, watching rom-coms, cuddling on the couch with Joanne (and now Boo), our bodies entwined beneath the sheets, me listening to him playing the piano at night before bed.

I took one last look back at my friends, heads huddled together as Ronald started the round: musical instruments. "First question," he said, "what is the name for the part of the piano that covers the keys?"

"Fallboard," I hissed, trying to telepathically send that

answer to my teammates.

Over the din of the crowd, I heard Mark say, loudly, "I think it's called a drop sheath."

"Damn it, Mark," I said through clenched teeth.

"You want to go back there?" Dax asked. "Is your legendary competitive spirit getting fired up?"

I gazed up into his laughing blue eyes. "No," I said, dragging him out of the bar and away from the competition before I could change my mind. Even if they lost, I'd make sure the rescue organization got the money. Dax was back, and I wasn't sure what that meant yet, how we'd fit into each other's lives, or whether or not we'd actually work as a couple. But none of that mattered, not now. We'd take it day by day, until maybe one morning we'd wake up and realize we'd made it to happily ever after.

I smiled up at him. "I'm sure they've got it handled."

ACKNOWLEDGMENTS

A huge thanks to my agent Louise Fury for believing in this book and encouraging me to write it as a single POV. I think it works! Thank you to my editor Stacy Abrams for all the great notes, which a lot of the time are "What is she feeling here?" because feelings aren't just scary for Annie, they're scary for me, too!

Thank you so much to Hannah Lindsay for catching my mistakes and to Myshala Liddick for her time and patience with this manuscript. I truly appreciate your perspective, and I am so proud of and grateful for Entangled's commitment to diversity and sensitivity. Thank you to everyone at Entangled for all of their publishing support. This is always such a wonderful team to work with!

I want to thank, in no particular order, Cathy Downing, Bernie Henry, Karen Alekna, Jackie Dreffein, LuAnn Baker, Jason Reed, Brittany and Jonah Von Spreeken, Mikey Vanlandingham, Brandy Rodgers, Nick Shannon, and Shannon Campbell. They know what they did, and it was spectacular!

Thanks to my dear friend Annie Martinez, who doesn't realize she helped with this book, but she should know that when I was asked to change the character's original first name and had to come up with a new moniker for this badass lady, "Annie" came to mind immediately. Many millions of thanks to another dear friend Amy Henning, who so kindly answered my doctor-related questions on this book and who has been so incredibly supportive of me since book one. You are two of my all-time favorite people, and I can't wait to hang out in person again soon.

Thank you to my family for their patience, always, and to Bucky for being the cutest and best distraction. I love you all!

Looking for more romance?
Entangled brings the laughs.

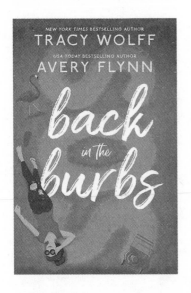

BACK IN THE BURBS

After a nasty divorce, Mallory's ready to leave NYC and start over. She decides to live in the house her aunt left her...in the suburbs. First rule of surviving the burbs? There is nothing that YouTube and a glass of wine can't conquer.

THE REBOUND SURPRISE

Carefree bachelor Aniel is the perfect guy to have a rebound fling with after organized and predictable Libby finds her fiancé defiling her linen sheets with the maid. Except, the fine print that says condoms aren't 100 percent effective is unerringly accurate.

Entangled brings the feels.

THE THINGS WE LEAVE UNFINISHED

Told in alternating timelines, *The Things We Leave Unfinished* examines the risks we take for love, the scars too deep to heal, and the endings we can't bring ourselves to see coming.

CONFESSIONS IN B-FLAT

Essence bestselling author Donna Hill brings us an emotional love story set against the powerful backdrop of the civil rights movement that gripped a nation—a story as timely as it is timeless...

Entangled brings the heat.

FOLLOW ME DARKLY

One chance encounter is all it took for Skye to find herself in the middle of a Cinderella story…but self-made billionaire Braden Black is no Prince Charming, and his dark desires are far from his only secret.

THE SPINSTER AND THE RAKE

The marriage game is afoot in this clever blend of *My Fair Lady* meets *Pride and Prejudice* with a twist!

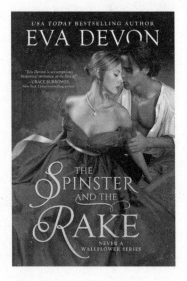

Entangled brings the heart.

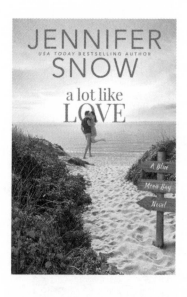

A LOT LIKE LOVE

Sparks start to fly between longtime crushes Sarah and Wes when they begin renovating the B&B her grandmother left her. But what happens when they realize each other's *real* reasons for restoring the landmark are at complete odds?

FOREVER STARTS NOW

Town misanthrope and diner owner Monroe decides to strike a deal with the hot Australian that just moved to Forever Falls to pretend to be his girlfriend for a price.

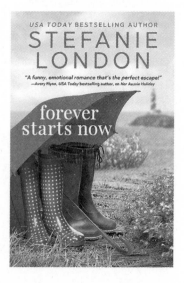

Don't miss any of the
exciting new romances
Entangled has to offer.

Follow @Entangled_Publishing
on Instagram and join us at
Facebook.com/EntangledPublishing

AMARA
an imprint of Entangled Publishing LLC